TWO
PARTS
BLOODY
MURDER

Previously published Worldwide Mystery titles by
JEN J. DANNA with ANN VANDERLAAN

DEAD, WITHOUT A STONE TO TELL IT
A FLAME IN THE WIND OF DEATH

TWO PARTS BLOODY MURDER

JEN J. DANNA WITH ANN VANDERLAAN

W⊕RLDWIDE®

TORONTO • NEW YORK • LONDON
AMSTERDAM • PARIS • SYDNEY • HAMBURG
STOCKHOLM • ATHENS • TOKYO • MILAN
MADRID • WARSAW • BUDAPEST • AUCKLAND

Recycling programs
for this product may
not exist in your area.

Two Parts Bloody Murder

A Worldwide Mystery/August 2016

First published by Five Star Publishing.

ISBN-13: 978-0-373-27951-7

Printed in U.S.A.

Acknowledgments

Once again, we are so immensely grateful for all the help we've received during the writing of this manuscript: Detective Lieutenant Norman Zuk of the Massachusetts State Police, Essex Detective Unit, for his continuing assistance to ensure our police procedures are correct. From taking the time for a personal meet-up in Boston, to ensuring any needed connections within the state police are in place, and then painstakingly going over all our technical questions and sharing his personal experiences on the job, his generous help continues to be invaluable. Detective Lieutenant Mike Holleran of the Massachusetts State Police, Crime Scene Services Section, for his insight into the inner workings of his department, and for sharing his personal experience on fingerprint collection and analysis. David Procopio, Massachusetts State Police, Media Relations Unit, for always assuring the support of the state police in our endeavors. James Marsh, Community Development Director, the City of Lynn, for kindly providing a tour of the High Rock Tower Observatory as well as information concerning its history. Dr. Tracy Rogers, Director of the Forensic Science Program at the University of Toronto, for technical consultation. Author Carrie T. Morgan, for sharing her insights into the emotional aspects of PTSD and its effect on soldiers.

From a writing perspective, we were once again joined by our incredible critique team: Lisa Giblin, Jenny Lidstrom, Margaret Isaacs, and Sharon Taylor. As always, you generously shared your time and considerable talents with us, and we're grateful for the stronger manuscript that is the result of your efforts.

We were aided once again by our editor, Gordon Aalborg, who always goes the extra mile to teach his authors how to think critically, and to assist them in finding ways to improve an already solid manuscript. Thanks also to our wonderful agent, Nicole Resciniti, who continues to support our endeavors in every way.

J.J.D. and A.V.

Thank you Paul and Shelly, you are the best son and daughter-in-law any mom could ever have. Your humor, encouragement, and enthusiasm brighten every conversation, chat, and email exchange. Well, at least until you start snickering at the autocorrect spelling absurdities I transmit while texting.

The Thundertail Tribe is a continuing challenge and an ongoing blessing. I have three wonderful pit bulls—Angel, Spike, and R Kane. Because of the Boys, I have more friends, help, and connection than ever before in my adult life. I have people I can rely on, people who rely on me, and a social network to advocate and help save lives every day.

Angel, a *Love-A-Bull* rescue alumnus, greets me every morning with a big pittie grin while pretending not to hog the middle of the bed. Fur brother Spike, a deaf dog from the same rescue, reminds me daily of the value of sign language and the futility of yelling at those who don't, or can't, hear. R—as in "Raising"—Kane is the newest Thundertail. This graduate of *Don't Bully Me Rescue* is the perfect "stubby dog": big heart, bigger head, and a tail that never stops wiggling his butt. In just thirteen months Kane has morphed from street dog into certified therapy dog volunteering to comfort AIDS patients, nursing home residents, and child victims of domestic violence.

A.V.

When someone who works full time commits to writing a book in a compressed period of time, it is often to the exclusion of almost everything else around her. So immense thanks are owed to my family—husband, Rick, and daughters, Jessica and Jordan—who allowed me to be "absent" for long periods of time while working on this manuscript. Rick, I could not have completed this novel without your continued support and willingness to carry part of my load. To Jess, thank you for endeavoring to teach me your considerable photography skills. To Jordan, my ever-willing victim—thank you for always being good natured when I need a stand-in to confirm skeletal positioning and mechanics. If our death scenes are realistic, it's partly because of the many times you've been "killed"! And thanks to my mother, Edith Danna, for giving me permission to hide a little piece of our family inside the history in this story.

J.J.D.

The title of this novel comes from *The Devil's Dictionary*, a series of satirical newspaper columns published by Ambrose Bierce (1842–1914) beginning in 1881. Originally collected and published in 1906 as *The Cynic's Word Book*, it was retitled as *The Devil's Dictionary* in 1911.

BRANDY, n. A cordial composed of one part thunder-and-lightning, one part remorse, two parts bloody murder, one part death-hell-and-the-grave, and four parts clarified Satan. Dose, a headful all the time. Brandy is said by Dr. Johnson to be the drink of heroes. Only a hero will venture to drink it.

PROLOGUE: BOTTLING

Bottling: the process by which a bottle is filled with wine or beer, and then corked, plugged, or capped.

Sunday, 3:10 a.m.
Many years ago
Lynn, Massachusetts

HE STEPPED BACK from his handiwork, the wooden handle slipping from his damp fingers as the tool fell with a clatter to the scarred wood floor. After wiping his gritty hands on his coarse wool trousers, he reached into the breast pocket of his threadbare shirt and retrieved a small leather pouch. He pulled out a cigarette paper, sparsely sprinkled on a ration of tobacco, and then rolled it.

It took three matches before he could still his shaking hands enough to light the end.

He pulled a deep draft into his lungs, feeling the smoke almost instantly calm his nerves.

It had to be done. It was only right.

He closed his eyes, still hearing the voice in his head—the curses, threats, and bribes that eventually changed to shrieks of terror. Until even those were finally muffled.

Not so brave now, are you? Take away your power and you're no better than the rest of us.

Standing before the wall, he calmly smoked the last of his cigarette. Then he dropped the butt to the ground, grinding it under the heel of his heavy boot. *There was still work to do.*

When he was finished, he stopped at the bar, eyeing the array of bottles. He contemplated for a moment, and then poured himself a large tumbler of pale, aged brandy. Turning back toward the tomb, he raised his glass in a final toast.

And drank deeply.

ONE: EIGHTEENTH AMENDMENT

Eighteenth Amendment: a constitutional amendment banning the manufacture, sale, import, export, and transportation of alcoholic beverages in the United States and its possessions beginning in January of 1920. Contrary to common belief, it did not prohibit the purchase, in-home preparation, or the consumption of alcohol. It is the only amendment to have ever been repealed.

Friday, 12:24 p.m.
The Adytum Building
Lynn, Massachusetts

THE WIND CAUGHT the door as it opened, sending it crashing into the antique brick wall hard enough to rattle windowpanes several feet away. Startled, Massachusetts State Police Trooper First Class Leigh Abbott braced a hand on filthy wood and glanced up from where she crouched on the floor. Raising her free hand to her forehead to block the glare from the tripod lights, she focused on the tall, burly man coming through the door. Then she pushed to her feet and stepped back from death.

"When I called the ME's office for a pickup, I wasn't expecting them to send you." Meeting him halfway, Leigh lifted one of the bags from his arms.

Dr. Edward Rowe cocked a single bushy, white eyebrow at her. "No one *sends* the medical examiner for the Commonwealth of Massachusetts, Abbott." His gaze shifted to the victim across the room. "But the call came through, and when I heard it was your case, I decided to follow up. It's been a few weeks since I attended to a case myself."

Leigh was well aware that standard protocol in Massachusetts was to send techs out to death scenes and for bodies to be transported without on-scene processing. Rowe was running a few cases on his own to prove to the funding Powers That Be that murder conviction rates improved with timely and thorough victim processing. But this was the first indication her victims were receiving special attention. Warmth at the implied compliment rushed through her. "Thanks. You know I'd always rather have you on-site than one of your techs."

"Don't say that too loudly. The tech will be in right behind me after he's parked the van." Rowe set another bag down on the dusty, debris-littered floor, fifteen feet away from the body. He opened the bag and pulled out a disposable Tyvek suit, shaking it out with a practiced *snap*. "But when it comes to working with cops, you and I always do well together. Better than most, in fact." His gaze quickly scanned the empty room as he tugged on the suit. "Although, I'm not used to you being on your own. After the cases you've run lately with Lowell and his team, it must feel odd working solo again."

Leigh gave him a crooked smile. She'd never admit it, but she was feeling the isolation of being without the team more strongly than she ever would have suspected. What started off as an unwilling alliance between herself and forensic anthropologist Dr. Matt Lowell had developed into a cohesive partnership. Add in Matt's three graduate students, and the team was complete. Compared to the mostly frosty relationships she had as the only woman in the Essex Detective Unit, working with her team felt like a homecoming. On a case like this, investigating solo, she missed not only the brainstorming and the way they played off each other to build the case, but also the camaraderie and the drive of a shared goal. "Only specific victims require the forensic anthropology team. Luckily this one doesn't, because Matt's out of town at a symposium, and won't be back for three days. Besides, he wouldn't know what to do with this victim. Too much flesh."

Rowe gave a short bark of a laugh. "Don't know if I'd agree with that. As an ex-Marine medic, Lowell knows his way around a body."

Leigh dropped her head to hide the warmth brightening her cheeks. *He certainly knew his way around hers.*

Rowe's voice interrupted thoughts not suited to a crime scene, jerking her back to the here and now. "What do we have here?"

"Something I wasn't expecting to find, that's for sure."

Rowe flicked a quizzical glance in her direction as he started to pull out gloves and his instruments. "You're a murder cop. What were you expecting if not a body?"

"I was expecting a body, just not one this fresh." Before he could ask, she raised a hand. "Let me back up. At the unit, if we have time on our hands, we work open reports and cold case files. I had a report of some old guy in a nursing home who repeatedly told a story about a body hidden in this building. The family didn't pay much attention—apparently he's ninety-six and tends to tell some pretty tall tales on a regular basis—except he kept retelling this particular tale. So they reported it to the local police, who turned it over to us since it described a murder. I had some time on my hands today during shift, so I came out to look the place over."

Daylight flared briefly into the room as the missing tech banged through the door, bags piled on his shoulders like a pack mule.

Rowe waved him in before turning back to Leigh. "Can we go ahead and do photos? I saw the crime scene boys in their van outside."

"Yes. They've done their initial work, even did a fancy 3D laser mapping of the room. They did body shots, but I know you like to do your own in case anything changes between the scene and the morgue. They cleared out until after you're done to preserve the integrity of the scene. I stayed to maintain it."

Rowe motioned the tech to get started. The tech put down his bags, pulled out a camera, and immediately started photographing the body *in situ*.

Rowe stepped back to stay out of his way. Hands on his hips, he tipped his head back to consider the high ceiling above them. Plaster crumbled in chunks from overhead, but the remains of intricate crown molding still circled the top of the walls. "This is a great old building. Must be a hundred years old."

"More than that actually. I took the time to look up the building's history because I was trying to get a feel for exactly how long the supposed victim could have been here. It was built in eighteen-ninety." She scanned the interior of the room again, taking in the worn wood floor, aged walls, peeling paint, and the water stain running nearly floor-to-ceiling beside a single window so grimy that only watery light filtered through. "It's been at least a decade since this part of the building was occupied. I talked to the owner, who was extremely skeptical at the suggestion of a body. The upper three floors of the building are now low-income senior housing. He said that those floors were totally gutted and refurbished about twenty-five years ago and they certainly hadn't found a body then. A few storefronts are still occupied but several are empty just like this space."

"If they only renovated the upper three floors, that still gave you some leeway for a search," Rowe reasoned. "Especially if the upper floors were always residential. It's doubtful they'd be able to hide a body up there with no one noticing."

"That's exactly what I thought. The owner wasn't willing to waste his time coming down here on a 'wild goose chase'—his words, not mine—but he gave me full consent and these"—keys jingled merrily where they hung suspended between her index finger and thumb—"and told me to help myself. I checked out the empty stores in front before coming back here. As soon as I got to the bottom of the stairs in the brick archway, I could see the door standing open. I called out my designation, but no one responded. I came in cautiously because I was expecting a homeless person squatting out of the cold nights. But instead I found him."

They both turned to look at the victim sprawled on the floor: male, probably in his mid to late forties. His clothes spoke of a lifetime of luxury and money—custom-made leather shoes, classic gold watch, and a perfectly tailored suit. He might have been asleep, if not for the dark blossom of blood over his heart and the waxy pallor of his skin.

Rowe stepped forward and leaned over for a better view. "That's no homeless person. He's wearing a Breitling watch that's worth more than many people in Essex County make in a year."

"I noticed that when the crime scene techs got the extra lighting set up." She looked up at the single light socket that hung from a cord in the ceiling, the base of a shattered lightbulb still embedded in the fixture. "I'm thinking the owner's estimate of this place being empty for a decade was conservative."

Rowe circled the body, surveying it critically. "Gunshot wound is the only obvious cause of death at first glance." After staring at the floor for a moment, he grasped one of the tripod lights and swiveled it around to shine into the dark corners of the musty, dank room. His gaze skimmed over the illuminated walls and floor. "Hmmm…"

"I know," Leigh said. "There's no obvious spatter or any other sign that he was killed here."

Rowe got the go-ahead from his tech and stepped up to the body. He crouched down and touched his fingers to the man's neck. "The body is well-cooled." He grasped one wrist and tried to lift it off the ground. The arm shifted by only millimeters. "Rigor is well-established. This man has been dead for hours."

"Was he killed here, or was he moved to this location?"

"I'll be able to give you my thoughts on that soon." He indicated the arms sprawled out to the side of the torso, the bent knee, and awkwardly twisted ankle. "If he was moved, it was before rigor set in. Let's get started. Ambient temp is 11.7°C." He pushed back the edge of the suit jacket and pulled the man's shirt from his waistband on the right side, raising it a few inches while being careful not to disturb the blood-soaked material. Leigh winced as he made a small, bloodless incision with a scalpel just below the bottom of the ribs before inserting the long metal probe of a digital thermometer deep into the body. "Liver temp at the start of the exam is 26.6°C." He pushed back his cuff to reveal a large luminous wristwatch. "Time-stamp it twelve-thirty-one." He glanced up at Leigh. "I'll do a second measurement before we pack him up to nail down the rate of cooling in this specific environment, but as a rough guess, considering the temp in the room, I'd say your vic has been dead for about twelve hours. Which is consistent with rigor."

Leigh pulled her notebook and pen out of her jacket pocket and jotted down the information.

"Wallet in the back pocket," Rowe commented. He deftly slid it out without rolling the body and flipped it open. "Driver's license lists him as Peter Holt, age forty-four." He rattled off a Boston address and then held the license photo next to the dead man's face. "That's definitely him. I'll get dentals to confirm, but I think you have your victim, Abbott. The question is—if he wasn't killed here, where was he killed and why was he moved?"

"Both good questions. I want to check out this room a little more closely and make sure we didn't miss anything. I'd like to be able to corroborate your opinion of whether the body has been moved. Are you okay here if I grab one of the lights?"

"Just leave me that one"—Rowe pointed to a tripod—"and that. Those will be enough for me to do the exam, then we'll start processing for trace evidence before preparing the body for transport."

"I'll leave you to it. I'm going to finish checking this room out, then I need to see if there's anything to the old guy's story."

"You know where to find me." Rowe turned back to his victim, and he and the tech got to work.

Leigh stepped out of the circle of light. Giving her eyes a moment to adjust to the shadows, she studied the room. She considered the shape of the building—a shorter, squatter version of New York's Flatiron Building. Built on the sliver of land between Union Street and the MBTA railroad tracks, the back of the building faced the old Central Square train station. Red brick and Italianate in style, it was only four stories tall. Facing Union Street, the ground floor hosted a few thriving shops and a café, but hard times had left several other businesses locked and permanently shuttered.

Since the elderly man's story implied the death had occurred decades before, possibly more than fifty years ago, it seemed unlikely that recently closed businesses or occupied living spaces could hide a body all that time. The chance of there actually being a body was close to zero.

Frowning, she turned back to where Rowe and his tech bent over her newest case. *Well, maybe not exactly zero.*

If you were going to hide a body, and have it remain undiscovered for decades, you'd have to put it somewhere so secret it wouldn't be found unless you knew exactly where to look. Leigh just wasn't seeing anything that set off warning bells.

She dragged the third tripod several feet away from the victim, turning it to direct the light beam at the back wall. Inching along the baseboard, she examined it closely, looking for any sign of blood spatter or bullet defect. The wall was discolored, making it hard to discern small spots, and several times Leigh leaned in with her forehead nearly scraping the plaster. Wrinkling her nose at the stale odor of neglect and hoping she wasn't inhaling some kind of toxic killer mold, she studied a splotch on the wall for a moment before deciding the dark stain wasn't something cast off by her victim.

She started to pull away when something further down the wall caught her eye. Stepping toward the center of the room made it disappear, so she leaned back in, staring along the length of the wall. The surface curved gently, but a small section bowed out from its surroundings a few feet away.

Going back to the tripod, she aimed the light more squarely at that area. Then she saw it: two barely discernible parallel lines, about three feet apart, running down the wall.

Heart thumping faster with each step, Leigh crossed to the wall and ran her hand along one of the lines. It definitely jutted out from the plane of the wall. Bending, she set her fingertips on the crack and ran them upward from the floor. At about seven feet, the outcrop disappeared from beneath her touch. Her breath caught as excitement surged in her. She couldn't see it but she started to search for any kind of defect to the right of where she lost touch with the crack in the wall. Stretching up on tiptoe, she ran her fingers along the wall, peeling paint disintegrating under her touch.

Come on, I know you're here. Then her fingertips slid into the subtle groove. *Got you!* She ran her fingers slowly along the crack until it veered downward. Dropping down to flat feet, she followed it down before stepping back.

It was a door, so perfectly inset into the wall and hidden by filth and peeling paint that you had to be nearly on top of it to see it. There were no hinges visible, so the door had to swing inward.

Bracing both hands just to the right of the offset crack, she gave it a hard push. The door shifted slightly. *Hinges on the right, door opens on the left.*

Pulling back a few feet, Leigh threw her body against the door, hitting the wall right where her hands had been and taking the brunt of the blow with her shoulder. She gave a small groan at the impact, but elation filled her as the door shifted further. She fervently wished Matt was here—his bigger body and rower's physique would make short work of the closed door. She stepped back to take another run at it.

"Abbott, what are you doing?" It was Rowe's voice behind her.

She turned around, surprised to see Rowe standing just feet away. In her excitement at finding the door, she'd totally forgotten the investigation going on behind her. "There's a door hidden in the wall. See it?"

Rowe nodded and then quickly pulled off his gloves and jammed them into a pocket of his suit. He pushed her gently to the side. "I have about seventy-five pounds on you. Let me try."

Leigh tapped the wall. "Aim here. That seems to be the sweet spot."

Rowe stepped back, eyeing his target. He turned sideways, grasped his right forearm with his left hand to hold it steady, and took a run at the door. With a squeal of wood on wood, it moved inward by a full inch. "Almost."

One more hard push had the door swinging open with an ominous creak to reveal a small landing with dust and debris lining the corners. A narrow wooden staircase to their left led down into the darkness below. The air was thick and stale after decades undisturbed.

Leigh reached into her pocket for the small flashlight

she'd tucked there before entering the building. Flipping it on, she leaned into the gap, shining the light down the stairs. Rowe leaned in behind her.

Cobwebs filled every corner and at least one of the steps looked dangerously rotten. The walls were painted a dark red, faded now, but with a hint of their former flair. The beam of light fell on a wooden barrel in the corner at the bottom of the stairs. The wood was aged to a dull gray and the metal bands encircling it were rusted, iron oxides leaching onto the wooden staves like a bloody smear. Just barely discernible, in black print between the rusted hoops, was the brand "Bushmills Irish Whiskey."

Leigh nearly dropped the flashlight as her hand went clammy, and she had to clench the cylinder tighter before it slipped from her grasp and tumbled down the steps. She steadied the light and blinked a few times to make sure she wasn't imagining the scene.

It was still there.

She turned to gape at Rowe, who wore the same slack-jawed, wide-eyed expression she imagined was on her own face.

They'd just discovered an old speakeasy, lost to time since the days of Prohibition.

TWO: BLIND PIG

Blind Pig: an alternate name for a speakeasy. Possibly called a blind pig because the establishment turned a "blind eye" to Prohibition, or because consuming the often-contaminated illegal alcoholic beverages sold there sometimes caused blindness.

Friday, 12:46 p.m.
The Adytum Building
Lynn, Massachusetts

"Abbott, do you realize what this is?" Rowe's awed words echoed strangely down the empty staircase.

"I think so." Leigh stepped back into the main room. "And I think I can confirm it before even setting foot on that staircase."

She hurried across the room, automatically circling the sprawled body on the ground and the tech kneeling beside it without really seeing either. Grasping the outer door, Leigh pushed it fully open against the wall.

She'd seen the small inset door at eye level on her way in. Seen it, but not truly registered it. And certainly hadn't appreciated its meaning.

She swung the door partially closed so she could look behind it. A small hinged cutout of the same wood was flush mounted into the door. Both the tiny hinges and the small metal bar affixed beside the cutout to lock it in place were rusted solid.

She knew about the speakeasies of Chicago, Detroit, and New York during the Prohibition years of the twenties and thirties. She knew local history and that Boston was a hotspot for rum-running during those years because of its ports and natural harbors. Her own great-grandfather had served the Boston Police Department as part of the elite Boston Liquor Squad, so she'd heard family stories about raids throughout Boston.

But she hadn't realized Lynn was a part of that history. Granted, given its proximity to Boston and the fact it was an oceanside town, it wasn't much of a stretch.

She tugged at the rusted knob on the metal bar. At first it didn't move, so she grasped it more tightly and pulled harder. There was an ear-piercing screech and then the bar slid back. Leigh pulled the cutout free of where it nested in the door, and looked out through the grille at blue sky and sunlit railway tracks beyond. She had a flash of a foggy night, a man with slicked-back hair wearing a dark suit standing on the doorstep, a stylish girl with bobbed locks and a fringed dress on his arm. A whispered password and the night was theirs.

She turned back to Rowe, who still stood at the passageway. "It's a speakeasy, all right. This room must have been their cover. If the cops ever barged through this door, they were safe as long as they could get the hidden door closed. I bet they even kept boxes or some other camouflage nearby to push in front of it in case of emergency."

"You think your body is down there?"

"Ten minutes ago I was thinking I should put money down on there being no hidden body here. Now I think

I might have lost spectacularly." She crossed the room and pulled out her flashlight again. "I'm going down."

"Shouldn't you call someone first? This is an amazing historical find."

"First and foremost, it's my crime scene. There's no way I'm having a bunch of academic geeks stomping through my crime scene." At Rowe's raised eyebrow, she clarified. "Unless they're *my* academic geeks, who I've already trained in crime scene protocol. Damn, I wish Matt was here. He'd love this."

"Find him eighty-year-old skeletal remains and he'll be here to love it, let me assure you. You're sure you want to do this?"

Leigh flicked on the flashlight. "Positive."

"Then you're not going down on your own." Rowe moved to one of the bags, pawing through it quickly until he pulled out another flashlight. "Ted, keep pulling any trace you can find and then hold the body. We won't be long." He nodded at Leigh. "Let's go, I'm right behind you. And be careful on those stairs. Some of the steps look pretty iffy."

Leigh stepped onto the landing. She slipped behind the door and then peered around the front of it. "As I thought. The door is wood, but they plastered over the front and then painted it to look just like the walls of the room. Sneaky."

"Back then, not getting caught was a big deal. Jail sentence aside, getting caught meant a huge loss of revenue for the owners. And for the Mob."

Leigh touched a toe to the first tread, a deep-set, narrow board of aged wood. "Maybe it wasn't a Mob joint." She leaned a small amount of weight on the step, and then still more. The wood groaned in protest, but held. Grasping the thick banister mounted to the wall, she stepped off the landing onto the step, pausing until she was sure it would support her weight.

"Back then, they were all Mob jobs. 'Mad Johnny' Orestes ran the city. He had his finger in every pie and was most likely providing the booze for this establishment too."

Leigh froze with her foot an inch over the second step and turned to peer up at him. "You sound like you know a little bit about this."

"Are you kidding? I love local history. It's kind of a hobby. And in Boston and the surrounding area, local history goes a long way back. But the Prohibition years were particularly colorful."

Leigh chuckled and continued onto the next step. "Good to know we have a resident expert on the team. It might come in handy."

"Why do you think I'm here with you instead of bent over that body upstairs? This is a once in a lifetime opportunity. And Ted has everything well in hand; I've already done the tricky stuff."

They crept down the stairs carefully, skipping some steps completely, with Leigh testing the others individually before Rowe would trust his greater weight on them. As they descended, the air became cooler and staler. "I wonder if this place was ever raided," Leigh said.

"If it were, I might be able to track it down. But you should ask Lowell about some local historians at B.U. too."

"That's a good point. He might know—" The step suddenly gave way under her weight. With a small cry Leigh started to pitch forward. Only her tight hold on the banister and Rowe's quick hand grabbing her jacket kept her from pitching headfirst down the stairs. With a ragged breath, she settled on the next step, glaring at the broken tread behind her. "That was close. Thanks."

"You're welcome. Just one of the reasons I didn't want you coming down here on your own."

Rowe eased himself over the broken step, stretching out his long legs to the next tread down before proceeding. They continued to the bottom of the staircase without further incident. At the bottom, they paused to examine the barrel.

Rowe grabbed the lip and rocked it back and forth several times. "Empty."

"You didn't think it would be full, did you?"

"Not really. But do you know what a cask of eighty-year-old Irish whiskey would be worth?" He grinned conspiratorially. "We could all comfortably retire."

"Tempting thought, some days."

"Amen to that…but not today." He stepped through the door at the bottom of the stairs, Leigh right behind him, both of them shining their flashlights into the open space.

Leigh gasped as Rowe went motionless beside her.

It was like stepping back in time.

Their lights slowly panned over the room, twin beams sliding over wood and glass.

Rowe whistled softly. "What are the chances there are working lights down here?"

"It's possible. The building is powered and the place must have had electricity. Unless mice have eaten through the wires, we might get lucky."

They turned their search toward finding a light switch. Leigh found several on the wall by the door—vintage paired buttons, inlaid with mother-of-pearl. She slowly depressed them one at a time. Two large ceiling-mounted lights with large round bulbs flickered on, tentatively at first, then stronger. One bulb in the fixture over the bar gave a sharp pop and winked out, but the one over the remains of the once polished dance floor stayed on. The next button push lit the scrolling Art Deco wall sconces mounted high on columns throughout the room.

Stepping away from the wall, Leigh turned off her flashlight and slid it into her pocket as she simply tried to take it all in.

A dark wood bar stood at one end of the room, its long smooth surface dulled by dust and grime. A tall square bottle with a yellowed label lay on its side, cork removed and precious contents long since spilled. At the far end of the bar, a sepia poster reading "Alfred E. Smith for President—Honest. Able. Fearless." hung over an open brass case with several disintegrating cigarettes still tucked inside.

Plaster columns topped by decorative capitals studded the outer walls. Tables were tucked between the columns, and the chairs around them—some tipped over, several broken—told a tale of rough handling and a rapid exit. A lone shoe—black leather with what must have been a scandalously high heel for the time—lay under one of the chairs shoved against the wall.

A blackjack table stood against another wall, scattered playing cards spread over the crumbling green felt surface, and a stack of chips still in the slots. Behind the table, a mural depicting Roman ruins splashed across the wall: crumbling archways, weathered statuary, and toppled Tuscan columns, all painted in cascading shades of blue.

A single forlorn music stand stood on a small raised dais in the back corner, as if waiting for the band to return.

Leigh circled behind the bar. Underneath, dusty shot glasses were stacked in rows, and two beer kegs were tucked under the long stretch of the bar, brass taps tarnished with age. Leigh grasped one of the smooth wood handles and pulled, but not even a single drop leaked out. Large glass jugs littered the floor behind the bar, some tipped over carelessly on their sides. Several wooden crates labeled by out-of-state wineries were stacked haphazardly in the far corner.

Seeing a slip of paper under one of the kegs, she tried to catch it with her fingertips. It took several tries before she drew out a two-dollar bill. Pulling out her flashlight, Leigh aimed it at the bill to study the details. "Get a load of this."

She passed Rowe the bill over the bar. He aimed his own flashlight at it, examining it carefully. "Two-dollar bill, series nineteen-twenty-nine." He looked up at Leigh. "That was the first year those bills were printed at their current size. Before that, they were quite a bit bigger." He flipped the bill over. "Look at that. Monticello on the back, not the Declaration of Independence. Probably not worth much on the open market, but worth an awful lot to a collector."

"Finders keepers as far as I'm concerned," she said, and then purposely turned her back on Rowe to examine a poster from the Salt Lake Brewing Company, extolling its Old German lager as "The American Beauty Beer" and promising a restful night's sleep, a stimulated appetite, and a "nourishing and strengthening tonic for mother and baby." That last left Leigh staring open-mouthed long enough that when she turned around, Rowe was standing alongside the blackjack table and the two-dollar bill was nowhere in sight.

Coming out from behind the bar, Leigh stood in the middle of the room. As she turned in a slow circle, she felt thrown back in time, a black and white movie playing in her mind as she scanned the room. A tall, broad man in a dark shirt with a white towel thrown over his shoulder stood behind the bar, backlit by rows of gleaming bottles of golden whiskey and ruby wine. Men in London drape suits holding lowball glasses sat at tables across from sparkling women sipping goblets of wine while brandishing long, slender cigarette holders. In the corner a four-piece brass band was blasting out the latest jazz tune. Women with short hair and shorter skirts crowded the dance floor, doing the Charleston and the Black Bottom. The smoky air was full of laughter and song.

"Abbott, I think you should see this."

Leigh shook her head and the music died away to a mere echo from the past. Her eyes focused once again on the dim, abandoned room. But there was no sign of Rowe and his voice was muffled, although she wasn't sure if it was from the music in her head or from his location. "Where are you?"

Rowe poked his head out from a swinging door behind the bar. "Over here. There's a storage room in the back."

She followed him into a flurry of tipped boxes and spilled bottles. She stopped in the doorway. "Wow. If we had questions before about whether this place was raided..."

"It was raided all right, no question. But I wanted to show you this." He pointed at the wall at the far end of the room.

Leigh picked her way through the crates to stand as close as possible. "What about it?"

"Did you notice that while the walls out there are plaster, the walls in here are just plain brick?"

"Sure. Why gussy up the storeroom when just plain brick will do?"

"Fair enough. But why is this wall different?"

Leigh stood back to look more closely at the room as a whole. The front and side walls of the room were composed of rough bricks in varying shades. But the back wall was uniform in color and texture, and the mortar was shades lighter in tone. "Good question." She ran her fingers over the bricks on a side wall and then over the back wall. "These bricks feel different. Smoother."

"I want to try something." Rowe slipped out of the room, returning moments later with a wooden baseball bat.

Leigh stared at him, dumbstruck. "Where on earth did that come from?"

"Behind the bar. I bet the barkeep kept it around just in case things got out of hand. In the rush to leave, it got left behind."

"Or after everyone was taken out," Leigh said. "What exactly did you have in mind?"

"I want to test that wall." Rowe put the bat down, tip to the floor, and casually leaned on the flat end of the grip. "Why would that wall be different?"

"It wouldn't be if it went up at the same time."

"Exactly my point." He picked up the bat, cradling it in both hands and frowned. "An antique Louisville Slugger. Now this is a crying shame." He tossed the bat in the air, deftly catching it in both hands, choked up, and swung it at the side wall. The bat hit with a loud *clunk* and a few flakes of brick fell from the surface to tumble out of sight behind a crate.

He moved to the back wall, tightened his grip, and swung again. The bat connected with the brick with a decidedly higher pitch. Rowe's raised eyebrows gave Leigh an *I told you so* look and moved on to the third wall, then the fourth.

They had their answer.

"Only the back wall sounds different," Leigh said. "Do you think it's because of the type of brick?"

"Possibly, but my money is on there being a space behind that wall. You want to find your hidden body? Try behind there."

"Your mind works in interesting ways, Rowe. Do you always see death everywhere you look?"

"Death is my thing. It's hard *not* to see it everywhere I go. But you came searching for it specifically this time, so I was watching for it. The difference in the bricks is pretty minor but nothing else seems out of place in here. Keep in mind I might be wrong and you might be trying to bring down a wall for nothing, in which case you'll piss off the historians in a big way. But can you afford to take that chance after coming this far?"

"You know I can't." Leigh pulled her cell phone from her pocket. "No signal down here. I'm going to head up. If Riley's at the unit, I'm going to have him pick up some tools and bring them here."

"Meanwhile I'll finish off with the body. Enough time has now passed to get my second liver temp. Then we'll package him up and send him on his way to the morgue."

Leigh led the way through the speakeasy and back toward the stairs. "Are you going to stay or are you heading back with the body?"

"I'm not missing this for the world. Ted can make

the transfer and put the body in the fridge. You're stuck with me."

"Happily." She took a cautious step back onto the stairs. "Let's do this."

Friday, 2:20 p.m.
The Adytum Building
Lynn, Massachusetts

"WHOA!" BRAD RILEY'S eyes nearly bugged out of his head as he stepped into the dimly lit bar. "This is amazing!" Riley was the squad rookie, and the one trooper in the unit Leigh was on truly good terms with. He'd heard the stories about Leigh from the other guys, but had decided on his own that she wasn't a bad cop. He'd even volunteered to help with her casework in the past. He was young and green, but they'd all been that at some point, and Leigh genuinely liked him.

Leigh grinned at his enthusiasm. "Yeah, it's pretty cool."

"The body is down here?" Riley swung the sledgehammer off his shoulder, carefully lowering it to the ground.

"Maybe. We're about to find out for sure. Through here." She led the way into the back, waiting patiently as Riley dragged his heels a bit, looking at everything as he came through.

"Do you want to do the honors?" she asked Rowe.

He stepped back, one hand raised, the other still weighed down with the crowbar he carried. "No, ma'am. This is the most fun I've had on a case in years, but this is your show. You do the honors."

Leigh accepted the sledgehammer from Riley, swinging it up to rest on her shoulder. "I'm thinking dead center to have the least amount of support from the surrounding structure. Agreed?"

"Yes. Not that you'll have much luck aiming with that, but try for the mortar joins. The mortar will give way before the brick."

Leigh got a good grip on the sledgehammer and then swung it with all her strength at the wall. It hit with a resounding *crash*, the reverberations shooting up both arms and straight into her shoulders. She let the sledgehammer fall heavily to the floor, narrowly missing her toes, before examining the wall. The bricks were all still in place, but mortar crumbled to the floor. Heaving the sledgehammer up to her shoulder again, she prepared for the second strike.

It took three blows to knock the first brick free and two more to make a hole big enough to see through. Leigh set the sledgehammer down against the wall, panting. "That…should do it." Stepping up to the shoulder-height hole, she pulled a loose brick free and tossed it onto the plank floor at her feet. She angled the light into the hole, crouched down to peer in, and froze.

The hidden space was approximately two feet deep and ran the length of the eight foot wall. She had to crane her neck to follow the narrow beam of light down to the floor. But after all the time spent with Matt and his students, there was no mistaking the pale flash of bones lying inside.

A tomb was hidden on the other side of this wall. But had the victim been alive or dead when he was bricked in so long ago?

Wordlessly, she stepped back and handed the flashlight to Rowe. He gave her a quick, searching glance, but then moved in to see for himself. He peered through the gap, squinting in the dim light and then spending a long moment taking in the remains. Finally, he pulled back and handed the flashlight to Riley before stepping out of the way.

Leigh met his solemn gaze. "Better call Lowell back ASAP," he said. "Looks like we're going to need him again."

THREE: BATHTUB GIN

Bathtub Gin: a mix of alcohol, glycerin, and juniper juice contained in bottles or jugs, usually filled in a bathtub because they were too tall to be topped off in a sink.

Friday, 8:05 p.m.
Abbott Residence
Salem, Massachusetts

LEIGH ROLLED HER shoulders as she trudged up her front path, feeling a slight twinge as her muscles protested. The sledgehammer hadn't felt heavy at the time, but there was stiffness in her shoulders now that wasn't there when she'd started the drive home. Maybe she'd go loosen up in the whirlpool tub with her favorite juniper bath salts… after she called Matt.

She glanced at her watch. It was just after five o'clock in San Francisco, so she might catch him between the afternoon sessions and dinner if she called now. Her step lightened in anticipation of his reaction to her news. No burned flesh, no mutilation. Just nice clean bones and a historical mystery. He was going to love this case. She was going to love working with him and the team again.

He'd been busy for the last few days, and she looked forward to catching up. She could picture him at the conference: a tall, muscular ex-Marine in a room of pale, skinny scientists. She chuckled to herself at her own use of the stereotype, but in her experience, most scientists weren't athletes. Matt hadn't been either when she'd first sat in one of his classes three years earlier. But that was before he and his father took up rowing. Now, their hard work showed clearly on both of them.

Leigh let herself in, automatically stepping over the mail strewn around the inside hallway from her mail slot. Bending, she started to collect the envelopes. *Bill. Bill. Junk mail. Real estate flyer.*

She flipped over the large white envelope lying face-down on the floor and froze as her blood went cold, bills and junk mail tumbling from suddenly nerveless fingers.

Not again.

This envelope was larger than those that had arrived previously. Like past packages, her name was neatly printed on the face in black marker with the same Boston postmark and no return address. But unlike past deliveries, this one had come to her house instead of her desk at the Essex Detective Unit.

As a police officer, Leigh kept her home address unlisted. But there were those with the computer skills or inside connections to find her anyway.

Clearly, whoever was sending the disturbing packages knew where she lived.

She carried the envelope into the living room, being careful not to shift her grip from its original hold in case there might be fingerprints to recover. She set it down carefully on the table and stepped back, as if staring at a coiled rattlesnake preparing to strike rather than mere paper and ink. Sometimes words and images could injure more deeply than fangs and venom.

The deliveries had started about a month earlier. The

first had sent her reeling—a crime scene photo of her father, killed while on the job, his broken body lying in the snow, surrounded by blood and brain tissue. The warning written on the back: *Your father wasn't the hero you think he was. He was a dirty cop. Soon the world will know it. And you'll be the one to pay for his crimes.*

The second envelope arrived a week later. It contained a grainy photo of her father and a man she couldn't identify meeting in the shadows near a seedy North Salem bar. A log of her father's cell phone was also included, highlighting several calls made to the same number. Since then, she'd determined the phone log was fake, but the highlighted number was real, assigned at the time to a burner phone, long since discarded. Another dead end.

The first time Leigh had opened an envelope, she was alone, with no one to help her bear the brunt of the brutal blow. But later that evening, she had found herself at Matt's front door. Only then, as he'd eased some of the weight from her shoulders, was she able to break free of her cocoon of shock and pain to start thinking like the investigator she was. When the second package arrived, they'd opened it together, his large body beside her, cementing her own strength and determination.

Now she was on her own again, and she wasn't sure she had the strength to face this new nightmare alone.

It had been weeks since the last delivery, and in some small part of her mind, she'd closed off the worry and the pain of her father's loss. But that door was wide open now, the pain rising to engulf her once again.

Struggling for calm, she picked up the framed photograph on the end table. It was her academy graduation photo, and she and her father were both in their Massachusetts State Police dress uniforms. Memories of that

day flooded back in a rush—entering the auditorium behind the pipes and drums, being inspected and then ad-
dressed by the governor of Massachusetts, followed by
swearing faith and allegiance to the Commonwealth of
Massachusetts, and the thrill of her badge being pinned
on for the very first time. Layered over it all was her father's pride that his only child was following in his foot-
steps. The Abbotts had been cops for nearly one hundred
years, and the tradition continued with Leigh.

Everything was so shiny and new back then. Before
mistakes were made. Before lives were lost and reputa-
tions were soiled forever.

The fingers of her right hand slipped inside the neck-
line of her shirt, unerringly finding the small circle of
hardened scar tissue above her left breast. Her head bent
low as heat and shame seeped through her, stopping her
breath and making her heart skip unevenly. Trooper Len
Morrison's words echoed hollowly in her head: *I don't
know how you live with yourself. You killed a cop, a fellow officer. You might as well have pulled the trigger
yourself.*

Her stomach clenched and her palms went clammy,
but she dug deep, pushing away the guilt and the sorrow.
*You did nothing wrong. The people that count know it
and that's all that matters.*

Leigh wondered if she told herself that enough times,
she might someday believe it.

Her gaze flicked back to the envelope, anger rising
like a hot tide, swamping shame and giving her a rope
to clutch before she slipped any further into the pit. Goddamn whoever was sending these packages. And goddamn her own weakness that allowed him to have this

kind of power over her. The only way to fight that weakness was to meet it head-on.

Someone was trying to sully her father's good name. She didn't know why, but really, the "why" didn't matter. What mattered was that she couldn't allow it. Wouldn't allow it. Sergeant Nathaniel Abbott was an honored member of the force, a man who had died in the line of duty, a man who was still talked about with reverence and respect to this day.

She'd do whatever it took to keep it that way.

Leigh sat down on the couch and pulled off her messenger bag. Digging inside, she drew out a pair of latex gloves and pulled them on before reaching for the newest envelope. She ripped open the end and tipped the contents out onto the coffee table. There were three file folders, each crammed with paper and encircled with an elastic band. Her clenched stomach relaxed a fraction. Nothing directly related to her father...yet.

She picked up the first file, sliding off the elastic band and flipping it open. Inside was a Salem Police Department case file of a drug bust in Salem four years ago. She recognized the area in North Salem, knew it was a high-crime neighborhood brimming with low-income tenements and high unemployment. The file outlined the case against Doug Palmer, arrested on charges of possessing both heroin and cocaine with the intent to distribute. But unlike the files crossing her desk every day, this file was sanitized—witness evidence was included, but names and identifying information, like addresses and phone numbers, were blacked out. Leigh flipped through the rest of the file: case photos, lab and fingerprint reports, court documents. It was all there, but the only relevant names in the file were the officers involved and the perp.

Leigh moved on to the second file. It chronicled another drug bust, this time of a pair of students from Salem State University for possession and distribution of marijuana. Again, the file was complete, but sanitized, and nothing stood out.

She picked up the thickest of the three files. This file had combined documentation from both the Salem P.D.'s Criminal Investigation Division and the Essex Detective Unit.

It was a case gone wrong in every way possible. Not only drugs, but also illegal firearms. Attempting to escape, the perps had opened fire on the Salem P.D. In the end, one suspect was injured and another lay dead. Tragically, so was an eight-year-old boy in the adjoining apartment from a bullet that pierced the paper-thin wall and lodged in the back of his head while he sat eating dinner. Surprise shivered through Leigh as she recognized a name. Both deaths were investigated by Trooper First Class Robert Mercer of the Essex Detective Unit.

Robert Mercer?

Trooper Mercer was another of the fallen. He'd died years ago during a high-speed chase, losing control of his patrol car on black ice and dying instantly when his car hit a bridge abutment, leaving behind a wife and four children.

It had been the death of Trooper Mercer that opened up a position in the unit. An opening she'd applied for and won.

This was the first connection to the Essex Detective Unit. She'd suspected all along that someone inside her own department might have something to do with these deliveries, but so far lacked proof of any kind. But now when proof finally surfaced, it was through a connection to a dead officer? That didn't make sense.

She thought of the file locked in her desk drawer at work. She'd just recently picked up the closed case file for the criminal investigation that led to her father's death. She'd been busy lately, but knew that her reticence to re-hash her father's death, to relive it over again in minute detail, was the real reason she'd not pursued this investigation. Clearly, it was time to remedy that. She packed up the files and jammed them back in the envelope. As of now, she was back on the case.

Reflexively, she reached into her pocket. She just wanted to hear the sound of Matt's voice, for his warm tone and calm logic to steady her. Her fingers brushed the smooth surface of her cell phone before she froze.

You can't call him. Not about this. Not now.

Her shoulders slumped and she sagged back against the couch. Matt gave his time freely whenever she needed him, always without question or complaint. Now, when he was finally dedicating an uninterrupted weekend to his own career, how could she call him? It was bad enough they had a case; if she told him about this latest delivery, there was no way she could keep him from coming home on the first available flight. He was an invaluable partner in their cases, but first and foremost he was a scientist with his own research. And this weekend, he was off the clock with respect to criminal investigations. For this weekend, she had to give him that time. And to do that, she would have to keep him in the dark about this particular issue.

She looked at the clock. Eight-thirty. Maybe having that nice long soak right now was exactly what the doctor ordered. It would not only wash off the dust of decades peppered with mortar grit, but would take long enough that by the time she called Matt, he'd be at dinner and she could just leave him a message. By the time he got back to his room, it would be far too late for him to come home. And if she left a message, she could be brief and he wouldn't hear the stress in her voice.

She shifted uneasily on the couch, trying not to think about how angry he'd be when she finally came clean the next time they saw each other. But she pushed the thought away. She would give him the pleasure of a new case he'd love, and not ruin the rest of his weekend with her personal angst.

It was for his own good.

FOUR: FERMENTATION

Fermentation: the process by which yeast converts carbohydrates into alcohol, acids, and carbon dioxide.

Friday, 6:15 p.m.
San Francisco, California

BOSTON UNIVERSITY'S DR. MATT LOWELL shut down his laptop and pushed back from the cramped desk. Wincing, he kneaded the knot of muscles in his lower back with the heel of one hand and glared accusingly at the hotel room bed. Only two more nights and then he'd be home and back in his own bed. Or Leigh's.

As if on cue, his cell phone rang. Picking it up from the bedside table, he flipped it over. A slow grin spread at the sight of her name displayed on his screen. "Hey."

There was a moment's hesitation over the line. "Hey, yourself. I was afraid I was calling so late I'd miss you. Isn't your dinner at six?"

"Six-thirty."

"Lucky me, catching you just in time then. How did your presentation go?"

Shunning the bed-from-hell, Matt flopped back into the padded armchair next to the sliding glass balcony doors. "Pretty well, I think. Sometimes it's hard to tell with the science crowd, but there seemed to be some real

interest in the Old North. I'm sure there'll be more discussion around it over dinner."

"Even for West Coasters, it's a well-known historic
site. *'One if by land, and two if by sea'* and all that. On
top of that, I'm sure most people don't know there are
a thousand sets of nineteenth-century human remains
tossed in a charnel house in a corner of the basement.
I've lived in the area all my life and *I* didn't know it."

"It was a definite surprise to some. And while a lot of
the conference revolves around new dating procedures
and forensics, this was one of the only talks with a heavy
historical theme. It was standing room only in the conference room and we had to cut off questions when we
ran out of time before the next talk." He rested his head
against the high back of the chair, his gaze skimming
over the room. What was it about hotel rooms that made
them all look so generic? He'd never been to San Francisco before and yet he could swear he'd been in this exact
room on several occasions. He closed his eyes to block
out the suffocating mundaneness. "But enough about my
day. Caught any new cases?"

"It's funny you ask…"

Matt's eyes shot open and he sat bolt upright, pushing his dark hair out of his eyes. "You have something
for us?"

"Believe it or not, yes."

He surged to his feet, heading straight for the alcove
where he'd stowed his suitcase. "Really? What's the con-
dition of the body? It will be hours before I can make it
home. Can they hold the scene that long? Do you need
me to send in Kiko and the guys now? I could trust her
to run the basics so we don't lose scene containment—"

He froze with one hand on the handle of his bag at the sound of her laugh. "What's so funny?"

"You." He could hear the smile in her voice. "At ease, soldier. We have the scene secured and held for you. I know you're not back until Sunday night but what's a few more days when we have someone who probably died eighty years ago."

Matt sat down heavily on the corner of the bed, all urgency leaching away. "Eighty years ago?"

"Well, it's a rough estimate, but I might not be that far off. We're looking at skeletal remains, so time since death may not be clear. But at first glance, this case is as cold as it gets. At least that part of it is."

"Wait, back up. It's a *partial* cold case?"

"That's one way to put it." Leigh quickly explained her day, starting with her newest fresh victim and ending up inside the speakeasy with a skeleton in the wall.

Matt listened with rapt fascination until she finished. "That's amazing. All that time in a building still partly occupied and no one ever stumbled across it?"

"I looked into the provenance of the building and specifically that part of it. The back area was rented out with one of the front-facing stores for decades. They used it for storage. I called the son of the guy who leased it, and he said for as long as he could remember that space was wall-to-wall crates and boxes. He said you couldn't see the walls, let alone a secret inset door. When his father retired, they sold the business and the space has been empty since then, so far as he knows. From what we found, it looks like the speakeasy got raided and shut down, and has been lost to time for the past eighty odd years."

"Until you found it."

"Looks like it. I insisted the remains be left untouched

until you and the team could get in there. You'll have to bring down the wall. Riley wanted to be helpful and take it down for you, but I wouldn't let him. I told him you needed to be there, on scene, to supervise."

"You sure you don't want me to cancel the rest of the conference and come home early?"

"Don't you have another talk to give tomorrow afternoon?"

"Sort of. It's a panel discussion."

"Then stay. Honestly, the remains aren't going anywhere, and we have the place locked down and then some. For most bodies, we wouldn't have this kind of freedom, but this time we do."

"I'll let the team know." He let himself fall backwards onto the bed to stare up at the ceiling. "I've missed you."

The soft breath of her sigh traveled over the line. "I miss you too. More than you know."

A thread of something mournful in her tone caught at him. "Everything okay?"

"Yes, just busy."

His eyes narrowed; she'd hesitated a beat before answering. "You're sure?"

"Yes."

His gut told him she wasn't being entirely truthful, but he couldn't effectively push from more than twenty-five hundred miles away. "If there is something, you know you can tell me, right?"

"I know."

"Okay." He glanced at his watch. "Damn, I have to get going." He rocked back to a sitting position. "And because of the time change, by the time I get back tonight, you'll be in bed already. I'll call you tomorrow."

"Deal."

"I'll let you know if I can shuffle my flights and get back early." When she started to protest, he cut her off. "If I can, I will. You know the scene should be dealt with as soon as possible. I'll talk to you tomorrow."

He hung up and reached for the fresh shirt he'd laid out for dinner. But his mind was already thousands of miles away, fixed on the possibilities of a new case.

FIVE: WINE BRICKS

Wine Bricks: a method to skirt the intent of the Eighteenth Amendment. Producing wine at home for personal consumption was not illegal during Prohibition. Wineries and vineyards dehydrated grape juice and compressed it into bricks. Buyers were reminded not to place the reconstituted juice in a cupboard for twenty days because it would ferment and turn into burgundy, sherry, claret, or some other type of wine.

Sunday, 8:44 a.m.
The Adytum Building
Lynn, Massachusetts

MATT RUBBED HIS gritty eyes and peered up at the red brick building through the windshield of his SUV. "Leigh said the entrance is around back." Craning his neck, he scanned the few cars up and down the street until he found hers. "There's her car, so she must be here already." He turned to Kiko Niigata, his senior grad student who rode shotgun. "You're sure she said nine? We're not late?"

"Trust me, she said nine." Kiko studied him, one corner of her mouth tipped up as she tied her long black hair into a ponytail. In contrast to the delicate features inherited from her Japanese ancestors, she was no-nonsense American in voice, attitude, and athletic prowess.

"You seem a little overeager. How much coffee have you had today?"

"Does last night count as today too, seeing as I haven't been to bed yet? In any case I've lost count." A snicker from behind had him turning to stare at the two men in the backseat. Paul Layne, tall and loose-limbed with short spiky blond hair and an irreverent manner, openly grinned. Beside Paul sat Juka Petrović, dark and solid, with only a thread of an accent from his early years growing up in Bosnia—when he actually talked, that is; Juka was an observer and preferred to let Paul rattle on. Juka solemnly stared at him with a straight face, only the twitching corners of his lips giving anything away. Matt leveled an index finger at Paul. "You try taking the red-eye with a shrieking toddler and see how *you* do. Coffee would be your best friend as well."

"Coffee is always my best friend," Paul quipped. "Screaming toddler notwithstanding."

"Of course it is." At this point, Matt would have sold his soul for just a fraction of Paul's energy, even if it was chemically induced. "Let's unload and take it all with us in one trip."

They piled out of Matt's SUV. Paul and Juka grabbed the heaviest of the backpacks and most of the tools, leaving Matt with a lighter load. They might cheerfully give him a hard time, but they were always there to carry more than their fair share if needed.

They circled around the back of the building, easily finding the brick archway from Leigh's description. Matt led the way up the stairs, pausing briefly to look at the speakeasy grille at the entrance, and then pushed into the building.

Leigh was just coming out of a passageway on the

far side of the room. Instead of the forgettable business suits and sensible shoes she usually wore on the job, she wore faded jeans that hugged her athletic body and a dark blue, long-sleeved T-shirt with the Massachusetts State Police logo. Her long blond hair was pulled back into a high ponytail that swung as she walked. Her face lit up at the sight of them. "You're early." She smiled for the group, but her green eyes locked on Matt.

"Matt's had a little too much coffee. He's lucky he didn't get pulled over for speeding." Paul hurried across the room and peered down the stairs. "This is awesome. Can we go down?"

"Sure. But be careful. The treads wrapped in crime scene tape are unstable and you have to step over them. Don't go past the main room"—Paul disappeared from view and Leigh had to raise her voice—"and don't touch anything!"

Kiko rolled her eyes at the empty doorway. "Don't worry, we'll keep him in line. Paul, wait up!" She and Juka followed Paul down into the basement.

Shaking her head at their usual antics, Leigh moved to follow them. Matt caught her hand, spinning her back toward him so she bumped up against his chest. His arms slipped around her, holding her in place.

She braced a hand against his shoulder. "Matt, we're supposed to be working."

"And we will be shortly. But I want thirty seconds to say hello first, seeing as I haven't seen you in five days." He lowered his head, brushing his lips over hers, feeling hers part in a smile under his before he dove in. Her hands slid up over his shoulders to link behind his neck as her body naturally curved against his. He forced himself to keep the kiss short, just enough to tide them over. Pulling away, he rested his forehead against hers. "Hi."

Leigh chuckled. "Hi." She brushed fingertips over his cheekbone. "You look exhausted. You didn't have to take the red-eye. We could have held the scene until tomorrow. What time did you land?"

"Left at nine-forty last night, landed at Logan just after six this morning. And I didn't want you to have to hold the scene any longer than necessary, when truthfully the last day of the conference was just breakfast, wrap-up, and networking. The only thing I really missed was last night's gala dinner and that's not a crisis."

"Aside from the fact that you're dead on your feet."

"It's not that bad. Nothing five or six coffees won't cure." When she rolled her eyes, he grinned at her. "And it's worth it to see you a day early. But now it's time to get to work." He forced himself to let go and step back. He extended an arm toward the open doorway. "Ladies first. I didn't hear any screams, so I assume everybody made it down in one piece."

Leigh led the way down the steps and into the main bar area. All three grad students were standing in the middle of the dance floor, eyes wide and mouths agape.

"This is seriously *cool*," Paul said. "It's like a real mobster's speakeasy."

"This isn't *like* a real mobster's speakeasy," Kiko corrected. "It's the real deal."

Matt wandered through the room, carefully skirting tipped chairs and chunks of crumbled plaster. He stopped at the blackjack table. "It's amazing to think the last hands to hold these cards are long dead."

Kiko crouched down beside the woman's shoe in the

corner. "And think of how the world has changed since then. Fashion, feminism, politics…"

"A World War," said Juka.

"Technology," said Paul. "All the scientific break-throughs of the last eighty years: penicillin, the polio vaccine, microprocessors, and landing on the moon. It's a different world."

"I think it's safe to say the people who lived in this world"—Matt swung an arm wide—"would hardly recognize the one we live in now." He turned to Leigh. "You said the remains were in a back room?"

"This way." She led them into the room behind the bar. Piles of crates were now stacked neatly against both side walls. "When we discovered the place, this room looked like a bomb had gone off. Crates and glass bottles everywhere. We had Crime Scene Services take photos first to preserve the original appearance for the historians, but once they were done, we boxed the bottles and stacked everything out of the way so you'd have room to work." She stopped in front of the small hole in the back wall. "This is as far as we got. Once we knew what we were looking at, we stopped and held the scene as is."

"Thanks." Matt dropped his backpack to the floor and searched through the contents. He finally pulled out a flashlight and stepped up to the tomb. Fishing an arm through the gap and flipping on the light, he pressed his forehead against the rim of bricks. There was a long moment of silence as he examined what he could see of the remains. "Single victim, fully skeletonized. Minimal clothing remnants, but leather belt and shoes are present. There's some kind of powder residue around the body. No obvious signs of trauma at first glance. Body positioning though…" His voice trailed off.

"What?" Leigh asked.

Matt's gaze shot to his students before sliding back to Leigh. "I'm not sure your vic was dead when the wall went up." The horror in her eyes was the same he felt in his gut. "I should be able to prove it either way, so let's hold that thought for now." He turned back to study the wall, and then wiggled one of the exposed bricks at the opening. "We're going to have to be careful bringing the wall down. When you made the initial break in the wall, some of the bricks had to go through, but we can't risk any more falling without possibly damaging the bones. We need to loosen the mortar and then use crowbars to pull everything toward us, moving the debris out of the way as we go. Kiko, you're small and flexible. If we get this hole just slightly wider and give you a boost up, can you squeeze your head and shoulders in there and get a full set of inside shots before we go any further?"

"Sure." Kiko knelt down and opened up her camera bag, drawing out the big SLR they used for crime scenes.

"The Crime Scene guys have already done that," Leigh reminded him.

"I'm sure they have, but I bet they were shooting the remains. I want those too, but what I'm thinking of is the wall. If the vic was alive when he was bricked up, there might be evidence of an attempt to escape. We'll destroy that evidence when we pull down the wall."

Leigh winced at the thought, but nodded.

"You understand what I need, Kiko?" Matt asked.

Kiko patted the body of the camera lens. "Help me get in there. I'll get your shots."

"Great. Now—" He stopped short when a voice echoed down the stairs.

"Hello!"

Leigh's wide gaze met his. "Rowe?"

They waited while the sound of clattering footfalls came closer. Seconds later, Rowe appeared in the doorway. "Am I late? You said you were meeting at nine."

"We got started early," Leigh said. "It's Sunday morning. I didn't think you were coming."

Rowe gave her a flat look. "You really thought I was going to miss this?"

"I guess not."

"Damn straight." Rowe crossed the room. "Just getting started, Lowell?"

"We are." Matt picked up a heavy steel mallet and a cold chisel by the handles and held them out to the medical examiner. "In the mood to get a little dirty this morning?"

"You bet." Rowe took the mallet, swinging it up lightly to rest on his shoulder.

Matt picked up the other set of tools. "Let's get started then."

Sunday, 9:27 a.m.
The Adytum Building
Lynn, Massachusetts

"THAT'S FAR ENOUGH!" Matt set down his mallet, head down, on the floor. "I don't want to lose any more of the wall if we can help it." Wiping the sweat from his brow, he dragged the mallet out of the way, leaning the handle against a crate.

Leigh eyed the wall; the remaining section was less than three feet high. "You think that's enough?"

"I'd rather leave it as intact as possible. It's low enough now I can climb over the top and get in there. I don't want to risk the wall losing stability and falling onto the remains. Kiko, one more round of photos, then I want to have a good look before we start packing the remains for transport."

They all waited while Kiko took the last set of pictures. "That should do it," she said, stepping back. "Matt, you're sure you don't want me to get in there? I'm the smallest of all four of us." His cheeks warmed as her gaze moved up and down his body, even though it was clearly a clinical evaluation. "You're going to have trouble fitting your shoulders in that gap."

"If I get stuck, I'll wave a white flag." He bent over to hide his discomfort, pulling out a Tyvek jumpsuit and concentrating on pulling it on over clothes now covered in grit from demolishing the wall.

"Just offering. You know where to find me if you change your mind." She grinned and bent down to put the camera away.

Matt zipped up the suit and then swung one leg over the threshold, carefully balancing on his toes. "Paul, give me a hand. I'm not sure how stable the wall is now and I don't want to knock it down." Paul moved to stand beside him and Matt braced his hand on the younger man's shoulder, keeping some of his weight off the bricks as he slid over the top. Reaching down with a booted foot, he found a clear section of wood floor and slowly transferred his weight. Swinging his other leg over, he settled into the tomb.

Carefully placing his boots, he crouched down on the balls of his feet, having to stay nearly parallel to the wall to allow his upper body to fit inside the two-foot gap. He glanced up at Kiko, who was smirking.

"Maybe you should lay off the rowing a bit," she suggested.

"Not going to happen." Finding his balance, he turned to the remains. The victim had been lying with the upper body partially rolled on its side at the time of death, one hand pressed to the wall, the lower arm thrown over its head. The ribs had fallen in a tumbled scatter as the body slowly settled and dissociated. The leg bones were stretched out, a few ankle bones still tucked into the uppers of cracked leather shoes lying pressed against the end wall. Delicate bits of cloth settled over raised sections of bone: dark, thickly woven wool from a suit and the fine weave of a cotton shirt, once probably white, but now stained and aged to a light mocha. He touched a gloved index finger to the edge of a piece of wool and it crumbled to dust. Scanning along the body to the phalanges of the right hand still pressed to the brick, his stomach dipped at the sight of deep shadowed gouges in the mortar of the outside wall and the small spots of dark staining on some of the lighter bricks. Picking up a distal phalange, he turned it into the light, immediately finding subtle abrasions on the very end. He tried not to imagine the horror of lying in the dark, feeling the grainy mortar squeeze through your trembling hands, clawing at the wall until your fingers bled and you scraped bone. Tearing and kicking at the four walls of your own tomb. He pushed the thought away, concentrating on the purely scientific appraisal of the victim before him as he set the small bone back into place.

"Better analysis back in the lab but here's your preliminary report." Matt paused as Leigh pulled out her notebook and pen. "The skeleton is fully articulated and appears to be totally intact. The long bones are all fused, so it's an adult, but I need to get a look the pubic symphysis and a better look at the skull sutures to be more specific about age." He studied the pelvis and then shifted to bend over the skull. "Definitely male. Dentition as well as nasal aperture and bridge suggest he was white. I'll confirm when I examine the palate."

"Shouldn't he have mummified behind a wall like this?"

Matt shook his head. "Mummification requires large amounts of dry air to desiccate the tissues rapidly before bacteria-induced putrefaction can set in. That didn't happen here. And walled off like this, it's doubtful any rodents or insects got to the body. He simply liquefied." He pointed at a thick line of white powder below the ribs before crouching down. "Juka, hand me a spatula and a sample jar."

Juka pulled the items from his backpack and handed them over the wall.

Matt loosened several small chunks of the dried powder, collecting them in the sample jar before handing it back. "We'll run it on the mass spec." He looked up at Leigh. "Back to the decomp process. We're assuming this is a murder victim."

"Doubtful it's a suicide," Paul mumbled to Juka. "Pretty hard to brick yourself in like that."

Matt gave him a narrowed stare before turning back to Leigh. "As a murder victim, the body wouldn't be embalmed, so decomp would have progressed normally. Do you see how this powder follows the contours of the body, almost like a chalk outline?"

"Yes."

"Whatever this is, it was either on the body or under it and as the body putrefied and liquefied, it puddled with the body onto the floor."

"But where did it all go? The…puddle… I mean."

Matt rapped his knuckles on the plank floor. "It drained through the gaps. There might be a dirt floor under this. If so, it just percolated into the soil. If it's a concrete foundation, then it settled there and dried. But notice the only scraps of material left are raised off the floor. And do you see this discoloration of the wood under the body? As decomp progressed, the putrefaction products on the floor became very alkaline. The puddle essentially dissolved all the natural fibers of the clothing and chemically burned the floor itself."

"Can you tell how long the remains have been here?"

"That one's going to be tougher," Matt said. "If this body is from Prohibition times, I can't use the atomic bomb curve because the bones pre-date it. But I could use a combination of uranium, polonium, and lead isotopes."

"Something doesn't make sense to me," Kiko said. "If he decomposed behind the wall, how was it no one smelled anything? A brick wall and wood floor…there must have been some gas exchange with the room air."

"I can go one further," Juka said. "How did no one notice a brand-new wall in this room?"

"I think I can answer that," Rowe said. "You guys missed what this room looked like when we found it on Friday." Reaching into one of the open crates stacked against the side wall, he pulled out an empty whiskey bottle. "This was a storeroom. Whoever put up the wall only had to move whatever boxes were against that wall, brick in the victim, and then move the boxes back so the wall was essentially invisible. Unless someone had a very sharp eye, they might not notice the room suddenly got a few feet shorter. And remember what it was like back then. If anyone smelled decomp, they might have just assumed a rat died in the wall. But I'll bet this place was always so full of cigarette smoke and sweat from all the bodies, the smell of decomp probably got lost. Certainly no one reported it back then."

"And clearly he didn't get out on his own." Leigh rested an arm lightly on the bricks and leaned in to peer over the edge. "Did he try?"

Matt set a hand against her shoulder, gently pushing her back. "Watch the wall. Kiko, did you get all the shots we need?"

"Yes."

Kiko's relaxed expression told him she must not have been able to visualize the gouges through the camera's two-by-three-inch display. *Just say it. There's no way to pretty it up.* "There are several significant gouges in the mortar and some faded bloodstains on the brickwork. It wasn't enough force to displace the bricks, but he knew what was happening to him and struggled to escape."

Kiko gave a small jerk, her face going pale. "That's *horrible*. Did he starve to death?"

"Assuming there wasn't any trauma," Rowe said, "which isn't ruled out yet, he likely asphyxiated first. We can calculate the oxygen capacity of that space and a time frame."

"As far as trauma goes, we'll have to examine the bones in the lab," Matt said. "There's no obvious fatal trauma, but that doesn't mean there isn't any traumatic damage." He noticed Juka staring fixedly at the remains of the wall, eyes narrowed and head tilted at a thoughtful angle. "Juka, what have you got?"

Dark eyes rose slowly to his. "Have you ever built a brick wall?"

"Myself? No."

"I helped my father do some repairs to our garage once so I have a little experience. Here's the thing—mortar doesn't set *that* fast. If the victim could claw at the wall, he probably could have pushed hard enough to displace the bricks and bring the whole thing down. So why didn't he?"

Paul leaned in to look again at the remains. "Any sign of rope remnants in there?"

"Implying his hands were tied?" Matt shook his head. "Nothing visible. We'll check under the remains once they're moved, of course."

"I think it's simpler than that," Rowe said. He rapped his knuckles against a wooden crate. "This was a storeroom so there were plenty of crates in here to use to stack against the wall. Maybe the victim was unconscious when the wall started to go up. If the killer was skilled as a master bricklayer, he could probably put up a wall like this pretty quickly. Then all he'd have to do is stack a series of crates in front of the fresh wall." He glanced upwards, squinting at the ceiling. "That's nine, maybe ten feet high? He'd need to stand on something to finish the job anyway. So he built his own platform as he worked, immuring the victim behind the new wall. The victim was trapped no matter what he did."

"Awful way to go." Stooping down again, Matt picked up a button from the floor by the ribs. "Shirt button?"

"Too big," Rowe said. "Maybe off a suit jacket?" He pulled on a pair of latex gloves and held out his hand for the button before turning it back and forth in the light.

"It's probably celluloid. Check out the gorgeous Art Deco styling. That by itself will help us date this man."

"Shoes and belt won't help," Matt said. "They look well made, but of standard style. Now this is off his shirt for sure." He handed a silver cuff link inlaid with black enamel over the wall to Rowe.

"Classy."

"Very." A flash of gold caught his eye and Matt gave a low whistle. "Now this…this doesn't look standard." He held a ring up to the light: a huge square cut, blood-red ruby set into a thick gold band, flanked by two square cut diamonds. A sunburst was carved into the gold band on each side.

"Whoa," Paul breathed. "That thing is huge."

Matt held it up into the light, using an index finger to scrape some of the white powder out from inside the band. "It took a bit of a beating from being on the floor and flooded with all those decomp products. But all things considered, it's in pretty good shape." He squinted down at the band, angling it into the light beam and rubbed at it again. "There are initials inside the band. It looks like… C.W.?"

Matt jerked when a hand clamped over his wrist. His gaze shot sideways to find Rowe standing just on the other side of the wall from him, his intense gaze fixed on the ring.

"C.W.?" Rowe's voice was strangely hoarse.

Alarm mixed with confusion surged through Matt's veins like ice water. "Does that mean something to you?"

Instead of answering, Rowe took the ring, holding it up to the tripod light.

Even though Matt was just on the other side of the half

wall, he only barely caught Rowe's mumbled words. *It couldn't be.* "Couldn't be what?"

Rowe turned slowly, the ring looped over the first knuckle of his index finger. "Have any of you heard of a big local politician during the Depression who pulled a Jimmy Hoffa?"

Leigh stepped forward and grasped Rowe's gloved hand, angling it so the old-fashioned dull facet cuts caught the light. "Pulled a Jimmy Hoffa?"

"Disappeared without a trace. His name was Charles Ward. Ward was a congressman and it was one of the worst kept secrets of the day that he had his eye on the White House. Even during the Depression, he had the money to take a run at it. He was also rumored to have ties to the Mob."

"You think this is Ward?" Matt stared down at the bones at his feet. "Buried behind a wall for all these years?"

"It would explain his disappearance."

"You think it was a Mob hit?" Paul asked.

Rowe frowned. "I guess that would depend on why they might want to kill him. But hidden behind a wall wasn't really the Mob's style. The Mob way back then was in the middle of the street with a Tommy gun. Any way we can trace this ring?"

Leigh held out an evidence bag and Rowe dropped the ring into it. She sealed the bag and stared at the ring thoughtfully. "I can try to see if there are any family members still around."

"They might have photos of him and we can see if he's wearing the ring," Matt said. "Maybe the B.U. archive would also have photos."

"Can you get me a better description of our vic? An

estimate of height and body build? Maybe a partial medical history?" she asked.

"I can do all of that back in the lab. And I'll get you an estimate of how long the bones have been here."

"I have a feeling finding out who he was may be the easy part." She looked over the wall at her newest victim. "What happened to you? And who hated you so much they'd bury you alive?"

SIX: THE UNTOUCHABLES

The Untouchables: a group of nine Prohibition agents recruited and led by Eliot Ness to fight organized crime in Chicago in 1929. The name "Untouchables" was coined by newspapers after multiple attempts by Al Capone to bribe members of the unit. Allegations of corruption in the unit likely stem from disbelief that agents earning $2800 per year would refuse $2000 per week in bribes, or that Frank Basile—Ness's friend, assistant, and driver—was a reformed convict. The Untouchables were disbanded in 1931 after Al Capone's conviction for tax evasion.

Sunday, 3:12 p.m.
Abbott Residence
Salem, Massachusetts

"YOU'RE SURE YOU don't want to take a nap?" Leigh asked as they entered her kitchen.

Matt set his duffel bag down on the floor by the door. "I'm fine." It was a bald-faced lie and he knew it. He suspected she knew it too, but he wasn't about to take an afternoon nap like a toddler, not when they were back together for the first time in days. "But I wouldn't mind more caffeine." His stomach gave a queasy, acidic roll at the thought of coffee, but he ignored it and pulled his laptop out of his bag.

"You're running on a mixture of adrenaline and caffeine already; no way am I giving you more. You need to ease back. How about something to eat instead? I have some leftover Chinese from last night I can warm up to hold us until dinner, since we never ate lunch."

"Sounds good."

They were just back from Boston, having transported the skeletal remains to Matt's lab at Boston University. Once the bones were secured in the lab, Matt sent his students home with instructions to be back in the lab the next morning at nine o'clock to get started on the real examination. He and Leigh then drove back to Salem for a quiet dinner together.

Matt pulled out a kitchen chair, more collapsing into it than sitting. Setting his laptop on the kitchen table, he booted up. "I'm curious about this Charles Ward character."

"I'm kind of half hoping it's not him," Leigh said from inside the fridge as she pulled out folded paper cartons.

"Why?"

"We had enough of a media circus in the Simpson case. The last thing I want is another victim that attracts attention."

Matt glanced up at her over the top of his screen. "You don't want to trip over that reporter again."

"Jason Wells? Absolutely not. I'd be happy to stay off his beat forever." She started dishing food onto plates.

"Here he is… Charles Ward. Born eighteen-ninety-six, no date of death. He was last seen by his wife on February fourth, nineteen-thirty-six. He went out that night and never came home. The wife had him legally declared dead in nineteen-forty-three but no trace of him was ever found. Look, here's a picture of him with Babe Ruth in nineteen-thirty-five before Boston's first home game of the season. That was Ruth's last year playing." He turned his laptop around to show Leigh the black and white picture of Babe Ruth in a Braves uniform and dark ball cap, holding the end of a bat and standing beside a man in a dark three-piece suit with slicked-back dark hair, oval spectacles, and a shrewd gleam in his eye.

Leigh paused in the process of loading the first plate into the microwave to squint at the screen. "He looks rich."

"He was rich. Rich, and, for his time, famous. And if Rowe is right, tied to the Mob." He turned the laptop back around and started to zoom in on the image. "Son of a bitch. Come look at this."

Leigh started the microwave before crossing the room to join him. "What?"

"Does that look like the same ring to you?" Matt pointed to the now grainy blown-up image. A heavy ring with a dark, square-cut stone encircled the fourth finger of Ward's right hand.

Leigh whistled and then glanced sideways to meet his gaze. "Could be. We'll need to find some more pictures and I need to contact any remaining family. But that'll have to wait until after I've informed Mr. Holt's next of kin about his death. We had trouble tracking down his dentist over the weekend, but Rowe is expecting the dental charts first thing tomorrow. Once we have the ID confirmed, I'll inform the family."

"Guess you won't need me this time? Since that's not my case and all."

"I've got this one, thanks. Coincidental locations don't make for connected cases."

He leaned back in his chair, crossing his arms over his chest and giving her a measured look. "But you don't believe in coincidences."

"True. But you're not going to tell me that the deaths of two unrelated people who died eighty years apart are connected, are you?"

"You have a point. Fact is stranger than fiction, but that one doesn't make sense even to me."

The microwave dinged. "Why don't you put that away for now," Leigh suggested. "Let's take this into the living room. You're going to drop if you try to push it much further. That way, if you doze off into your plate, you're already on the couch."

Matt closed the lid of his laptop and pushed it a few inches away. "Normally I'd be all for a few extra hours of work, but right now my concentration is shot."

Leigh handed him a plate of steaming rice, stir-fried vegetables, and pepper steak. "Go on, I'll warm up my plate and be there in a minute."

Matt's steps dragged as he wandered down the hallway. He misjudged the turn into the living room, scraping his shoulder against the door frame. Rolling his eyes at his uncharacteristic clumsiness, he set his plate down on the coffee table, pushing a large white envelope sealed in a clear plastic bag out of his way. He started to straighten and then paused, his gaze going back to the envelope. *Looks like an evidence bag.* Curious, he flipped it over.

Shock and disbelief left his mouth sagging slackly. Having seen the other envelopes, he knew exactly what it was. The end was ripped open—clearly Leigh already knew the contents—but she hadn't felt it important enough to share with him? They'd been together all day. He could understand that she wouldn't want to mention it in front of the students, but they were alone before starting the recovery. She could have mentioned it. Or after the drive back to Salem. There was more than enough time then.

Leigh's uncharacteristic hesitation on the line during Friday night's call suddenly sprang to mind. Surely this was the reason—this little emotional bomb that likely arrived in Friday's mail. Which meant she'd left him in the dark on purpose.

An unexpected, illogical fury rushed through Matt, drowning exhaustion under a wave of temper. Gripping the envelope in a white-knuckled fist, he stormed back to the kitchen. Leigh's back was to him as she took her plate out of the microwave. "What the hell is this?"

Leigh whirled, startled by his tone of voice. "What is wh—?" She stuttered to a halt at the evidence in his hands, color rising in her cheeks. "Oh…that. It came a few days ago."

"And you weren't going to tell me about it? I thought we were a team. Maybe even more than that."

"We *are*." Her eyes went to slits as her voice rose. "But just because we're a team doesn't mean that I need to share every single thing that comes into my life."

"That's what partners do, Leigh. They help each other share the load. You shut me out." His words lashed out, the tone razor-sharp.

"Give me some credit, will you?" She twisted her hands together, the skin mottling in patches of white and red under the growing pressure. "Maybe I was trying to do you a favor."

"How, exactly?"

"Believe it or not, I was trying to respect the fact that you have a life and responsibilities of your own. You always make yourself available when I need you. This time, you had your own work."

"I was three thousand miles away. I wasn't going to just pop in," he snarled. "You purposely kept me in the dark."

"You know very well that you'd have come home if I'd asked. You probably would have come even if I said not to. You were willing to jump on a plane just because of the case. So if I'd told you that another package arrived, you'd have been on my doorstep for sure."

"Wouldn't it have been nice if you'd let *me* make that choice? Yes, my work is important to me. But apparently you think you aren't?"

"That's not what I'm saying!" In frustration, Leigh turned back toward the counter, bracing her hands against the edge and leaning on stiffly locked arms, pausing to take several deep breaths. "Look, this is getting us nowhere," she said to the cupboards in an attempt at a more measured tone. "I made a judgment call, knowing that you were going to be coming back soon and I could show you then. But I wasn't expecting you until tonight at the earliest, and I didn't think I'd see you until tomorrow."

"Which is why you carelessly left it on the table. Leigh, this came to your *house*." He tossed the envelope onto her kitchen table with more force than necessary, and it slid nearly all the way to the far edge. "They know where you live. You shouldn't be the only one who knows about this. You should have told me."

She whirled on him, her eyes snapping with anger. But something else hidden behind the anger caught at him, something darker and heavier, something that weighed on the soul. "Don't you understand that I wanted you here? That every time one of these packages shows up, the bottom drops out of my stomach and I break out in a cold sweat? That I'm afraid to open the package because I don't know if I'm going to be able to breathe after seeing what's inside? Do you know what it took for me *not* to call you and beg you to come home, to be with me when I opened it?"

Matt's anger drained away in the face of such bleakly naked pain, leaving him hollowed out in its wake. He reached out a hand as if he could touch her through the fifteen feet separating them. "Leigh—"

But she continued as if she hadn't heard him. She didn't meet his eyes and her hands were clenched into fists at her side, her body stiff. "You were my courage the second time around. Having you beside me let me draw from your strength when it felt like I didn't have any of my own. And there you were on the other side of the country and I was alone and I didn't know if I could do it without you and—"

He simply couldn't take any more and crossed the room to pull her against his chest. His arms wrapped around her, one hand cupping the back of her head, stilling her words as he pressed her face against his throat and rocked them both from side to side. "Leigh, no more. For the love of God, no more. I'm here now." He closed his eyes, bending his head low to press his cheek against hers. "Shhh…"

For a moment she stood rigid in his arms, and then hers wrapped around him, her hands catching great fistfuls of his shirt and hanging on. For long minutes he rocked her, holding tight and rubbing her back slowly with his free hand. Finally, a great warm sigh gusted against his throat and she started to pull back. He let her go, but only far enough to cup her face and search her expression.

Most of the color had left her face, accenting the dark shadings of stress and exhaustion under her eyes. He ran his thumbs softly over her cheekbones. "I'm sorry." He bent and pressed a soft kiss to her mouth. "I'm overtired and I was way out of line."

She sighed quietly, capitulation heavy in the sound. "I haven't been sleeping well since this arrived and I've been feeling guilty about not filling you in on Friday night and—"

Matt laid an index finger over her lips. "No harm, no foul. But next time, give me the option. If you don't want me to come, tell me and I won't. But don't leave me in the dark. You could have even had me on the phone with you. Or Skype. Anything. We can always find a way to work it out."

Her head tipped downward and she nodded.

Slipping a finger under her chin, he angled her face back up toward him. "And I don't want to hear you say you don't have the strength to do it on your own. You're one of the strongest people I know. Clearly, you did have the strength. But next time, don't put yourself through it. Now, can you tell me what's in the envelope?"

She took a deep breath and let it out slowly. "Nothing too horrifying this time, thank God. Three drug bust files, two from the Salem P.D. Criminal Investigation Division but there's one file from the Essex Detective Unit involving Trooper First Class Robert Mercer."

"You've never mentioned him."

"That's because he died in the line of duty shortly before I joined the unit three years ago." She hesitated, gnawing on her bottom lip. "I know you want to see this stuff, but can it wait? I'm tired, and you're exhausted. I'd rather look at it again when we're both fresh. I promise we will. Just…not tonight."

"All right, not tonight." He glanced down the hallway toward the living room where his meal was getting cold. "Let's eat and then grab a shower. We're both covered in mortar dust. Then let's relax for the evening and we'll start again fresh tomorrow."

"Sounds good. Go get your plate and I'll warm it up again."

At the doorway, Matt looked back into the kitchen, taking in Leigh's pinched lips and furrowed brow. They needed to get to the bottom of this investigation into Leigh's father. It was taking too much out of her, always catching her unawares and keeping her on edge.

Maybe it was time to pull in the big guns. And when it came to sneaky and under the radar, from what he'd heard, there was only one man for the job.

Rob Tucker.

Sunday, 4:36 p.m.
Abbott Residence
Salem, Massachusetts

"Now that you're showered, would you like a glass of wine? As long as you don't think it'll make you fall—" Freshly showered and dressed casually in yoga pants and a fleece hoodie, Leigh stopped abruptly in the living room doorway, the words dying in her throat.

Across the room, Matt lay stretched out on the sofa, one of her throw pillows stuffed under his head and held in the crook of his arm. His eyes were closed, his lashes throwing shadows over the already dark smudges under his eyes as his chest rose and fell rhythmically.

The caffeine had run its course, and the last thirty-five hours plus their argument had finally caught up with him. He was asleep.

Tiptoeing across the room, Leigh lifted the warm woven throw blanket from the back of the couch. She shook it out and then gently laid it over him, tucking it around him. Bending down, she pushed his damp hair aside and dropped a light kiss onto his temple, just above the scar he acquired during a firefight in Afghanistan. He mumbled something unintelligible, the last word drifting off into a soft sigh.

Picking up her book from the end table, she sat down in a nearby wing chair, tucking her feet up under her. With one last look at her exhausted partner, she opened her book and settled in, keeping watch as he slept.

SEVEN: ROOT BEER

Root beer: a nonalcoholic beverage first developed in the eighteenth century by Temperance activists in the naïve hope that it would replace real beer in popularity.

Monday, 2:15 p.m.
Beacon Street
Boston, Massachusetts

THE ICY WIND whipped the last of autumn's dried leaves around Leigh's feet as she climbed the front steps of the magnificent four-story brownstone. Here in Beacon Hill, she was surrounded by some of the grandest houses Boston had to offer. Hunching her shoulders against the cold, she knocked on the door and then quickly jammed her fists in her pockets. Winter's chill was already in the air, and she regretted leaving her gloves behind on the kitchen counter when she left the house that morning.

As the seconds dragged by, she found her gaze drifting across the street to where the historic Boston Common stretched down the hill toward the Public Garden. Over the years, the Common had been a cow pasture, a gathering place, an execution site, an Army campground, and the Central Burying Ground dating from 1756. Now the oldest city park in the United States, it was nearly deserted on this gloomy, breezy afternoon with only a few lone figures hurrying through, stooped against the wind and clutching Starbucks coffees. Through the denuded trees, Leigh's gaze found the soaring Soldiers and Sailors Monument, a tall neoclassical column dedicated to the men of Boston who lost their lives in the Civil War.

The sound of a lock sliding back caused Leigh to turn back toward the house. The heavy green door opened to reveal a young woman in neat black pants and a tailored white shirt, her hair in a perfectly coiffed, conservative bob. "May I help you?"

Leigh proffered her badge. "Trooper Abbott of the Massachusetts State Police out of Essex. I'd like to speak with Evelyn Holt."

"I'm sorry, Mrs. Holt is not receiving callers this afternoon."

The woman started to close the door and Leigh slapped her palm against it, holding it open. "I'm sorry, perhaps I wasn't clear. This isn't a social call. I'm here on police business and need to see Mrs. Holt immediately."

Leigh watched the internal struggle reflected in every nuance of the other woman's expression, but she held her ground. She wasn't leaving until she had informed next of kin.

With a restrained sigh, the other woman stepped back, opening the door wide. "Come in. I'll see if Mrs. Holt is available."

She will be, Leigh thought as she entered a foyer of elegant Venetian plastered walls, rich hardwood floors, and a sweeping mahogany staircase. She tried to not look awed by her surroundings, but the moment the woman disappeared down the hallway, Leigh spun in a slow circle, goggling at the quiet opulence. Easily one hundred and fifty years old, the house's owners had meticulously maintained the nineteenth-century accents—high ceilings, ornate crown moldings, intricate wainscoting, and gleaming wood as far as the eye could see.

Leigh managed to close her mouth and stop gaping like a tourist just before the woman returned.

"Madam will see you now. She's working in the library, but has consented to a short visit."

Leigh followed the other woman down the hall, past a richly furnished living room that looked out over the street and the green space beyond. They continued down the corridor until they reached a closed door. The other woman opened the door just far enough to lean in. "Trooper Abbott, ma'am."

The older woman didn't even raise her head from where she bent over her writing desk. "Thank you, Hilary. You may bring the tea now."

Hilary waved a hand for Leigh to enter and she stepped into the room. The door closed behind her with a quiet *click*.

For a moment, the room remained silent except for the scratch of pen on paper as the older woman continued her writing. Trying not to grow impatient at the obvious slight, Leigh let her gaze drift over the room. It was a classic English library, paneled in satiny dark wood. Mrs. Holt's wide writing desk sat before the window, the late afternoon light falling over neat stacks of cards and envelopes. A fireplace of gold marble stood between towering built-in bookcases crammed with leather-bound books, and a heavy iron chandelier hung from the ceiling, filling the room with a subtle glow enhanced by pairs of sconces on each side of the mantel. When she continued to be ignored, Leigh wandered over to the classically styled globe mounted on a tall wood pedestal and gave it a gentle spin with her fingers.

Mrs. Holt set down her pen and turned slightly in her chair. "My apologies, Trooper. We had a charity fundraiser for the Boston Children's Hospital and I'm still writing thank you notes for organizers and contributors a week later. Now, what can I do for you?"

Leigh took a seat in an overstuffed armchair near the desk, finally getting her first real look at the older woman. Mrs. Holt appeared to be in her mid-seventies, but the brightness in her eyes reflected a much younger mind. She wore an elegant silk blouse and her steel-gray hair was swept back into a neat chignon. Clearly an afternoon at home was cause to dress formally, even when company wasn't expected. "Ma'am, I'm sorry to bring bad news, but your son's body was discovered in an abandoned storage space in downtown Lynn on Friday. My condolences on your loss."

Mrs. Holt's face pursed with confusion. "I'm afraid that you must be mistaken, my dear. Peter is fine. In fact, he's meeting me at L'Espalier for dinner tomorrow night."

Leigh leaned forward, the insistence in her tone punctuating the serious nature of her message. "I'm afraid there's no mistake, Mrs. Holt. We've confirmed identification by dental records." The woman froze in apparent shock, and Leigh forced herself to gentle her voice, to soften the blow. "But you're more than welcome to identify the deceased. Some victims' families find it gives them closure when such a sudden death occurs. I can arrange that for you."

For a moment the older woman simply stared at her blankly, her back ramrod straight and her only movement an occasional flutter of her eyelids. When she finally spoke, there was a tremor behind her words. "I don't understand. 'Victims' families'? Was he mugged? Kidnapped for ransom? There was no request for money."

"I don't know why he was killed, but my team and I are hard at work on this case. Your son was found in a building down by the Central Square train station in Lynn. He was found with his wallet in his pocket and still wearing an expensive watch, so it doesn't appear to be a robbery. But he'd been shot."

The facade of cool sophistication crumbled slightly as the older woman's hand rose shakily to cover her mouth and her eyes went wide.

"Can you tell us if your son was having any difficulties in his personal or business lives? If he had perhaps argued with anyone lately, or disagreed with anyone publicly or privately? Anyone at work or in the family?"

"No, not that I know of." Bracing one hand on the desk, Evelyn Holt rose unsteadily on slender high heels and crossed the room to the circular brass bell pull installed near the door under an aged black and white photograph of a man in a dark suit and stiff white collar. As she pulled on the handle, the faint peal of a bell shimmered through the air somewhere down the hallway. Returning to her chair, she sank down, some of the starch leaving her as she sagged back weakly.

A moment later the door opened and Hilary leaned in. "Yes, ma'am?"

"Bring the Hennessy with the tea."

The younger woman's brow furrowed with concern, but she simply said, "Yes, ma'am." She disappeared from sight.

Mrs. Holt took a breath, a deep, jagged inhalation. "Peter was an only child and we have no other family in this area anymore. It was just the two of us after cancer took my husband ten years ago. Peter was a good man and an even better son. Some might have considered him boring, but he was truly dependable and reliable. He was just never one to blow his own horn. I would consider that admirable, not boring." She paused for a second, her fingernails digging into the arm of the chair as she fought for control. And won. "He was in finance, working at Rutherford and Fisk. Well-respected in his community and by his coworkers, but he wasn't a risk taker. It wouldn't be within Peter's personality to have a problem with anyone that could lead to murder. He wasn't aggressive enough." A shudder went through her at the last word. "You're sure it was…murder?"

"Yes, ma'am." Leigh pulled out her notepad and pen. "What about his personal life? Friends, lovers…is there anyone who might wish Peter harm?"

"Peter was married once when he was in his twenties, but he and his ex-wife went their separate ways after only a few years. She was killed in a boating accident about six years ago. Nice enough girl, but she wanted more than Peter was capable of giving, would ever be capable of giving. But it scared Peter off marriage. He's had a casual girlfriend for years—Cheryl Ballantine—but it's not anything serious, more a relationship of convenience. Someone to take to company functions, that sort of thing. We Holts are an independent lot, and we're usually happiest in our own company." Her eyes closed briefly and Leigh imagined that she was realizing that her own company was all the family she had left now.

Hilary entered the room and set the tea tray down on the desk. She deftly poured tea into a delicate china cup for Mrs. Holt, adding a large splash of amber brandy from a crystal decanter before handing it to her. The cup rattled violently in the saucer, sloshing tea over the rim before the older woman set it on the desk. Raising the cup to her lips, she took a long sip.

"No, thank you." Before Hilary could even ask, Leigh waved her off, and then waited until they were alone again. "Mrs. Holt, there's another aspect of this case I wanted to discuss with you. The lack of evidence at the location where your son's body was discovered indicates that he was killed elsewhere and then moved."

The china cup clicked sharply as it lowered to the saucer. "Why would someone do that?"

"We're looking into that. But does the location mean anything to you?" Leigh rattled off the address on Union Street, her heart sinking at the expression of confusion on the woman's face as she shook her head.

"I'm not familiar with it. Peter spent all his time in Boston; there was no reason for him to go back to Lynn."

Leigh drew in a breath to ask her next question when a single word struck home. "Go *back* to Lynn?"

"My family was from Lynn. I was born there. But my father died when I was a young girl. In the years following, as the Depression continued, as factories closed and the unemployment rate skyrocketed, my mother didn't like being so close to the water and away from the center of town. She felt we were isolated and could be the target of a desperate laid-off factory worker or even a drifter. So we moved to Boston to be close to her family. When she remarried, we stayed. I still own the family home back in Lynn. We used to use it as a summer home for trips to the beach but it's been over ten years since we've gone there. Lately there's never been any reason for us to go, and certainly no reason for Peter to go on his own. It's so…blue-collar."

Some of Leigh's sympathy dissipated as irritation rose at the thread of snobbery in Evelyn's tone. "And so it was beneath him? Even though it was your hometown?" The questions slipped out before Leigh could stop herself.

"It was a different city when I lived there. Before the Depression, it was a booming business town. After the Depression, after the jobs disappeared, it became the lower-income area it is today. There's nothing wrong with the working class. We just have so little in common with them. They don't move in the same social or financial circles as we do. Peter would have had no connection to any of them." At the sound of her son's name on her own lips, the older woman swayed for a moment and laid her hand on the desk to brace herself. Leigh half-rose to her feet, but Mrs. Holt held out a hand to hold her back. "I'm sorry, but I find that I am unwell. You understand that this news has been a shock. I'd like you to go now."

Leigh quickly crossed the room to the bell pull and gave it a quick turn. Returning to the woman's side, Leigh leaned over her, genuine concern for the woman spiking at the sight of her pale face and dull, glassy eyes. There was no mistaking the genuine distress. She pulled a business card from her pocket and laid it on the desk. "This is my contact information. Please call me later and I'd be happy to connect you with the medical examiner's office. Can I get you anything in the meantime?"

"No." Mrs. Holt rose shakily to her feet, just as Hilary came through the door. "Hilary, please help me upstairs. I'm not feeling well."

Leigh stood by helplessly as the younger woman wrapped an arm around Mrs. Holt and firmly grasped her elbow. The older woman leaned on her, practically slumping into her arms. Hilary started to lead her out of the room, Leigh following slowly behind.

Hilary looked back over her shoulder. "Can you find your own way out?"

"Of course." Leigh followed them to the door and was nearly out of the room when the framed photograph on the wall over the bell pull caught her eye. Surprise stopped her dead in her tracks.

The photograph was of a man in his thirties, with slicked dark hair and a confident bearing. But she'd seen those oval spectacles and that shrewd gleam in his eye before. He sat, straight-backed, in a formal armchair, his hands folded neatly in his lap.

It was the man in the photograph with Babe Ruth. And he was wearing the ruby ring they'd found with the remains.

"Wait!" Leigh leaned around the doorway. Hilary and Mrs. Holt were several feet down the hallway, but Hilary stopped and half-turned. "Who's the man in the portrait here? The one by the door."

Hilary stared at her as if she'd lost her mind. "That's Mrs. Holt's father. Mr. Charles Ward. Now, if you'll excuse us…" Turning her back, Hilary continued down the hallway, leading Mrs. Holt toward the back of the house.

Leigh stepped back into the library, pulled out her cell phone, and snapped a quick picture of the portrait. Then she stood slack-jawed in front of the image of Charles Ward, her heart tapping like a military drummer against her ribs.

This changed everything.

EIGHT: FORESHOTS

Foreshots: the first distillates coming off the still containing methanol and impurities with boiling points lower than ethanol. For this reason, old-time moonshiners would always discard the first bit of shine that came off the still. This part of the run, known as the foreshots, smells like high-powered solvent, tastes even worse, and is potentially poisonous.

Monday, 4:03 p.m.
Boston University, School of Medicine
Boston, Massachusetts

"RIGHT HUMERAL HEAD is 49.1 mm." Matt waited while Juka noted the measurement before moving to the opposite side. He was just adjusting his calipers around the bone when the lab door opened and Leigh entered the room. Straightening, he set the instrument down on cold steel. "How did it go this afternoon?"

"You remember our discussion last night about how I don't like coincidences?"

The hair on the back of his neck rose in response to her tone. "Yes."

"I don't like them. *At all.*"

The bottom dropped out of Matt's stomach at Leigh's tone. Something was very wrong. "What happened?"

"I just told Mrs. Evelyn Holt that her son was found shot in an abandoned storage space in Lynn."

"And...?"

"She was very upset. Her son lives alone, so she had no idea he was even missing. She still thought she was having dinner with him tomorrow night. So, it was a shock. But that's not the important point. As I was leaving, I happened to notice a framed photograph on the wall. Black and white, circa early nineteen-thirties." She pulled out her cell phone, called up the photo, and extended it. "If you hadn't shown me that picture last night I wouldn't have caught it, but this is the same man. And I don't mean Babe Ruth." She paused, as if unwilling to deliver bad news. "Charles Ward was her father. Holt is her married name."

"No way!" Paul pushed back from his workstation and surged to his feet. "The two vics are related?"

"Grandfather and grandson." She leveled an index finger at the remains. "Assuming this is Charles Ward, which we haven't proven yet. But we're considerably closer considering the man in this picture I just saw was wearing what looked like the ruby ring we found."

Matt circled the gurney. "There's no way it's a coincidence if this really is Ward."

"No way at all," Leigh agreed. "And now we have a whole different case."

"We sure do." Kiko rose from the bench where she'd been studying the skull under the brilliantly lit magnifying lens. "We thought this victim was just a historical mystery. Now it has to be more than that."

"This victim could be the key," Juka said.

"Exactly what I'm thinking. His mother described Peter Holt as dependable and boring, not the type to enrage anyone to the extent that they'd want to murder him. So we're left with the question of why he was killed." Leigh slid her messenger bag off her shoulder and dropped it on Matt's desk before turning to the remains. "I thought this case was going to be a fun challenge—a case with limited evidence and no witnesses, but no real rush because anything older than seventy-five years isn't really considered a relevant police case. But if this murder is the key to Peter Holt's death, the lack of evidence and witnesses could hobble us."

"Hold on," Matt said. "We have a witness. Or at the very least, we have a source of information."

"Yes, we do. Whether he's a witness or not remains to be seen." She pulled a file folder out of her bag, flipping it open. "The original story came from Mr. Samuel Kain."

"How old is he?" Kiko asked. "You said he's in a nursing home, right?"

"Yes. He's ninety-six."

"Can we assume that at ninety-six he's not responsible for your most recent victim?" Matt asked. "He wouldn't have the means or the opportunity."

"Or the strength to carry the dead weight of a body," Leigh said. "Rowe did the autopsy this morning and he's sure the body was moved after death. No way would a ninety-six-year-old man be capable of that."

"But he could have been responsible for the man behind the wall." Juka circled the table to join the group. "If he's ninety-six…" He paused for a moment as his eyes narrowed and went unfocused. "He was born in nineteen-sixteen."

"Charles Ward was last seen in February of nineteen-thirty-six, right?" Matt looked to Leigh, who nodded in confirmation. "Kain was twenty in nineteen-thirty-six."

"He could have done it," Paul said. "But did he have the skills to brick him up behind a wall? I suspect you won't be able to ask him any of these questions."

"It doesn't sound like he's lucid most of the time." Leigh flipped through the pages in the folder. "I have some of the family contact names so it's a place to start. But that's for tomorrow." She closed the folder. "Have you got anything on the remains to prove this could be Ward?"

"We've been at it all day, so we have quite a bit." Matt motioned her over to the gurney.

Leigh tossed the file onto Matt's desk and crossed the lab to join the team. "Was the preliminary information you gave us on Sunday correct? White adult male and all that?"

"Yes, although now I can be more precise with the age. And it fits right in with what we might expect if the remains really are those of Charles Ward. Pubic symphysis, the sternal end of the fourth right rib, and skull sutures all corroborate an age at death between thirty-seven and forty-five. Palate confirms race as white American. Victim height was approximately one hundred and eighty centimeters or five-foot-eleven."

"That photo—he was shorter than Babe Ruth by several inches. Anyone know offhand how tall Babe Ruth was?" When the room stayed silent, Leigh's gaze darted over the three male faces. "I thought you were good ol' American boys. Don't you learn these things at your daddy's knee?"

Juka shrugged. "I was born in Sarajevo. For us it's all about soccer."

"Hold on, I've got this." Paul broke away from the group to return to his writing station. He flipped his laptop open and in a few clicks and keystrokes had his answer. "Professor Google says Babe Ruth was six-foot-two."

Leigh turned to Matt. "That would be about right, wouldn't it?"

"Pretty much right on. You know, to definitively nail this down, we're going to need to do DNA analysis. You have a living breathing relative right there. If we could get a DNA sample from her, we could compare it to DNA extracted from this femur. Wouldn't hurt to take a sample from the grandson for comparison."

"If we're building this as the story, we should make it as complete as possible. I'll let Rowe know you want a sample from Peter Holt. You talked about doing a test for determining the age of the bones. We need to know if we're looking at the right time period. Maybe whoever this is has been in there since nineteen-twenty-eight, so there's no way it could be Ward."

"I'm not going to be able to get you so close that you'll be able to differentiate over the span of less than a decade. This is a tricky time period. Some isotopes measure well in the last fifty years, post-bomb curve. Others, like carbon-fourteen, are supposedly good from fifty years, but really test at their best when it's hundreds or thousands of years in the past. We're in that awkward in-between time frame, but I'll do what I can. We haven't had a chance to pull samples yet because we've been looking at victim ID and cause of death instead." He grinned when Leigh lit up like a kid on Christmas morning at his words.

"You have cause of death? I thought you couldn't see any trauma?"

"I couldn't then, squeezed into that tiny space with insufficient lighting and the victim partially rolled over.

But once we got decent lights and a microscope on the bones here all that changed. We have two locations of injury, so let's start with the fatal blow. There are two score marks visible from this injury—one on the inferior surface of the left clavicle and one on the superior surface of the first left rib." Matt picked up the clavicle from where it lay above one of two arcing columns of ribs. He turned it so the gentle double curves faced Leigh and ran his index finger past the upper edge of a depression that followed the line of the bone. "It's right here, just beyond the groove of the subclavian sulcus, a muscle attachment point."

Leigh leaned in, squinting. "It looks like some kind of abrasion."

"Exactly. This will get a lot clearer when you see it under the microscope." He moved to a microscope and flipped on the light source before adjusting the focus. "We've talked about kerf marks and how different tools leave different shapes. Knives and axes leave a V-shaped trough in the bone, although the kerf a knife leaves is much narrower. Saws tend to leave a squared-off trough." The defect came into view. *There you are.* He paused for a moment, fine-tuning the focus before stepping back and holding out a hand, inviting Leigh to look.

She bent over the scope, examining the defect Matt had seen only moments before—a trough cut into the bone with smooth, squared sides. "He was killed with a saw?" She glanced up from the scope at him. "It must have been pretty narrow to fit in there."

"I kind of set you up there. No, it's not a saw. Saws leave a similar kerf mark, but because of their teeth, they leave striations in the bone. Do you see how smooth the sides of the walls are?"

Leigh turned to look again. "Now I do. Not a saw then."

"No. Also note the physical characteristics of the kerf mark. Deeper on the anterior side—toward the front of the body—and shallower on the posterior side. Since we're seeing the same type of kerf mark on both the rib and the clavicle, that suggests a blade that slants in on both sides."

"It's some kind of angled blade? How wide is that groove?"

"1.4mm."

"So narrow, but without a knife edge. What kind of odd blade is that?"

"One that isn't really meant to be a blade. Now, keep in mind we aren't going to conclusively prove it by finding the murder weapon because that's likely long gone, but Kiko has a great idea as to what it might be."

Leigh stepped back from the microscope and turned around to find Matt's senior grad student by the gurney. "Okay, I'll play. What are you thinking?"

Kiko retrieved her laptop from her workstation. "Remember, I'm an artist, and one of the things in an artist's toolkit is a palette knife. It's a small trowel, about four or five inches long with a wooden handle and a pointed triangular blade. That made me think about other times I'd seen something similar but bigger in size. Juka helped me track it down." She brought up a picture on screen of a trowel with a pale wooden handle connected by a short metal arm to a wickedly pointed triangular blade. "This is a bricklayer's pointing trowel. It's used for applying and smoothing mortar when laying bricks."

"Ouch." Leigh stepped closer, bracing a hand on the desk and leaning in closer. "That looks sharp as hell."

"It would be," Matt said. "Sharp enough to do the job.

Also, very sturdy and strong, which I think was needed for the second injury."

"The same tool was used for both?"

"I think so." He picked up two vertebrae from the lower back and led Leigh over to the lighted magnifying lens, setting one of the bones down on a stainless steel tray on the counter. "Come in close, because I'm going to have to angle this so you can see it. Now, this is T-12 or the last of the thoracic vertebrae. Normally, it's oriented like this, with the body of the vertebrae facing toward the anterior side and the spinous process projecting out the back on the posterior side of the body. This hole in the middle, the vertebral foramen, is where the spinal cord runs through all the vertebrae in sequence." He angled the bone under the bright light. "Can you see the defects around the spinous process?" He indicated the narrow bony projection angling downward from the posterior side of the bone.

Leigh moved in close, resting her cheek against his shoulder as she leaned in to look through the magnifying lens. "I don't see what you're… Wait, yes I do. Those nicks in the bone?"

"That's them." He turned the bone over. "This is the inferior side, or the bottom of the bone. This is a little tougher, do you see that scoring?" Her head moved in a nod against his shoulder. "Do you see how it goes right under the body of the vertebra? That's going to be key." He set down T-12 and picked up the next vertebra. "This one is L-1. Take note that this bony projection, the superior articular process, is chipped on the right side and shows several nicks that I'd describe almost like false starts with a saw. Additionally the superior surface of the body is scored. Put it all together and we have a good idea of what happened." He flipped off the bright light and Leigh stepped back.

"We've taken samples from both locations to look for trace evidence, but at this point, I'd be willing to testify that one weapon was responsible for both injuries. The back injury came first." Matt turned around, using an index finger to draw a line over his back, slightly below his kidneys. "Vertebrae T-12 and L-1 are right here. The killer used the pointing trowel to immobilize his victim, using it as a blade to cut the spinal cord between those two vertebrae."

Leigh winced. "He used a trowel to cut the guy's spine? Wouldn't that be hard to do?"

"It wouldn't be easy," Matt said. "For starters, the bony projections on the vertebrae are not only for attachment of the back muscles, but also to protect the spinal column. The chips and nicks in the bone are testament to multiple attempts to force the blade through. Also, because of the presence of the spinous process, he'd have to come at the spinal column slightly from the side. But the scoring on the bone goes clear past the vertebral foramen to the body, so it's clear that the tool passed through the spinal cord, severing it."

"That would take pure brute strength," said Paul. "And a very sharp trowel."

Kiko picked up one of the vertebrae, examining it. "I think the only way to make it work was to have the victim facedown on the ground. One or two downward thrusts with the blade and he'd be able to get it through the spine if he really leaned on it. But even still, the killer must have been strong."

"Aren't we assuming he was a manual laborer?" Juka asked. "If he was a bricklayer, he had to be strong since he'd be lugging sacks of mortar and piles of bricks for a living. A pampered politician who probably never did a day of manual labor in his life would be no match at all for him."

Leigh moved back to stand at the head of the gurney. "So the killer paralyzes his vic. That gives him the time to brick him in because the vic can't walk away."

"But he could move his arms," Matt said.

"The gouges in the wall. He was paralyzed from the waist down, but he still tried to claw his way out. Although he never had a chance because of the crates shoring up the wall." Leigh looked back up at Matt. "So if the man was trapped, why the fatal injury? Rowe said he would have asphyxiated inside that wall. Why not let him die slowly?"

"Because it would have been too slow. Imagine you were the killer," Matt said. "You could kill the man outright and then hide the body, but instead you keep him alive during the process. Why?"

"Revenge," Paul said. "It's the only thing that makes sense."

"I agree. If it's the kind of death we think it was, the killer wanted his victim to suffer and know exactly what his fate would be. But, the killer also didn't want the vic lasting until morning when someone might come in and hear yelling from behind a bunch of crates and a brand-new wall. I think he tried to find a middle ground. That was the fatal blow. Not deep enough or angled enough to hit the aorta or the heart, but it could easily have hit the internal thoracic artery. Now, I don't for a moment think our bricklayer had that kind of anatomical knowledge. He probably was simply trying to miss the heart itself, and, in doing so, missed most of the major vessels as well."

"It had to be a little nick," Kiko said, "or else Ward would have bled out fast and we know that didn't happen."

"Agreed. But he would have been gone for sure inside an hour or two, probably less. And during that time, he gets bricked in. Then the killer camouflages the new wall and simply walks away while the victim dies, then later decomposes and liquefies. Which reminds me, I know what that powder around the remains is. I dropped it off with a colleague first thing this morning to run it on the mass spec and he sent me the results about an hour ago. It's pretty simple stuff. Calcium oxide." When Leigh simply stared at him blankly, he said, "Maybe you've heard it by its common name: quicklime."

"Uh…no?"

"Then Paul's going to be your man on this one because he's been researching it since we found out." Matt turned to Paul. "What have you got?"

Paul leaned back against the benchtop and casually crossed his ankles, basking in the attention. "A couple of interesting things, actually. For starters, the most important aspect of quicklime chemically is its ability to bind sulfur compounds."

"That totally explains it," Matt said.

Kiko and Juka murmured in agreement.

Rolling her eyes, Leigh waved a hand. "Sorry, but the dummy in the room doesn't get it. What does that totally explain?"

"First of all, you're *not* the dummy in the room," Matt said. "You're just the only one without a science degree."

"That makes me feel so much better," Leigh muttered with a sideways glare.

"And none of us have a degree in criminal justice, so you can run circles around us there. Okay, let's put this in perspective for you. Remember Tracy Kingston?"

"I'm never going to forget Tracy Kingston."

Early during their first case together, the team had stumbled across Tracy's mutilated and decomposing body when they interrupted the murderer digging her grave. The scar puckering Matt's right biceps was testimony to the life and death struggle that had ensued.

"Let me be more specific. Do you remember just before the firefight, when I stopped you because I could smell the decomp gases coming off the body?"

Leigh nodded. "Putrescine and cadaverine. I remember."

"Exactly. Those are among the sulfurous compounds produced during decomposition."

The light dawned in Leigh's eyes. "Ohhhhh. That totally explains it."

Matt patted her shoulder and grinned. "There's an echo in here."

"Quicklime has actually been used in open burials for centuries," Paul continued, "and likely for just as long in clandestine shallow graves to hide the smell of decomposition. Calcium oxide binds with the sulfur in those compounds to produce calcium sulfate, a totally non-odiferous compound. That still leaves all the nitrogen-based compounds and a few others, but it will knock down the worst of the smell."

"So whoever put the vic behind the wall dumped in

the quicklime knowing the body would decompose back there and not wanting anyone to be able to smell it." Leigh looked down over the expanse of pale bones. "I hate to say it, but that was clever."

"It was," Paul agreed. "Now, there's one extra piece to the puzzle. Keep in mind how the body was hidden behind a fresh brick wall. So whoever hid the body was familiar with masonry. And up to the time of the Second World War, quicklime was one of the major components of mortar."

"Add this to the murder weapon and all the dots connect." Leigh started ticking points off on her fingers. "A bricklayer would know all the components of mortar and would have those materials on hand. He used a tool at hand to kill and then to camouflage. He had the strength to carry it out."

"And then he walked away," Matt said, "his crime completely undetected. What are the chances the old guy did it?"

"After all this time? He might have simply been an accomplice after the fact who knew about the body's location. Remember, he never said exactly where the body was. And we don't even know that he *was* a bricklayer. Maybe he was just told about the body, but not responsible for it himself. I'm going to have to talk to him, but I'm not sure what reliable information I'll get. It might be a better idea to talk to his family."

"Let's do both," Matt said. "Can you arrange it?"

"I can. You want in on it?"

"Do you even need to ask?"

"Then I'll set it up. Can you get DNA going ASAP? ID on this vic is going to be a crucial point for the Peter Holt case."

"You get me comparison samples and I'll get you your answers right away." He grinned at her. "And in the meantime, let's take Samuel Kain on a walk down memory lane."

NINE: PROOF

Proof: refers to the alcohol content of a beverage. In the U.S., proof is equivalent to twice the alcohol content as a percentage of volume. Thus, a 100-proof beverage is fifty percent alcohol by volume. The term originated in the eighteenth century when the rum used to pay British sailors was "proofed" by mixing it with gunpowder to see if it contained enough alcohol to burn.

Tuesday, 1:32 p.m.
Office of Chief Medical Examiner
Boston, Massachusetts

"I'M READY." EVELYN HOLT squared her shoulders, her expression coldly set as she stared resolutely at the shuttered glass separating her from her son. Dressed all in black, with her hair scraped back into a tight bun that erased any trace of softness from her face, she exuded an air of brittle stoicism.

A silent spectator, Matt leaned against the wall on the far side of the viewing room beside the only furniture—a small nondescript couch and an end table with a box of tissues and several pamphlets on grief counseling. He'd asked to attend the viewing, and, to his surprise, Leigh had agreed. Only moments before, Leigh had escorted Mrs. Holt into the room, but the older woman had looked neither left nor right, and his presence remained unremarked.

Leigh stepped up to the small intercom on the wall, pressing the small white button. "Open the blinds, please."

The blinds immediately slid open to reveal a small, spare room on the other side of the glass. A single table in the center of the room held a form under a long white drape. A technician in green scrubs and a white lab coat stepped away from the window to the head of the table. She looked over at Leigh, who nodded. The technician pulled back the drape and folded it neatly over the chest of the corpse.

Evelyn Holt's back was to Matt so he couldn't see her face, but her single sharp indrawn breath cut through the silence as she swayed slightly on her feet. Concerned she was about to collapse, Matt pushed off from the wall to take a single step toward her, but the older woman reached out a shaky hand to steady herself on the windowsill and he froze.

Leigh gave him a single small shake of her head and he stepped back.

"Mrs. Holt," Leigh said gently, "can you confirm that this is your son, Peter?"

"Yes." The single word was hoarse and laden with unshed tears. "That's Peter." Giving up the pretense of indifference, she dropped her head into her hands and started to weep.

Leigh nodded through the glass at the technician who quickly covered the body again. Taking her arm, she helped the older woman over to the small couch, settled her onto the cushions, and passed her the box of tissues. For a moment, the room was quiet except for Mrs. Holt's jagged breathing as the elderly woman struggled to pull herself together.

Leigh laid a hand on her arm, rubbing lightly. "Mrs. Holt, is there anything I can get you? Anyone I can call for you?"

"No, thank you." Mrs. Holt wiped her face and daintily blew her nose. "Is there anything else you know at this time about Peter's death?"

"Nothing so far, but I will be talking to Peter's coworkers and to Ms. Ballantine either later today or tomorrow."

"If there's anything I can contribute, anything to help speed up the process, you'll let me know, won't you?"

Leigh didn't even blink in the face of an apparent bribe. "That won't be necessary, Mrs. Holt. I have all the resources I need, but thank you for the offer."

Mrs. Holt wilted slightly at the rejection. "When can I get…when can the funeral home come to get Peter?"

"As soon as they can arrange it. He can be released right away. We have some personal effects that were found at the scene. We'll need to hold onto them for a little while longer as evidence but I'll let you know when they can be returned to you."

Mrs. Holt blinked owlishly at Leigh for a moment, as if she was having trouble following the conversation. "What personal effects?"

"What he was carrying at the time of his death. His wallet and keys, his cell phone. What appears to be a pair of antique cuff links. They look like a family heirloom and are probably valuable, but they're well-protected here and I'll get them back to you as soon as possible."

"Cuff links? We don't have any heirloom cuff links in the family."

"They're small gold ovals with inlaid blue stones depicting a Roman ruin. But perhaps—Mrs. Holt!"

Matt jumped forward as the older woman started to
topple off the couch, catching her shoulders even as Leigh
tightly grasped her arm. Together they eased her back
on the cushions.

The older woman was already starting to push their
hands away. "Are you all right, Mrs. Holt?" Leigh asked.

Mrs. Holt closed her eyes as if fighting a wave of pain.
But when she opened them moments later, her expression was blankly composed. So alarmingly so that Matt
drew back in surprise at the woman's control.

"Thank you." She shook off Leigh's hand and stood.
She regally straightened her spine, once again fully in
charge of her emotions, despite her tear-streaked cheeks
and red, watery eyes.

"I'll walk you out," Leigh said.

Jaw clenched, Matt balled his hands into fists to keep
from reaching out, repeating the mantra in his head as
his one chance walked toward the door. *Throw it away,
throw it away, throw it away.*

The two women slowly crossed the room. Mrs. Holt
paused briefly at the door, carelessly dropping the used
tissue in the wastebasket near the doorway. Then they
were gone.

Matt sagged back against the wall in relief. Victory
snatched from the jaws of defeat at the very last second.
He strode over to peer into the garbage can, satisfaction
spreading warmth through his chest at the sight of the
single tissue sitting in the otherwise empty can. *Gotcha.*

Leigh reappeared, pulling back sharply as she nearly
ran into Matt standing so close to the doorway. She put

a hand out to brace against his upper arm. "What are you doing?"

"IDing our vic." Matt reached into his pocket, pulling out a pair of latex gloves and sliding them on.

Hand on hips, Leigh narrowed her gaze on his jeans. "Do you always carry gloves?"

"Lately, yes. I never seem to know when I'm going to need them since I met you." Bending over, he picked up the discarded tissue. "But I admit this time I planned it."

Leigh's look of confusion suddenly cleared, her expression taking on a sly cast of understanding and approval. "That's why you wanted to be here. You wanted to see if we could get her DNA."

"Considering why she was here, it didn't seem unlikely to me. Unless she was hard as diamonds, she was going to be emotionally shaken by the sight of her dead child. It's natural. And since you didn't seem to want to come out and tell her about the possible identification of the remains behind the wall…"

"I'm going to have to tell her if it really is Charles Ward. But right now, while we're looking at two members of her family dead and I'm not sure what the connection is, I'm leery to give anything away until we know for sure. And she *was* hard as diamonds. Did you catch her reaction at the end there?"

"I caught it, all right. I thought she was going to pass out for a moment and then, five seconds later, she's cool as a cucumber. It was kind of creepy."

"Show no weakness, I guess. But to be fair, she's not exactly a young woman and seeing her own child on a morgue table had to be a shock."

"I'm not disagreeing with you there. Luckily, she broke down long enough to need a tissue. And since she discarded it and it's perfectly legal to test any sample re-covered from it, I think this is our best angle right now." He pulled a small evidence bag from his pocket, securely sealing the tissue inside before stripping off his gloves and discarding them in the garbage can. "I'm going to take this in now. I've already dropped off the femur DNA sample and the sample from Peter Holt, so I'll get this added into the analysis ASAP. Are we still on for the nursing home tonight?"

"We are. It's time to finally meet the man who started this whole case."

TEN: JAKE LEG

Jake leg: a little known Prohibition-era affliction affecting the spine, causing partial paralysis and an inability to walk normally. A nationwide epidemic resulted from the use of ortho-tri-cresyl phosphate by drug manufacturers to denature Jamaica ginger extract, a late nineteenth-century patent medicine that was more than seventy percent ethanol by weight.

Tuesday, 7:02 p.m.
Saint Joseph's Nursing Home
Lynn, Massachusetts

"THANK YOU VERY much for agreeing to meet with us on such short notice. Please, sit." Leigh sat down on the loveseat in the small reception room. Matt settled beside her as members of the Kain family all found seats around a room decorated in soft pastels with rolling landscapes dotting the walls. A room meant to soothe, Leigh supposed. She scanned the array of faces staring back at her. "We appreciate so many of you being able to come out."

"We're happy to." Barb McDermott, a stout woman in her mid-forties wearing a brightly patterned floral dress, had established herself as the spokesperson for the entire family from the very first handshake. "Once you told us something had come from Grandpa's story, we were all dying to know more. He's never really said much about his early life."

All twelve of them were crammed into one of the nursing home's small family rooms, a room really meant for no more than six. Younger relatives sat on couch arms or the floor, leaving the more comfortable seating for their elders. Family members ranged from their early twenties to their late sixties: a daughter, several grandchildren and their spouses, and a cluster of great-grandchildren. Three generations come to talk about a fourth.

Barb sat forward in the large wing chair she had selected to accommodate her girth, but also one conveniently adjacent to Leigh—what she no doubt saw as a place of honor. "You were a little vague on the phone. You actually found a body? He was telling the truth all this time?" Excitement tinged her voice.

Leigh imagined this was probably the most exciting thing that had happened to this family in a long time. "We did. But the story gets a little more complicated. We actually discovered the body in an abandoned speakeasy from the nineteen-twenties or thirties."

The family members gave collective gasps and murmurs of surprise before questions started coming at Leigh from all sides. She raised both hands for silence. "One at a time, please."

She dealt with their questions patiently, describing the speakeasy and the body found in the storage room, but carefully leaving out the fresh body and the location of the remains behind the wall. Once the family worked through all their questions, the room finally became quiet again.

"If it's all right, I have some questions about your grandfather before we go see him."

"Great-Grandpa's not in trouble because of this, is he?" Connor, one of the younger family members, spoke up from the floor. Dressed in a dark polo shirt and neat khakis, he sat with his back against the pale, mint-green wall.

"It's honestly hard to say at this point," Leigh said, trying to balance the truth with reassurance so the family would remain open to her questions. "All we have right now is the story about a body in a building and those remains. We have absolutely no evidence of who committed the crime."

"You are sure it's a crime?" Barb asked. "There's no way it was an accident?"

"None." Matt had stayed quiet up to this point, letting Leigh handle the questions and steer the conversation to suit her needs, but now he stepped in. "That's my part of the investigation, and it's very clear the victim was murdered."

"Are you like one of those CSIs on TV?" This question came from Heidi, another one of the younger family members. She smiled widely at Matt, her gaze slipping boldly down to run over him.

"Yes, but we do it in better lighting and with realistic time frames," Matt said dryly.

"Do you get to carry a gun? Is it really as cool and exciting as—"

"Let's stay on topic." Leigh cut the young woman off, telling herself it wasn't from irritation that the girl was openly flirting with Matt, but rather to keep the investigation on track. "We wanted to ask about the elder Mr. Kain's life here in Lynn in the nineteen-twenties and thirties."

"We're happy to tell you what we know." Ethel, Samuel Kain's youngest daughter and only surviving child, sat just beyond her daughter, Barb. A slender woman, she had the frail appearance characteristic of many older people; Leigh was afraid a good wind could knock her down. A tremor shook the winkled, arthritic hands in her lap as they clasped and unclasped. "But, as Barb said, Dad wasn't ever very willing to talk about his past. He had a hard life and didn't like to dwell on it. Bad memories and all. And now we may never hear about it. He was diagnosed with Alzheimer's about ten years ago."

"Actually, he's done rather well," Matt said. "Most Alzheimer's patients survive only about seven or eight years after diagnosis."

Sadness tugged at the edges of Ethel's lips and reflected in blue eyes cloudy with glaucoma. "I lost my best friend to it in less than that. But I think Dad's time with us is coming to an end."

"Is he aware of his surroundings?" Leigh asked. "If we wanted to ask him some questions, would he be able to answer them?"

"Like most patients here, he has good days and bad days," Barb said. "So it will depend on what kind of day he's having. Most of the time, you only get his attention for a short time, so don't beat around the bush. It will also depend on what your questions are. If you want to know what he had for lunch last week, you're out of luck. But if you want to know about his years on the front lines during World War Two, he might be able to remember that. Often the old memories are clearer than the recent ones."

"And some days it's all gone," said David, Barb's husband. "It's kind of a crapshoot."

"Fair enough," said Leigh. "I guess we'll find out

shortly. Can you give me some family history? Your father identified that specific building, but was he living in Lynn at the time?"

"Minus his time overseas or with the Civilian Conservation Corps, Dad lived all his life in Lynn," said Ethel.

"The Civilian Conservation Corps? What's that?"

Leigh turned toward the voice. Even in this overcrowded room, the young man in the corner seemed a solitary figure. He certainly appeared to be the square peg in the round hole—his ripped fatigue pants and unkempt hair brushing the collar of his ratty T-shirt were a stark contrast to the rest of the neatly dressed and involved family. She'd noticed that when the barrage of questions had come earlier, he'd been the only one to remain silent, a watchful sneer on his face. He'd been introduced as "Eric" by his father, but had offered neither a smile nor a handshake during the greetings.

"Didn't you ever pay attention to anything Great-Grandpa said?" Connor's derisive tone only highlighted the irritated glance he threw at his cousin. "Considering your obsession with the Army, I would have thought you'd have at least paid attention to that. It was a government program during the Depression to train and employ manual laborers. They built state and national parks, planted trees to increase the country's forestlands, built bridges, buildings, roads, and airports."

"Did they build your precious astronomy tower?" The snide comment was accompanied by a curled lip.

"Aren't you paying attention now? I said *during the Depression*. High Rock was built in nineteen-oh-four, decades before." His eyes drifted to the window. High above them on a hill in the center of town, spotlights lit the tall, square Romanesque Revival tower. "And you should never make fun of gainful employment. At least I'm contributing to society, which is more than you can say."

"Not now, boys," snapped Craig, Eric's father, speaking to both young men, but only sending a searing glare toward his own son.

Eric returned a poisonous look while Connor dipped his head in apology.

Noting the family dynamics and filing it away for later reference, Leigh glanced sideways, meeting Matt's gaze and holding it. She didn't need his words to know they both focused on the same point. *Built bridges and buildings.*

Leigh turned back to Ethel. "Do you know what he did with the Corps?"

"I don't know what specific projects he did, but I do know that's where he trained to be a master bricklayer."

Beside her, Matt's body went very still. She shifted slightly, hiding the press of her hand against his thigh as she pulled out her notepad. *Play it cool.*

"They trained him during the Depression," Ethel continued, "and then in the late thirties and early forties, when the economy picked up again and construction jobs became more plentiful, he started working for a local contractor. He did one tour of duty overseas with the infantry in World War Two after Pearl Harbor, but came back to bricklaying when he returned. He married Mom when he was back stateside and they started a family. That was how he supported the family in the boom years following the war. They couldn't build fast enough. In later years, when the lifting and carrying got to be too much for him, he became a construction foreman."

"You mentioned he married," Leigh said. "Is your mother still alive?"

The room went deadly silent, so much so that the hair on Leigh's arms stood up as if the electrical charge in the room had suddenly shifted.

It was Barb who finally broke the silence. "I guess you don't know."

"I wouldn't have asked if I did," said Leigh. "What don't I know?"

"Grandmother was murdered in nineteen-seventy-five. It was a home robbery gone wrong and the man responsible was convicted several years later. We don't like to talk about it," Barb finished stiffly.

"My condolences." Leigh made a mental note to look into Mrs. Kain's death since clearly no more information would be forthcoming. "Let's go back to the Depression. Mr. Kain helped to support the family with his position in the Corps?"

"No, he was on his own by then," said Ethel. "He's never spoken of his father, so we've always assumed his mother was never married. We do know she raised him on her own and died when he was fifteen. That was nineteen-thirty-one, at the height of the Great Depression."

"Do you know how she died?"

"All he would say was she was sick. Medical care was pretty much unavailable for many back then."

"Did he go into the system?"

"At fifteen?" Ethel shook her head sadly. "Back then, the public system couldn't afford to feed infants and toddlers, so they wouldn't even look at a teenage boy who was considered a grown man back then. No, he was on his own, and out on the streets."

"Is that when he joined the Civilian Corps?" Matt asked. "Would they take them as young as fifteen?"

"You had to be eighteen to join the Corps. Besides, they didn't start the program that early. He was on the street for three years before joining the Corps, but he won't talk about those years. It must have been a horrible time for him."

"Back then, in those circumstances, I'm sure survival was his only goal," Matt said.

"One more question before we go talk to him. Is there anything else you can add to the report you filed with the Lynn Police Department? Any details that you might have remembered since then?"

"It took us a long time to file that report," Barb said. "Honestly, we thought it was just nonsense because so much of it is—like his latest story about Heidi. He said someone had kidnapped her, tied her to the top of a moving train, and then they went through a low tunnel and she got scraped off." She patted her daughter's knee where she perched on the arm of her chair. "As you can see, Heidi is alive and well. Since this is what we hear from him on a regular basis, we tend not to put much stock in his stories."

"But the one about the body kept coming up again and again," David said. "I finally convinced them all it wasn't our call to make. If the story was real, the police would make that determination. And you did. But when we filed the report, everyone added any details they could remember."

"Then I think we're ready." Leigh stood, Matt rising to his feet to join her. "Let's go see Mr. Kain."

Tuesday, 7:24 p.m.
Saint Joseph's Nursing Home
Lynn, Massachusetts

THE OLD MAN IN the bed was a frail shell of the bricklayer he'd once been. Weighing at most one hundred pounds, his body was reduced to papery thin skin, ropy veins, and protruding bones. A nasal cannula delivered oxygen and an IV snaked over the bed, the needle piercing the near-translucent skin on the back of one gnarled hand. His chest barely rose and fell, but the wheeze coming from his parted lips reassured Leigh he still lived.

Leigh paused just inside the door, Matt at her back. The private room was small and bare bones, but the family had brought in personal items to make it more comfortable: family photos crowded the bedside table, a child's bright painting was taped to the wall beyond the foot of his bed, a homemade throw was draped over his feet, and a goldfinch feeder was suction-cupped to his small window, its perches empty in the dark. A pencil sketch of High Rock Tower stood propped against a short stack of books, a faithful representation of the glowing tower visible from the bed through the window.

They'd left most of the family downstairs with the promise of full details upon their return; now it was only Ethel and Barb who accompanied them. Connor and David had stubbornly lobbied to come along, but Barb held firm, concerned the nursing staff would ask them all to leave if too many people tried to crowd into this small room.

Ethel crossed to the bed, laying her hand on her father's shoulder and bending low toward him. "Dad? Dad, it's Ethel. Barb and I are here and we have some people who'd like to see you."

After a few moments of silence, Leigh let out the disappointed breath she hadn't realized she'd been holding as the steady wheezing continued without change. "Is he asleep?"

"Not so much asleep as just out of it," Barb murmured to her. Raising her voice, she said, "Let me try." She circled the bed to stand on the other side. "Grandpa, are you awake? A police officer is here and wants to talk to you. Remember your story about the body hidden away in Lynn? Well, she found it."

The old man gave a low groan and his eyelids fluttered open. He blearily focused on Barb.

"I thought that might do it," Barb said. She waved Leigh over before raising her voice again. "Grandpa, this is Trooper Abbott of the Massachusetts State Police." She stepped back so Leigh could move closer.

"Mr. Kain, I'd like to ask you some questions." Leigh spoke slowly and clearly, not sure how much the old man could understand. He blinked at her slowly, which she took as a good sign. "Your family reported what you told them about a body hidden in the Adytum building. I went and checked out the location. I found what's left of an old speakeasy."

"Connor…" The word came out as a rasp, rough bark over sandpaper.

Leigh glanced back at Barb, who stepped forward and leaned over the bed. "Connor's not here now, Grandpa. Maybe he'll come in later." She tipped her head toward Leigh. "He loves Connor," she said in an undertone. "He's always been a favorite. Grandpa used to take him to ball games and he taught him to work with his hands. Connor's love of astronomy came from Grandpa. They have a special connection." Barb gave her a gentle push toward the bed. "Try again."

"Leigh, you may not have his attention for long." Matt spoke up from the other side of the bed, his eyes not on Leigh, but critically evaluating the old man. "Cut to the chase."

She leaned low, staring intently into his face. "Mr. Kain, what can you tell me about the man in the basement? About the man behind the brick wall." There was a flicker of recognition and shock in the watery brown eyes, so she pushed harder. "How did you know about the man behind the wall, Mr. Kain? What is his name and how did he get there? What do you know about the speakeasy?"

The old man's mouth moved, his lips trying to form words, but all that came out was a wheeze. Leigh bent down, her ear to his lips, trying desperately to catch the slightest thread of sound.

Blue ruin.

Not sure she'd heard correctly, she started to pull away to question him, but a gnarled hand snaked out, closing with surprising force around her wrist, his fingers ice-cold on her skin. The shadows cleared from his eyes and Leigh recognized for that brief moment that Samuel Kain was with her.

"Deserved to die." A harsh cough rattled in his chest, breaking through the hoarse whisper. "Too many gone... his fault."

"Who deserved to die?" she pressed. "By whose hand?"

"Justicccccce…" The word stretched out like a snake's hiss, venom dripping from the tone.

"Vigilante justice? For what?"

Suddenly, the hold on her wrist loosened. The intensity went out of the old man's eyes, all animation draining from his face as his lax hand fell limply back to the bed. His eyelids slipped closed over eyes rolling up into his head.

Matt stepped in, slipping two fingers along his neck, expertly finding the pulse. "Pulse is thready and tachycardic. Better get a nurse. This might have been too much of a shock to his system."

Barb bolted from the room with a lightness of foot unexpected in a woman of her size.

Leigh looked down at the old man, sure that while she had some of her answers, she was left with more questions than when she'd entered the room only minutes before.

Tuesday, 7:57 p.m.
Saint Joseph's Nursing Home
Lynn, Massachusetts

"SORRY IF IT seemed like I was pushing you in there," Matt said. "I didn't like the look of him. His fingernails were blue, even with the supplemental oxygen, and his respiration was too shallow. Then when he went under, I was worried he might go into cardiac arrest."

They were heading toward Leigh's car, along a walkway lined with neatly trimmed boxwoods and studded with solar lights, illuminated parallel lines guiding their way to the parking lot.

Leigh glanced sideways. Matt's face was mostly in shadow, but relaxed, absent of the strain memories of his time as a medic often conveyed. Relief loosened her shoulders. "I knew you could hold him until the cavalry arrived, but I'm all for not making use of those skills if we don't need to."

"I'm with you there. They're right; he's not in good shape. I thought the low oxygen alone guaranteed he wouldn't be lucid."

"For a very brief window, he was more lucid than I expected. For just a few seconds, he was right there with me." Leigh sighed. "And then he was gone."

"Can anything he said be used as evidence?"

"I could try, but a decent lawyer would rip it to shreds on the grounds of diminished mental capacity. I couldn't swear for most of the conversation that he even knew what I was saying. Except for that one moment."

"You realize that what he said tonight cements our theory of a revenge killing…if you'll pardon the pun."

She gave him a flat stare. "That joke wasn't even worthy of Paul. But you're right. It supports the revenge killing theory, but doesn't absolutely mean he's responsible for it. He still might only have knowledge of the event."

"What does your gut say?"

Leigh considered for a moment, aimlessly jingling her car keys in her hand as she worked it through again in her head. "My brain says I can't logically be sure. But my gut recognized the bone-deep hatred in his eyes during that moment of lucidity. He remembered the act, remembered why he did it, and reveled in it. He's not ashamed of it; he's proud. But I'm never going to be able to prove it. No witnesses, no DNA to corroborate or tie him to the crime, and a probable killer who won't even survive to the time of a trial."

"A killer who sounds like justice was served as far as he's concerned."

"But I have no idea why. I may never be able to charge Kain, but I'm more and more convinced the death of the man behind the wall is what set this whole chain of events in motion. We need to know why, because the gap in time between the two deaths makes no sense right now. Only then can we build the rest of the case. By the way, do you have any idea what 'blue ruin' is? That's what he whispered to me when I bent down."

"Never heard of it before. Are you sure that's what he said?"

"I *think* that's what he said. Rowe seems to be up on his history. If it's something to do with those times, he might know. I'll ask him tomorrow." They stepped off the walkway into the well-lit parking lot, heading for her car at the far end. "Are you going to stay tonight, or do you have to go back?"

"I need to head home tonight. I have a departmental meeting tomorrow at seven-thirty, so I'll get a faster start from there. Besides, this way I can go remind my father to be nice to me because I'm going to pick his nursing home. Maybe I can talk him into making filet mignon to butter me up."

She couldn't help the chuckle. "You're the worst."

"The way to a man's heart is through his stomach. Apparently it's also the way to ensure your kids treat you right once they're in charge. Oh, speaking of nice dinners, I meant to tell you. Do you remember me telling you about Father Colin Reid, the unit chaplain when we were overseas?"

"I remember him. From your tarot reading—he was your Golem, your loyal friend in times of trouble."

"That's the one. I took your advice. I contacted the V.A. and asked if they had any contact info for him. They did, so I gave them my information and asked them to pass it on to Colin. I got an email from him this morning. He's coming into town this weekend and asked if he could stop by to see me on Saturday."

Leigh stopped dead in surprise, instinctively reaching out to grasp his forearm. "Did you answer him?"

Matt shuffled his feet awkwardly, his gaze falling to the pavement. "Not yet. I'm not sure what to say."

"Say 'yes.'" Leigh shook his arm for emphasis. "Wouldn't it be wonderful to see him again after all this time, to catch up with him?"

"Probably." His head came up, his conflicted hazel gaze meeting hers. "But I haven't seen any of the guys since I left the Corps. It just feels a bit...awkward."

"Forget awkward. This is a friend you're talking about. Okay, so you've lost touch. This is your chance to fix it."

"I was thinking about asking him to the house for dinner, assuming it doesn't interfere with the case."

"I'll do my best to make sure it doesn't."

"If you're free, would you come? If I'm going to do this, I'd like you to meet him." Naked entreaty shone in his hopeful expression.

Her hand dropped down to his, intertwining their fingers to grip tightly. "I wouldn't miss it."

ELEVEN: BRAND NAME

Brand name: a proprietary name. The term originated, in part, from the practice among American distillers of burning ("branding") their names and emblems onto their wooden kegs before shipment.

Wednesday, 11:10 a.m.
Boston University, School of Medicine
Boston, Massachusetts

"THANKS. I'LL MAKE sure Leigh gets this." Matt took the file folder from Rowe. "You didn't need to run this over. I could have sent one of the students." He opened the file and flipped through the autopsy report before his narrowed gaze returned to Rowe. "Or you could have emailed it."

Rowe threw up both hands in surrender. "Okay, I confess. I needed an excuse to get out of there. The bureaucracy is going to kill me. If I have to attend one more meeting…" His gaze found the ceiling as if begging for strength from above. "I went into pathology to help people find answers. Now most of the time all I do is drown in paperwork."

"Tell me about it. After all those years in the lab and out in the field, it feels like I spend most of my time on the mind-numbing bureaucracy of grant applications, peer panels, grad student committee meetings, lecture schedules, and university regulations."

"But you have *this*." Rowe turned and crossed the lab to stand at the gurney, the remains laid out on cold steel before him. "This is fascinating. History and intrigue all wrapped up in a single package." His gaze flicked to Matt. "May I?"

Matt set the folder down on his desk. "Of course. Pay special attention to the inferior surface of the left clavicle, the superior surface of the first left rib, and both T-12 and L-1."

Matt stood back while Rowe donned gloves and started to examine the remains. He had to admit that Rowe had a point. It was too easy to lose the joy of pure science under the administrative demands of being a university professor, and the thrill Matt experienced from real scientific research threatened to painfully fizzle and die.

The woman who put that thrill back into his life chose just that moment to appear in the lab doorway.

Leigh crossed the room toward them. "And once again, I didn't expect to see you. You're like a bad penny—you keep turning up," she said to Rowe, returning his grin as he set the clavicle back into place.

"I'm playing hooky." Rowe raised a gloved finger to his lips. "Don't tell." He waggled bushy eyebrows at her and turned back to the remains.

"Wild horses couldn't drag it from me." Leigh turned to Matt, her amused expression sliding toward quizzical at the look on his face. "What?"

"Remind me to thank you later."

"For what?"

"I'll explain it to you then."

Leigh's gaze darted from Matt to Rowe and back

again, and she shook her head, clearly baffled at the oddity that was the male species. "Actually, Rowe, I'm glad you're here so we can pick your brain. Does the term 'blue ruin' mean anything to you?"

Rowe straightened, the T-12 vertebra cupped in his left hand. "Sure does, especially if you mean in reference to the speakeasy. It's an old slang term for what was commonly known in the twenties and thirties as 'bathtub gin.'"

"Bathtub gin? Isn't that a slang term in itself?"

"Not as much as you'd think. Bathtub gin was basically homemade booze. In its simplest, non-distilled form, it only needed a day or two to age, so you could make it and drink it fairly quickly. It's a method called 'cold compounding': mix grain spirits with something for flavor, like juniper berries—thus the reference to gin—and maybe something as exotic as citrus peel if you had it, and then dilute it out by adding tap water. But they made it in such large containers, they couldn't fit the bottle under the kitchen faucet, so they'd use the bathtub instead. Thus, 'bathtub gin.' If you had the equipment, you could distill this same mixture, which was much safer. If there was any methanol contamination in the mix, it evaporated first during distillation."

"It sounds awful." Leigh wrinkled her nose in disgust.

"It was awful, but it could get worse. For many, if they couldn't get their hands on grain spirits, they used denatured alcohol."

Now it was Matt's turn to wince. "That could be a death sentence."

"For many it was. Or you could get off lightly and just go blind."

"People were that desperate for alcohol they'd drink poison?" Leigh asked.

"A lot of them didn't know they were drinking poison. But many of them knew they were taking their chances and did it anyway. It's hard to describe the desperation of people back then, especially during the Depression. The chance to escape the misery of their daily lives, even if only for a little while, was simply too big a temptation. The worst of it was the Feds got involved in it too."

"How?"

"They knew what was going on. Distilling alcohol was illegal under the Volstead Act but it happened anyway. But because alcohol was needed for scientific research and the production of dyes and fuels, the Feds knowingly poisoned some of that alcohol to discourage it from being used for human consumption. People drank it anyway and died by the tens of thousands. And then the Feds had the nerve to label them 'deliberate suicides.'"

"Unbelievable," Matt muttered.

"Believe it." Rowe set down the vertebra and pulled off his gloves. "It was a different time back then and the Feds had the power to do whatever they pretty much wanted."

"My dad used to tell stories about those days," Leigh said.

"Whose stories?" Matt asked. "Your dad was too young to have been involved himself."

"Dad wasn't born until well after Prohibition, but his grandfather was with the Boston Police back then and served on the Liquor Squad. I've seen a picture of him with four or five other guys, all dressed to the nines and ready for a night on the town on New Year's Eve. In reality, it was the group getting ready to go out and start raiding parties." She drummed her fingers over the edge of the gurney, a steady sequence of repetitive beats. "That picture was in a box of stuff that used to be in dad's attic."

"A box of stuff from your great-grandfather's days on the Liquor Squad?"

"My memory says it was a mixture of things from his life. But where is that box?"

"Could it have gotten tossed out?" Rowe asked. "When you sold Nate's place?"

Matt started at the familiarity of Leigh's father's name falling so easily from Rowe's lips, before he remembered Rowe knew Nate Abbott from his days in the Essex Detective Unit.

"That wasn't a great time for me, but I wouldn't have tossed out a box of family history like that. I couldn't deal with a lot of stuff at the time, so I probably put it up in my attic. I haven't seen it in years."

"Could be some interesting stuff in there," Matt said, curiosity piquing his interest. "Real details from an officer back then. How far back do you Abbotts go in police work anyway?"

"I'm the first woman, but fourth generation."

"No wonder your dad was so proud."

"You have no idea," Rowe said.

That got Leigh's attention as her laser-sharp gaze focused on Rowe. "What do you mean?"

"Your dad and I were pretty good friends for a long time. We got on well together, just like you and I do. Similar personalities and work ethic, that sort of thing." Rowe smiled gently down at her. "He also had the same stomach for autopsies you have and the same backbone to stand through them no matter what. We were both working our way up the ranks, but we bumped into each other during investigations all the time. When I met him, you weren't even in high school, but he was already talking about how smart you were and how he knew you'd make a great cop."

The color rose in Leigh's cheeks and she swallowed hard, blinking several times.

"It's funny," Rowe continued. "I don't think he ever doubted you'd join the force. There was never a question in his mind. When I asked him if you'd expressed an interest in police work, he'd just say 'not yet, but she will.' And then, one day, there you were, graduating from the Academy to join him. He was so proud of you." He chuckled. "You couldn't get him to shut up about it."

Matt ran his fingertips over Leigh's back, her ribs jumping under his touch on a jerky indrawn breath as she struggled to keep herself together. But Rowe's levity seemed to buoy her and when she spoke her voice was even. "That was Dad. Family was everything to him."

"He was a good man." As if sensing Leigh's need to move away from this topic, Rowe turned back to the bones spread out on the examination table. "I see what you mean, Lowell. Definitely scoring at those specific locations. You have an idea about the weapon used?"

"More a tool than weapon, but we think it was a bricklayer's pointing trowel. The killer severed the spinal cord between T-12 and L-1 and also nicked the internal thoracic artery. The victim slowly bled to death, not able to move, as the wall went up in front of him."

"Nasty," Rowe said. "And where are we on ID of this vic?"

"I haven't had a chance to update you," Leigh said. "It turns out we agree with you that this is likely Charles Ward. We've seen more than one picture of Ward wearing the same ring we found on Sunday. Good call on that, by the way."

"You're welcome." Rowe regally tipped his head toward her in a small bow.

"But what we didn't expect was that our fresh victim, Peter Holt, is actually Ward's grandson."

Rowe's air of pride at having named Ward dissolved in apparent shock. "*What?*"

"Yeah, that was our reaction too. We'll be confirming that connection—that's why Matt asked for that DNA sample from Holt—but we're pretty confident already. We'll be comparing Evelyn's DNA to her son; we'll also be comparing both to this gentleman here."

"It's being run now," Matt said, "with the usual duplicate samples going to the state labs. We'll have our answer soon, but in the meantime, we're running with the theory this is Charles Ward."

Rowe circled the table, staring at the pale bones. "Grandfather and grandson both found in the same place? With the grandfather only discovered because we were specifically looking for a clandestine body? Clearly, someone took the time to set up this scenario. You think it's the old man? The one whose story sent you to the Adytum in the first place?"

"Yes and no. I think he's responsible for this." Leigh waved a hand over the skeletal remains. "My gut says he did it, even though I can't prove it. But he's not responsible for Peter Holt's death. He's dying of Alzheimer's and doesn't have the mental or physical capacity to murder anyone anymore."

"Leigh said you found evidence during the autopsy that the body was moved?" Matt asked.

"Yes. He was killed in the two hours between ten p.m.

on Thursday and midnight Friday, and then the body lay on its right side for up to approximately four hours. Tissue compression indicators within the areas of livor mortis suggest the body lay in a curled position during that time."

Matt's gaze flicked to Leigh to see if she understood the technical term for blood settling by gravity into the lower tissues of dead bodies, indicating the postmortem position, but she was already nodding in understanding.

"We found him on his back. The autopsy confirmed livor mortis over the back as well as on the right side, indicating the body was moved before the blood fully congealed," Rowe continued.

"So the body lay curled up for a few hours and was then moved to the Adytum where he was laid on his back." Leigh's gaze flicked up to Matt. "I bet the body was kept in the trunk of a car. Killed somewhere, maybe wrapped in plastic or some other covering to be moved, transported by car, and then the perp waited until the coast was clear to move the body inside. He was killed before midnight and moved during the middle of the night. Then I found him around noon that day."

"That theory works for me," Rowe said. "I'm still waiting on trace reports from the fibers we pulled off the body. If the body was transported by car and there aren't car carpet fibers, then that supports the idea the body was wrapped. That's your copy of the file over on Lowell's desk, by the way."

"You hand-delivered a copy? Why didn't you just email the report?"

"I did that too. But I wanted some air so this gave me an excuse to get the hell out of the office."

Leigh's gaze flicked from the remains to Rowe. "You

wanted to find out where we were on the remains," she accused.

"Okay, yes, I did. It's not my case, but it's on the outskirts of my case and I have a vested interest at this point."

Matt clapped him on the shoulder. "You're welcome in the lab anytime. God knows my students and I invade your morgue often enough."

Rowe glanced around the mostly empty lab. "I thought it seemed quiet around here. Where are your students?"

"Down at the Old North in the charnel house. We're waiting on tests that are out of our hands right now, so it gave them a chance to get back to their own projects in the interim." Matt turned to Leigh. "Have you talked to any of Peter Holt's contacts?"

"Actually, I just came from his office. He was an investment officer at Rutherford and Fisk. Everyone there seems genuinely devastated by his loss. His mother described him as 'boring' but his coworkers appear to have respected him. He was steady and solid with a very level head. I spoke at length with one of the vice-presidents and he said they hadn't had any problems with Holt, either inside the office or with any clients. He hadn't lost any accounts and his portfolios were all in good shape. Before that, I spoke to Cheryl Ballantine, who his mother described as his 'casual girlfriend.' In reality, it was more of a friends-with-benefits arrangement. She was upset about Holt's death, but it was clear she considered him more of a friend than a life partner. They were friendly, but there wasn't enough invested there, at least on her part, to lead to murder."

"Both work and personal issues seem less likely when you consider the tie between the two victims. I think we're not seeing the motive for the death because we don't have the whole picture yet," Matt said. "I think we need to go back to the nineteen-thirties to figure out how this whole thing started. Then maybe it will make more sense."

"Let me do some research at home tonight," Rowe suggested. "Assuming we're looking at Charles Ward, let me see what I can find on him in any of my books." He pushed back his cuff and grimaced at his watch. "And that's it for my playing hooky today. I have a lunch meeting I can't miss." He started for the door. "I'll let you know if I find anything relevant." And he disappeared out the door.

Leigh shook her head in bemusement at his rapid exit. "I can't believe he snuck up here."

"He's the medical examiner for the Commonwealth of Massachusetts. He can do whatever he damned well wants. His office is just across the street, so it wasn't that far out of his way. And he didn't sneak. I know what it's like to be involved in only part of the investigation, so if he wants in on this, I'm not going to object. He's an excellent resource at any time, but especially now."

"I agree." She gazed up at him. "So…feel like a tour of my attic tonight after dinner?"

"You bet. I'm fascinated by what you might have up there."

"I may only have massive spiders and piles of dust. Just be warned."

"I promise not to shriek like a girl every time I see one of your massive spiders."

"That makes one of us," Leigh said dryly. "But let's give it a shot. Maybe Great-Grandfather can help us solve a case from the grave."

TWELVE: IZZY AND MOE

Izzy and Moe: a very effective team of Prohibition agents. While disguising themselves as vegetable vendors, gravediggers, streetcar conductors, fishermen, icemen, opera singers, and Democratic National Convention delegates, Isidor "Izzy" Einstein and his partner, Moe Smith, made 4,932 arrests and confiscated an estimated 5,000,000 bottles of illegal alcohol. After a busy day rousting Prohibition scofflaws, Izzy and Moe liked to sit back and enjoy their favorite beverages—beer and cocktails.

Wednesday, 8:48 p.m.
Abbott Residence
Salem, Massachusetts

"Ready?" Leigh looked down at the old wooden steamer trunk they'd just dragged from the corner of her dim and dusty attic. Solidly built of sturdy wood, it was banded with steel straps.

"Let's do it." Matt flicked open the rusty latch that secured the contents.

They each grabbed a corner of the lid and eased it up. Inside, the trunk was filled to the brim with books, clothing, documents, and pictures. A worn, olive-drab uniform jacket, the metal buttons dulled with age, lay on top of the pile.

Matt freed the sleeve to reveal the double chevron patch sewn onto the top of the sleeve. "A corporal. How long was he in the Army?"

"Less than a year. He was twenty-one when he was drafted and sent over in the summer of nineteen-eighteen to take part in the Second Battle of the Somme. It's where he earned this." She extracted a small leather box. It opened with a squeak of disuse, revealing a circular bronze medal depicting the winged form of Victory holding a shield and a sword hanging from a short, rainbow-hued ribbon. A narrow bar clasped across the ribbon read "Somme-Offensive." Leigh lifted the medal gently from the box and handed it to Matt. "It's the Victory Medal—the Silver Citation Star—for gallantry in battle."

"Leigh, this is amazing." He turned the medal over and Leigh read the words "THE GREAT WAR FOR CIVILIZATION" and the names of the Allied countries listed on the back. "Why is it up here in a trunk? You should have it framed and displayed."

"You think so?"

"I would. It's not just a piece of history; it's something to be proud of. Your great-grandfather was quite a guy—served in the First World War and then came home to become a cop."

"Speaking of which…" Leigh reached in for the small softcover book that peeked out from the pile. "I remember the story behind this." About three-by-five inches, the navy front cover had a circular hole near one corner that penetrated deep into the body of the book. "He was carrying this book in his breast pocket the night he got shot." She held the book up over her heart. "It was in the early nineteen-twenties when he was new to the Boston P.D. and was still walking the beat. There was a Mob gunfight down the street and a stray bullet caught him in the chest as he ran toward the sound of gunfire. He got hit right here." She poked her index finger into the defect left by the bullet before handing the book to Matt.

He opened the small volume, spreading the pages wide. At the top of both pages was the title "BOSTON STREET DIRECTORY." Underneath, a running list of names streamed down the page in alphabetical order, accompanied by their street address and occupation. "The bullet made it about three-quarters of the way through before it was stopped." He looked up to meet her eyes. "It must have been partially spent to be stopped by this, but he was still lucky. Considering where he carried it, if the bullet got into one of the intercostal spaces between his ribs and entered the thoracic cavity, it could have killed him."

"Which would have been the end of me," Leigh said. "He was only newly married at the time. My grandfather was the second of five children and wasn't born for a few more years." Rising up on her knees, she started carefully sorting through the trunk contents, removing unrelated items one at a time. "I know some of his stuff from his time on the Boston Police Liquor Squad is in here. Ah…here we go. This is the photo I told you about this morning."

She handed Matt a black and white photo, the paper yellowed with age. In it, five men in tuxedos sat on wooden chairs in front of a row of metal lockers. "That's him, second from the left." She tapped the photo above the head of a slender man with thinning hair and sharply intelligent eyes. His tuxedo jacket was pulled back to reveal the law enforcement badge pinned to his waistcoat. "This is part of the squad on their way to check out some New Year's Eve parties at a couple of swanky Boston hotels."

"They were a separate department within the Boston P.D.?"

"Yes, one specifically mandated to bust rum-runners, club owners, bootleggers, and the Mob—anyone who was heavily involved in booze back then. They tended to work closely with the Feds, who were tasked with enforcing Prohibition." She bent back over the trunk. "I'm sure there's a journal in here that will be useful to us."

"Like a diary?"

"More like the notepad I carry. He kept his notes in it. I don't think he specifically held onto it after he retired from the force, but, after his death, it was found in a drawer, tossed in with a bunch of papers. The family had moved from Boston to Salem by that time, and my grandfather was already with the Massachusetts State Police. The journal meant something to him, so he held onto it. I know it's in here somewhere because last time Dad and I went through this trunk—" She lifted out a photo album and her pulse skittered. A leather journal lay on top of a short stack of books. "Got it."

She settled back on the dusty wood floor beside Matt. Once dark brown, the worn leather was faded to a soft coffee color, the front and back covers tied closed with a tattered ribbon. Leigh carefully slipped the ribbon free and opened the book. Scrawling dark ink covered the lined pages.

Matt leaned in to study the writing. "Looks like it starts in nineteen-thirty-four. Bootlegging...hijacking... firearms too. Was that part of their investigation?"

"Not specifically, but it was all part of the Mob mentality. Find the booze, find the guns protecting it." She started to slowly flip through the pages scanning for names and locations. "There are names I recognize here. J.L. Lombardo for one. He was involved in Mafia activity in this area and the B.P.D. knew it. And look at the clubs they were watching: The Cocoanut Grove. The Cotton Club." She flipped a page to a section of notes and a large diagram. "Look at this. The Faneuil Hall Club. The owners kept their booze in sacks in another building across the alley. When a customer wanted a drink, they got a big, long stick and reached across the alley, catching one of the sacks and hauling it over. After the drink was poured, they pushed it back. Whenever they got raided, there wasn't any stock of booze on-site. But clearly the cops figured it out. Look at this drawing." She pointed to a rough sketch of a room outfitted with pulleys and ropes. "This must have been how they managed it."

"Pretty damned ingenious."

"Remember how much money was at stake. People would really go the distance to get a drink and were willing to pay for it." She flipped to a page with names listed under the title "Wanted for Questioning." She ran a finger down the page, stopping about halfway down and letting out a low whistle.

"What?"

"Look at this. Charles Ward is listed here on a list of potential suspects wanted for questioning."

"But this was for the Boston P.D. Didn't Ward live in Lynn at the time?"

"He did. But he also probably spent a lot of time in Washington when Congress was in session. There must have been a reason the Boston Liquor Squad wanted to question him." She flipped several pages. "I don't see anything else on him, but we have to go through this carefully. There might be something useful for us in he—"

Her phone rang. Sliding the book into Matt's lap, she shifted her weight and pulled her phone from her back pocket. "Abbott."

Wednesday, 9:06 p.m.
Abbott Residence
Salem, Massachusetts

MATT PICKED UP the journal, leaning in to study the yellowed pages. The old-fashioned handwriting was narrow and slanted, making the content hard to distinguish, but if he stared at it long enough, the lines and dots coalesced into words.

Leigh laid a hand on his thigh, drawing his attention from the journal. "Can I put you on speaker?" she said to her caller. "It'll save me explaining all this to Matt. We're in my attic right now, going through my great-grandfather's records from his days with the Boston P.D." Leigh set the phone on the corner of the trunk. "Go ahead, Rowe, you're on speaker."

Rowe's voice was slightly tinny, but his usual vigor came through loud and clear. "First of all, you remember I explained what 'blue ruin' was?"

"Bathtub gin," Leigh said. "We remember."

"Well, apparently this time it's a bit more than that. It's also the name of that club."

Leigh went absolutely still beside him. "The speakeasy?"

"Right. All the clubs had names, but the hidden ones didn't hang a sign over the door. Although if you think back, this one had a sign of sorts."

Matt scanned his mental image of the room. The bar. The open dance floor. The small stage. The blackjack table—

Leigh beat him to the answer. "The mural. The one of the Roman ruins behind the blackjack table."

"That's it," Rowe said. "The *Blue Ruin*. That was their sign and their advertisement, all in one."

"Pretty smart," Matt said. "And if the cops came and if they could hide the booze, it would just look like a downstairs jazz club."

"Apparently that didn't work out so well for them," Rowe said. "Now, I have some info on both the club and Ward. It took me a while to connect the name of a Prohibition-era club to that location specifically, but after that I hit the Boston Public Library. They have newspapers that date back to that time."

"Find anything good?"

"Quite a lot, actually. First of all, Charles Ward disappeared as originally suggested on February fourth, nineteen-thirty-six. The papers made quite a fuss over it then, and, as you might imagine, fingers were pointed toward the Mob. But as we said before, this doesn't have the feel of a Mob hit. They investigated, but I think the cops knew that too."

"It was too quiet," Matt said. "When the Mob killed, it wanted to make a point."

"Exactly," Rowe agreed. "And felt free to make that point often. In Chicago alone, by the time Prohibition was repealed, over eight hundred were dead in bootlegging-related shootings."

"Rowe, a question. I'm not from here, so I'm not as up on the local history as you and Leigh. Who was running the show back then when it came to the gangs?"

"Originally, it was the Irish. The Gustin Gang had a hand in almost everything—gambling, larceny, prostitution—and then when Prohibition came along, they got into rum-running and hijacking. They'd dress up like federal agents with fake badges and stop trucks at intersections, hijacking the vehicles and then selling the contents. Until they hijacked the wrong truck."

"Let me guess, they picked off booze belonging to a rival gang."

"Filippo Buccola and Joseph Lombardo, to be specific. Fifty thousand dollars' worth. Frank Wallace, head of the Gustin Gang, and Lombardo agreed to a meet in the North End where the Italians ruled Boston."

"Still do..." Matt said. "And have some of the best restaurants in town."

"Wallace, his brother, Steve, and their enforcer, Bernard Walsh, went to the meet. Wallace and Walsh died in a hail of bullets, Steve barely escaped. The balance of power in Boston tipped, and the Italians were on top for the next fifty odd years, especially after the Boston and Providence crime families merged to create a New England crime family with Buccola as boss. At the time we're talking about, the mid- to late-thirties, it was the Italians running the show."

"So where does Charles Ward fit into this?" Leigh asked.

"We know he was a congressman at the time. But you have to understand how politics and crime families sometimes rubbed shoulders back then."

"Back then?" Matt cast a sideways glance at Leigh who nodded in agreement. "I don't think it was just back then."

"Good point. But the issue here is that there was a lot

of give-and-take between the Feds, who were in charge of enforcing Prohibition, local police departments, politicians, and the gangs themselves," Rowe said. "Even now, the FBI makes deals with gang members to turn evidence or inform on rival gang members. It's a complicated relationship every which way. Politicians put pressure on the Feds or the cops, who sometimes look the other way when things are going down or when evidence gets lost. Many of these guys never went to jail when they absolutely should have, or only served a very short time."

"So then where does Ward fit into this mess?"

"I think this is the kicker. I found some indications that Ward owned property in Lynn, and I'm not talking about his house. In one article, he was directly tied to the Adytum Building."

"He owned the *Blue Ruin*?" Leigh asked.

"Maybe he was a law-abiding politician by day and a booze peddler by night. He wouldn't have been the first. The money involved in these activities was significant."

With a jerk of shock, an image suddenly shot into Matt's mind: intricately inlaid Roman columns and arches, meticulously crafted from tiny pieces of blue enamel, and carefully set into gold ovals, their luster dulled with age.

"Hold it." Matt's hand shot out, closing over Leigh's wrist with enough force that she winced. He immediately loosened his hold. "Sorry. I just had a thought and I think it's a big one. The mural of the blue Roman ruins… it occurs to me that we've seen something else with that theme before but didn't really account for it."

"What?"

"I saw the photo of the cuff links found in Peter Holt's pocket in the case file. Think about it—blue ruins. Ward owns a club called the *Blue Ruin* and his grandson is found carrying cuff links depicting blue ruins. We've gone off coincidences for this case, right?"

"Bloody hell." Rowe's voice exploded from the phone. "I didn't even think about that and I pulled them out of his pocket. They're old, Abbott, easily old enough to have been Ward's. And their styling—very Art Deco. What if they were Ward's private advertisement about his club? Or his way of flaunting his ownership in a clandestine way? Almost like he was thumbing his nose at society?"

"But if they were Ward's and then got passed down to his grandson after his disappearance, why didn't Evelyn Holt recognize them?" Leigh asked.

"Maybe she did." When Leigh stared at him blankly, Matt continued. "Think about her reaction. I thought she was going to pass out when you described them to her."

"That's true. I chalked her reaction up to the stress of the experience, but maybe it was the stress of that moment. But what's the significance of her son having a family heirloom like that? And why deny knowledge of it?"

"I'm not sure. Let's just keep it in mind as something that seems out of place. Now, back to Ward himself. If he owned the *Blue Ruin*, do you think that's why the Boston Liquor Squad wanted to talk to him? Rowe, in the notes we've found here, Boston P.D. had a list of individuals to bring in for questioning and Ward is on that list. Someone must have suspected some shady dealings on his part."

"Tricky thing, bringing down a congressman. They'd have been treading lightly."

"Especially considering all those complicated relationships. If we're lucky, there's more on it in the journal. We'll keep looking to see if there's anything else."

"This could be why he was killed. Even if he owned the club, he should have been buying his booze from Buccola and company. Unless he found another source."

"Wouldn't the Mob just have hit the competitor instead of the buyer if that was the case?" Matt asked.

"They might have. On the other hand, what if they wanted to make an example of Ward? A warning to other owners to remember who held their leash?"

"But didn't we just say that Ward's death was too quiet?" Leigh asked. "I thought that wasn't the Mob way."

"Normally, it isn't. But considering who the guy was, it makes me wonder if they took a different tack. Killing another mobster is one thing; in some ways the cops would thank you for whacking a bad guy. But brazenly kill a congressman and you'll bring down a world of hurt and unwanted attention on your head. Kill him and hide the body, and things might go smoother for you."

"They got attention from the disappearance anyway," Matt pointed out.

"They did," Rowe agreed, "but not for long. Without a body, nobody could actually prove Ward was dead, and there was zero evidence leading directly back to the Mob. So the cops had to let it go. But now that we're looking at it with the benefit of time and perspective, we may find something else."

"Do you really think that Peter Holt's death was a Mob hit, related to Ward's death all those years ago?" Leigh asked. "I find that hard to believe considering the state of the New England crime family now. It's a shadow of what it used to be."

"I admit it doesn't seem likely, but can we discount it?"

"I guess not. But my gut just isn't going there."

"Let's keep it on the table, but look for other options.

I'm going to try to narrow in more on Charles Ward. I'll let you know if I find anything else."

"Us too. Thanks for the update, Rowe."

"My pleasure. Really. Talk to you later." Rowe clicked off.

Leigh climbed back on her knees and spent a moment sorting through the remaining trunk contents. "I think that's everything that will be useful to us. Let me put all of this back and then let's take the journal downstairs to look at it in better light over a glass of wine." Leigh carefully repacked the trunk, and then climbed to her feet and started toward the stairs.

Matt started to trail after her and then abruptly stopped as he realized that she'd barely taken a step. Following her gaze, he noticed the boxes piled in neat rows on the far side of the attic. "What's that?"

"Boxes from Dad's house." Her voice was flat, and his heart ached for the pain she always tried so hard to hide when it came to her father.

"There's quite a few." He attempted to keep his voice casual, to keep the concern from his tone. He wasn't sure he pulled it off.

"I didn't sort through it at the time. I just boxed it all up and put it away, so there may be stuff I could get rid of."

Put it away for four years? Locked all the pain and misery away in boxes in the attic and never dealt with it? Matt caught her arm and turned her around to face him. Leigh's gaze fixed on the top button of his shirt, clearly not wanting to meet his eyes, but he slipped one hand under her chin to tip her face up. At first, she resisted, but he kept up a gentle pressure until she finally raised her face. Her eyes were dry but unease roiled in their depths.

"You never went through any of it," Matt said quietly.

"No. It was just too hard back then. Too...final." She glanced sideways toward the boxes that were all she had left of her father. "And there wasn't a rush. It wasn't like he needed any of it."

"Leigh." He ran a warm palm up and down her arm. "Maybe there's something in there you'd like to have." Another angle occurred to him and he stared intently into the shadowed corner. "Maybe there's something in there we can use."

"For what?"

"Against whoever is sending you those deliveries? You keep a notepad, your great-grandfather kept a journal. What did your father keep?"

"I don't remember there being anything like that, but I admit I boxed up his office without really looking. He used to work on cases from home at night, but all of that was on his computer."

"You can take files home and work on them at night?"

Leigh colored slightly. "Well...it's not exactly department policy. And I don't think he was taking evidence or active files home. But sometimes the work gets into you and your shift might be done, but you're not. I found him working on stuff at home more than once. For Dad, the job didn't stop when he walked out the unit door."

"Like father, like daughter," Matt said. "You said you kept his hard drive because there were personal files and family photos on it?"

"Yes. It's one of those things I was always going to get to, but somehow managed to continue putting off. And then when the packages started to arrive, it should have moved up my list, but there was always something else that needed doing first." She scowled and tapped her thigh with a clenched fist.

"It's not like you've been sitting with your feet up for the last few weeks. You've been busy."

"Not so busy that I couldn't make time for it. Let's be honest; part of me doesn't want to deal with this."

"Which is totally understandable. Where's the hard drive? Somewhere in that pile of boxes?"

"Probably. Why?"

It's now or never. "I want you to bring someone else in on your father's case," he said flatly. When she immediately started to protest, he cut her off. "We need help and from what you've said, he's a good guy."

Hands on hips, Leigh narrowed her eyes on him in suspicion. "Who?"

"Rob Tucker."

She opened her mouth to speak and then snapped it shut again as if reconsidering.

"You said he's a computer genius. You said he's solid and can be trusted. You have your dad's hard drive and who knows what's on there? If there are deleted files, Tucker could probably recover them. We need to find out more information about the case your father was working on when he died, and I bet Tucker could help. I've been thinking about it for a few days, but I wasn't sure how to bring it up." When she stayed silent, he started to second guess himself, started to back down. It had to be her decision in the end. "Terrible idea?"

"Actually, no."

Surprised relief rushed through Matt, loosening the knot in his gut.

"You may have a point," Leigh continued. "And I think we can trust Tucker. We can't do anything at the office;

I'd need him to come here for us to explain it to him. And I'd need to find the drive. It's over there…somewhere."

"Then let's do it. Leigh, it's time to go on the offensive. Let's not wait for that bastard to send something else. Let's go after him instead."

For the first time in what felt like a long time, hope flickered in Leigh's eyes. Squaring her shoulders, she marched over to the boxes and started pushing through them, reading the neatly printed labels on each container. She glanced back at Matt, who still stood near the trap door that led down to the second floor. "Well? What are you waiting for? Get over here and help me find that damned drive."

With a wide grin, he ducked low and joined her.

It was time to put an end to this.

THIRTEEN: DISTILLED SPIRITS

Distilled spirits: ethanol that is separated by heating fermented products, such as crushed grapes or mash, and then condensing the resulting vapors.

Wednesday, 10:15 p.m.
Abbott Residence
Salem, Massachusetts

THERE WERE THREE sharp knocks at the front door.

Leigh put down her glass of wine and started to push up from the couch but Matt was already on his feet. While trying to look casually relaxed, he'd been practically perched on the edge of the couch, waiting for Rob Tucker to arrive. He waved her back down. "I'll get it."

Matt strode down the hallway. He wanted a moment to size up this new team member before they started handing over sensitive information to him. And he wanted to put the guy at a slight disadvantage while doing so by keeping Leigh out of sight. Tucker had been incredibly helpful in his first case with Leigh—he'd been the one to identify the killer and provide his location—but he was Leigh's contact and still something of an unknown commodity to Matt, despite the fact Matt had lobbied to include him. He'd heard a lot about Rob Tucker, all of it good, but he'd yet to actually meet him.

He'd anticipated an uptight computer geek, but when

he opened the door, the man on the other side could have just walked out of a college dorm. Tucker looked more than a little disheveled—his shaggy red hair was sticking up like he'd been running his fingers through it, and his loosely tied sneakers were scuffed and worn. An open ski jacket revealed a faded black T-shirt declaring *There's No Place Like 127.0.0.1* worn over equally faded black jeans.

At the sight of Matt, suspicion streaked over Tucker's face and his gaze shot over Matt's shoulder to search the hall behind him. "I'm looking for Leigh Abbott."

Matt stepped back and held the door wider. "You're in the right place." He held out his hand. "Matt Lowell."

Tucker's eyes were blank for just a millisecond, and then understanding dawned. "You're the scientist that helped her crack the Bradford case." The two men shook hands. "She's here, right?"

"She is." Tucker's eyes darted left and right, clearly searching for Leigh, but Matt didn't move, essentially trapping Tucker in place. "Look, she's going to share some pretty personal stuff and I need to know it's not going to go beyond you. If you can't be trusted with this—" Tucker's eyes went wide, clearly offended at the suggestion, but Matt barreled on. "—then it stops now."

Tucker drew himself upright, unmindful of the fact that he was a good five inches shorter than Matt. "I don't know who you think you are—"

"A friend. One that won't stand by and see her get hurt."

Tucker took a step back, coolly appraising Matt with a critical gaze. Then his expression relaxed. "Good enough for me. I like Abbott; she's solid. Never believed any of the crap I hear about her from the guys." He met Matt's gaze. "Is she in trouble?"

Any tension Matt felt about Tucker dissipated at the genuine concern reflected in the younger man's eyes. "Not right now, but it's hard to say where this will go. She'll explain it all to you. Just realize this is going to be hard for her."

"She's always been fair with me. Rides my ass when I don't get her info fast enough to suit her, but she's always fair. If I can help her out, I'm in."

"Appreciate that. This way." Matt led the way down to the living room to where Leigh sat stiffly on the couch in front of the roaring fire. Tucker's gaze darted from the fire to the two empty wine glasses on the coffee table to the low lighting. He shot a sideways look at Matt. "Friends, huh?" he muttered under his breath.

"No one knows, so keep it under your hat," Matt replied in a low tone.

"Nobody talks to us computer geeks anyway." Tucker raised his voice. "Abbott, still doing your best to have me at your beck and call at the worst possible time? I have a life, you know."

Leigh cocked a single brow at his bravado. "There's no football game on tonight. Nerds are infamously lonely, so I thought I was doing you a favor. I wouldn't want you to resort to trying to find a date on the BBS."

Matt flicked a surprised glance at Leigh; he never would have guessed she was familiar with computer bulletin board systems.

"Damn it, how do you know about that? I thought only us geeks knew the wonders of the BBS still. Now I may have to kill you."

Watching the repartee, Matt quickly understood that banter seemed to be the main form of normal communication between these two.

"But no BBS for me tonight," Tucker continued. "I was just kicking back with my code and a beer. And I was all right with that. Until you called me and ruined a perfect evening." The sarcastic tone left his voice, leaving him somber. "What's going on? Lowell made it sound serious."

Leigh sent Matt a narrowed glare and he returned it with a flat stare. He would do whatever needed to be done; vetting someone new coming onto the team was well within his purview.

"Lowell can step back a bit," Leigh said pointedly.

"Not a chance." Matt sat back down beside her and indicated the armchair for Tucker. "Not considering what's going on. I'm just being…cautious."

"You know I can look out for myself. I don't need you to—"

"Wait a second." Flopping loosely into the chair, Tucker interrupted before they could wind themselves up. "You've got an issue and I'm here to help. Rather than going a few rounds when we're really all on the same side, how about you fill me in." He glanced at Matt, who returned a single nod of thanks.

Leigh sagged back against the couch, as if suddenly exhausted. "I'm… I'm…" She stopped and looked at Matt. "Damn it, I don't even know what to call it. I'm not being blackmailed."

"Yet," Matt replied succinctly. "Leigh's received several unmarked packages in the mail. Two were delivered to the unit last month; this week one of them came to the house. They're mailed from Boston, but have no return address. I've run DNA each time and it comes back negative."

"I've dusted for prints, which also was negative," Leigh said. "So whoever it is, they're taking precautions."

"You say you're not being blackmailed," Tucker stated. "Then what's being sent?"

Matt simply looked at Leigh, letting her take the lead as they got into deeper waters. Leaving it up to her to decide what she wanted to reveal.

She rubbed a hand over tired eyes and then met Tucker's gaze. "Information about my father. The first package contained a crime scene photo from his shooting. On the back of the picture was the warning that he was a dirty cop and I was going to be the one to pay for it."

"Nate Abbott a dirty cop?" Tuckers smirked in disbelief. "I never met him—I joined the unit after his death—but the man is a legend. If he was a dirty cop, then every man in the unit is wrong about him."

"He wasn't dirty," Leigh snapped out. Then she bent her head and rapped both fists on her knees. "Sorry, I'm slightly oversensitive about all of this. Every time this stuff gets discussed, my back goes up."

Tucker gave an easy shrug. "No worries. So are the deliveries supposed to provide evidence of his indiscretions on the job?"

"That started in the second delivery. There was a photo of him at a meeting with someone I don't recognize." Leigh picked up one of the two manila envelopes on the coffee table and passed it over to Tucker. "This is what came in the first two deliveries."

She looked away as Tucker pulled out the crime scene photo from the first package. She didn't need to see it; it was already burned into her brain.

Tucker's gaze flicked once to Leigh and then he set the photo facedown on his thigh. He pulled out the second photo, the one that had arrived in the second delivery. "Who's the guy with your dad?" He flipped around the photo of Leigh's father and another man meeting under a glowing sign lit with the words *Bruno's Tavern*.

"That's one of the things we don't know. Think there's enough in the photo for facial recognition?"

Tucker turned the photo back to face him, eyeing it critically. "Only a small bit of profile to work with, but I may be able to finesse some magic out of it. Facial recognition from a profile is nearly impossible, but assuming the guy's face is symmetric, I can use software to essentially clone the one side to generate the other and then rotate the image to get an anterior view for comparison."

"How long will that take?" Matt asked.

"At least a few days, depending on how the extrapolation goes and how lucky I am running it through the system. And, of course, that all depends on what blows up at work in the meantime."

"Will the force know you're running it?"

Tucker laughed. "Me? No," he said scathingly. "You've come to the right place if you want something done under the radar. No one knows those systems better than I do."

Leigh shifted uncomfortably in her seat. "What happens if you get caught?"

"It's pretty simple—I won't get caught." He was silent for a minute, studying the picture thoughtfully. "Another question that leaps out at me is where did this shot come from?"

"It looks like a still from a security camera," Leigh said.

The hand that waved in her direction clearly conveyed the fact that he didn't expect more from a mere intellectual mortal. "That's a given. It's pretty crappy quality,

but four years ago a lot of those cameras were analog re-
corders using VHS tape, so I'm not surprised. Even if we
could get our hands on the original media, there'd be no
metadata to draw from, date and time, that sort of thing."

"But there's already a time stamp in the photo," Leigh
pointed out.

"That was either embedded in the video stream at the
time of recording, or was added later. I'll analyze the
photo and look for tampering. But back to my original
question. *Where* did the shot come from?"

"Clearly, it's from across the street," Matt interjected.
"From the angle of the shot, you might be able to ex-
trapolate back to where the camera was located. Then
it's a matter of trying to get the actual footage. But four
years later, how likely is it that you'll be able to recover
anything? If it was really captured on VHS, it's likely
been taped over dozens of times, if the tape itself even
exists still."

"It's going to be a challenge, I agree. But whoever sent
this somehow got his hands on it." He pulled out the remaining sheet of paper from the envelope. "Now…a cell
phone log. Real?"

"No," said Leigh. "I determined that much already.
You need a subpoena to get a cell carrier to provide this
kind of info. No subpoena was filed and the company has
no record of supplying the log. It's faked, but the highlighted number was real. It belonged to a burner phone
that's been out of service for years."

Tucker was nodding, his eyes on the log. "I might be
able to get you more information there. I can take this
stuff with me?"

"Yes. The log is a copy. The photo is the original because I knew you'd need that."

"Thanks. I'll get it back to you once I've got it scanned into the system and I'll keep it safe in the meantime." He slid the photos and the log into the envelope. "That's only two of the deliveries. What about the third?"

Leigh picked up the thicker envelope and slapped it against her open palm a few times. "This is the one that came to my house." She met Tucker's gaze and his eyes narrowed at her hesitant expression. "This is where things might get a little tricky. If any of this makes you uncomfortable, I'll understand if you want to step away. No hard feelings. I'd just ask that you keep what you know confidential."

Tucker held out his hand, wiggling his fingers for the envelope. "You've got me, Abbott. I'm not backing out. Gimme."

"But things get kind of murky from this point. You need to understand that."

Tucker extended his hand even further. "I've got it. Now *gimme*."

When Leigh paused again, Matt leaned forward and plucked the envelope from her hand. "He understands, Leigh, and he's with you. Now let him do what he can to help." He handed the envelope to Tucker.

"Thanks, man." Tucker opened the envelope and took out the three case files. He quickly flipped through the first two, his eyes scanning quickly down the pages as his heel jiggled a rapid beat against the floor. He opened the third file and Matt knew the moment he hit the connection to the Essex Detective Unit as his leg suddenly went still. Tucker's head tipped up slowly, his gaze finding Leigh's. "You think someone from the unit is involved?"

"I don't know. But right from the start it looked like

an inside job. This is just the first real indication that the unit is linked into this somehow."

"From this it looks like Trooper Mercer just investigated the two deaths in this case."

"It also looks from the picture outside Bruno's Tavern that my dad is having a drug meet. Sometimes things aren't what they appear. And Trooper Mercer isn't here to declare his own innocence seeing as he died three years ago." Leigh pushed off the couch to stand in front of the fireplace, staring up at the watercolor painting. The small girl running through the churning sea waves with her black Lab puppy was Leigh herself. The small signature in the corner—Grace Abbott—had been painted there by the mother Leigh lost to cancer when she was barely older than the child on canvas.

Tucker swiveled to face Matt. "I can look into all these cases. Let me see what's there to find."

"That's what we need you to do. Check the official records and make sure they match what Leigh's being sent. After the phone log, we can't know for sure that this is reliable information. And we have something else for you too." Matt stood and crossed to the end table to pick up the hard drive. "This was from Nate Abbott's home computer. Leigh thinks there might be copies of some of his files on here from when he used to work on them at home."

Tucker whistled. "So if tampering in the files is a concern, that drive might be our only evidence of the truth from back then."

"That's what we're thinking." Matt handed it to Tucker.

Tucker ran a finger over the drive's metal case. "Then let's give the little lady a whirl."

"You're probably going to be looking for deleted files. Can you recover them?"

"Damn straight. Sometimes it takes a gentle hand to convince these girls to hand over their treasures, but they always do." He gathered the envelopes and the drive and stood. "Abbott, give me some time. I guarantee I'll find something for you."

She finally turned back to the men. She was worrying her lower lip and had jammed her hands in her pockets, hunching her shoulders. "I don't know what to say. I don't know how to repay you for this."

"There's nothing to repay. It's what friends do." He perked up. "Unless you want to convince Harper that I need another fifteen big ones in my budget. There's a sweet server I'd love to have." He grinned at her, bright-eyed.

Leigh laughed, her shoulders relaxing fractionally. "Yeah, let me see what I can do for you there. Harper always comes to me for budget recommendations." She scuffed a toe against the carpet. "But seriously, Rob, thanks."

Tucker touched two fingers to his right temple in a salute. "Happy to help. I'll see myself out. 'Night."

In a flash he was down the hall and out, the door crashing shut behind him.

Matt studied Leigh as the color slowly eased back into her cheeks. "That went pretty well."

"Better than expected, actually."

Her whole body drooped with exhaustion, so Matt dropped onto the couch and caught her hand, pulling her down into his lap to catch her when she more toppled than sat. He pulled her in, resting her head on his shoulder. He waited as she pulled in a long breath, let it out, and finally sagged against him, her muscles going slack.

"You have more friends at the unit than you think."

"Really? Have you been chatting with Morrison lately and know something I don't?"

Matt nearly snorted. "Morrison? *No.* But think about the last few days. Riley shows up early on to help out with the scene and did you hear what Tucker said? 'The drive might be *our* only evidence of the truth.' He's with you on this. They both are."

She looped one hand up over his neck, stroking the hair at his nape, more to soothe herself than him, he suspected. "I just wasn't sure."

"About trusting Tucker enough to bring him on board? Or whether he'd stay and not bail?"

"Both."

"You influence those around you more than you realize. You have friends, Leigh. Let them help. You'd step in to help them if they asked, wouldn't you?"

"Well…sure."

"Then give them that same chance. I can't wait to see what he finds. I have to say, he's an interesting guy."

"What makes you say that?"

"His mannerisms and the way he seems to take in everything at once. I get the feeling he's not just smart, he's one of those scary smart guys who's always miles ahead of everyone else in the room."

"That's Tucker. Sometimes I have to make him back up and explain things to me again because he's twelve steps ahead of me."

Matt chuckled. "I know some people on campus like that. He's a lot more normal than most of them. I think we're in good hands."

"God, I hope so."

Matt tightened his arms around her and settled back more comfortably on the couch, watching the flames dance in the grate.

For now, all they could do was sit back and wait, but he had a good feeling that Tucker could be the key to all of this. They just needed to give him time to work his magic.

FOURTEEN: DENATURE

Denature: the attempt to prevent ethanol consumption by adding nauseating or poisonous substances to make it undrinkable.

Thursday, 1:22 p.m.
Lowell Residence
Brookline, Massachusetts

"MATT, LEIGH'S HERE." Mike's voice floated up the stairs.

Matt yanked a clean T-shirt over his head and left the master bedroom at a jog. Leigh and his father were talking at the bottom of the steps. He recognized the two plain brown boxes beside the wheel of his father's chair.

He stepped down from the staircase and nudged the bottom box with one foot. "Is that all of it?"

"No. There's one more in my car."

She turned to the door, but Matt was already slipping into the sneakers he'd left on the front mat. "I'll get it. It's unlocked?"

"Yes. Just lock it up when you're done."

"Back in a flash." Matt ran out to the midnight blue Crown Vic in the driveway, returning moments later with the last evidence box in his arms. He set it down on top of the others. "It's a good thing we have reinforcements coming. This is a lot of material."

"I'm grateful for the help, even though there's not

much evidence by today's standards, considering the crime," Leigh said. "A home invasion and a murder. But back then they didn't collect the same types of evidence we do now."

"DNA wasn't even remotely on the horizon in nine-teen-seventy-five, nor was a lot of the chemical analysis done routinely today." Matt turned to his father, who sat near the newel post. "You mind if we take over the kitchen for the afternoon? We could use the counter space."

"Not at all." Mike deftly whirled his wheelchair around to face his son. A car accident a decade before had taken both his wife and the use of his legs. It had also ended Matt's military career in the Marines when he'd left post–9/11 Afghanistan on a hardship discharge to take care of his father in the wake of his mother's death. "Do you need a hand? You're going through an old case file? Something related to your current case?"

"Probably not," Leigh said. "But we've sworn off co-incidences in this case, so we're not leaving anything unexplored." She turned to Matt. "You've filled him in?"

"Uh…yeah." After a handful of cases together, Leigh understood Matt often kept his father abreast of his work, but that information never left their house.

"The wife of the old man who started the whole investigation was killed in nineteen-seventy-five during a home invasion. But when I asked the family about it, they clammed right up. I understand murder is horrible, but over thirty years after the fact they still didn't want to talk about it to a homicide cop? The kind of person who'd best understand both the process and what they've gone through? That's a bit unusual and raised some red flags for me. And after two apparently unconnected deaths suddenly became very connected, I'm not letting anything slip by. If Samuel Kain murdered Charles Ward, and eighty years later the body of Ward's grandson is left in the same location, then these families are linked and we have to look at everything. Especially when it involves another murder. So, if you have time to help us sort through evidence and run through files, I'd be grateful for the extra set of eyes."

The sound of a motorcycle engine suddenly broke the silence as it roared up the street. Matt opened the front door just in time to see Paul pull into the driveway, followed closely by Kiko and Juka in Kiko's little hatchback. After stowing his helmet under his seat, Paul joined Kiko and Juka on the front walk.

Matt elbowed Leigh lightly and tipped his head toward her. "Kinda makes you want to borrow it again, doesn't it?" he murmured.

She glanced at him sideways and gave a low laugh. "I'm not sure you could convince Paul again. You barely managed it the first time. You could always buy your own, you know, if you miss it so much."

"Don't tempt me. I'd forgotten how much fun it is."

Kiko, Paul, and Juka trooped up the front steps, their familiarity with Matt's father evident in their casual greetings. In the midst of handshakes and hellos, the sound of nails on hardwood heralded Teak's arrival. A K-9 wounded in Iraq when an IED exploded during a search that cost him both his left eye and ear, and almost his life, the Belgian Malinois was now Mike's faithful service dog. Man and dog were firmly bonded—the walking wounded finding comfort in each other. Teak eagerly wound through legs and around boxes, greeting each new arrival individually and receiving scratches and pats in return.

When Matt noticed Leigh taking in the group with wide eyes and a baffled expression, he sidled a little closer. "They come over a couple of times a year for dinner or a barbecue, so they know Dad and Teak." When her gaze narrowed on him, head slightly cocked in contemplation, he squirmed self-consciously. "What?"

"You're a good boss. Not all bosses invite their staff home with them like that. They maintain a separation between work and personal lives."

"I have the advantage of being in an academic setting. No strict business rules. It's very casual."

"That may be, but you still do it better than most. In many ways, they're your extended family." She turned back to where Paul was in an animated conversation with Mike as Kiko and Juka both bent down to pet Teak. "It's time to get this going or we'll spend the whole afternoon in the front hall." Leigh cleared her throat and raised her voice. "Guys, let's take this into the kitchen."

Matt, Juka, and Paul each grabbed a box and the group moved into the kitchen, Teak trotting eagerly in their wake.

Leigh motioned to the floor at one end of the counter. "Put it all there." She waited while boxes were set down and the men moved back. "Thanks for offering to come out this afternoon to give me a hand. There's a definite advantage to working as a group when doing these big case reviews. Did Matt explain to you what we're doing?"

Kiko nodded. "Looking into the murder of the wife of Samuel Kain." She leaned in conspiratorially, a gleam in her eye. "You've met him now. Do you think he killed Charles Ward and bricked in the body?"

"I may never be able to prove it, but, yes, I do."

"I'm not sure I understand why we're here." Juka sat down on one of the kitchen chairs. Teak immediately laid his muzzle on Juka's leg and gazed up at him imploringly with his single eye. "You don't think this death is related in any way, do you?" He scratched around the dog's intact ear. Teak gave a noisy sigh of contentment and leaned against Juka in bliss.

"I don't know. Kain lost his wife, Anna, to a home robbery that went badly wrong, according to the official report. But I couldn't get anything from the family besides that, so I wanted to look into it further." She laid a hand over the lid of the top box. "It's all in here. I haven't even had time to crack open the lids. Let's run it like we always do—when you find something, no matter how small, speak up."

"Let's get started then." Moving to the counter where mugs, cream, and sugar were set out, Matt looked up to find Paul already eyeing the full coffee pot. "I don't even need to ask you. Anyone else besides Paul want coffee?"

For the next few minutes, he and Leigh maneuvered around each other delivering case files and coffee mugs. Finally, he set two mugs down and pulled a tall leather barstool up to the breakfast counter. He pointed to one of the two mugs before patting the empty stool beside his. "Sweet and light, just the way you like it."

She handed him a file and settled in. "There you go. Hit me with some groovy nineteen-seventies science."

"I'll do my best."

Leigh picked up her mug, cradling it in both hands, and took a long sip, letting out a satisfied sigh as she set it down. "Thanks."

"For what?"

"For the kitchen and the coffee."

"The coffee was bait to get Paul on board."

"I heard that." Without even raising his head, Paul's voice came from the kitchen table where he sat, bent over a file, between Juka and Mike.

"You're a cheap date," Matt retorted. "And predictable." He turned back to Leigh, grinning. "But you're welcome."

The room settled into a comfortable silence for a few minutes.

Kiko was the first to break that silence. "It looks like I have the responding officer's report," she said. "Trooper Bern responded to the call from the Lynn Police Department. Mr. Kain had come home from work to find his wife dead in the hallway leading to the front door. She was lying facedown and he rolled her over to administer CPR."

"What time was that?" Matt asked.

"About five-fifteen."

Matt winced inwardly. He could imagine the man coming home to his dead wife, rolling her over to try to save her, only to find her body stiff and her skin ice-cold beneath his hands. "Autopsy report lists the time of death between ten a.m. and two p.m. The body would have been cold by then with rigor setting in already."

"I have the scene photos," Mike said. "The body has definitely been shifted judging by the original blood puddle on the floor. Mrs. Kain is lying face up and there appears to be a gunshot wound to the chest and another to the abdomen."

"Gut shot. It's an excruciating way to die." The edges of the autopsy report crumpled under his grip and Matt forced himself to loosen his hold. Forced himself to push back memories of dying comrades lying on the hot sand amid rubble and bomb debris. "That was the first shot. The ME estimated approximately five minutes between the two shots, based on blood loss and the extent of bruising while the heart was still beating."

"Blood spatter on the kitchen wall, as well as one bullet casing in the kitchen, indicated that was the site of the initial shot," Kiko interjected. She looked up from her report. "The second shot was in the hall."

Matt looked across to his father. "The chest shot in your photo is actually an exit wound. The entrance wound is in the back. She was in the hall trying to get away when the second bullet pierced the superior vena cava. She went down and bled out pretty quickly after that."

"That second shot had to have played into the sentencing," Leigh said. "The perp…hold on, where is his name…" She ran a finger down her file. "Here it is. Santino Cabrera. He's still in jail over thirty years later. I looked into that before leaving the unit."

"He murdered someone," Juka said. "Wouldn't we expect him to still be in prison?"

"We would if it was first-degree murder. But most home invasion deaths are charged as second-degree murder due to the lack of planning and initial intent. Second-degree is usually life with the chance of parole after fifteen years. Now, maybe he hasn't been a model prisoner. Or because the murder occurred during the commission of a felony and because of the shot in the back, it might have been bumped up to first." Leigh stopped and tapped a nail beside an entry. "Or this could have done it too. It was his second home invasion charge. We're serious about armed home invasions. Do it a second time with an illegal firearm—there are several firearms charges here as well—and kill the homeowner? That would be life with no chance of parole for sure. So, he broke in during the middle of the day when she was alone. I wonder if he'd been watching the house."

"Or he might have been trailing her from outside the home." Mike held up a color crime scene photo depicting paper grocery bags tipped sideways on the counter, their contents spilled and rolled to the four corners of the room. Shattered pieces of broken glass and china littered the countertop. "Looks like she'd just come in from doing the groceries, and there was some sort of scuffle on this side of the room."

"According to the police report, there were two tea-cups on the table," Kiko said. "There was also an ash-tray with several cigarette butts in it. One of the lipstick prints on the butt matched a color Mrs. Kain wore but there were several more with a color that didn't match anything she had."

"So a friend stopped by that morning?" Juka suggested. "Maybe unexpectedly? Before she'd had a chance to put away her groceries?"

"Mr. Kain's statement said his wife always did the groceries on Wednesday mornings," Paul said. "It was just the two of them by that time. All their kids had grown up and moved out. She filled a lot of her time with charity work and often had ladies over to discuss projects. That was nothing out of the ordinary. But with her husband at work, the house would have been empty when she went out. It could have been a random attack, she could have been followed from the store, or maybe it was someone who knew her schedule."

"Do we have any idea who was inside the home first?" Matt asked. "Maybe it was someone who knew her regular routine and tried to gain entry while she was gone. Then she came home earlier than expected and it all went to hell."

"Looks like he got there first." Kiko waved her report. "The back door was jimmied open. Back then, a lot of people would leave their doors unlocked if they were home. So this sort of implies the perp got in first while she was out. If she came in the front door, she'd never have known there was someone else in the house until it was too late."

Matt flipped through his file. "It looks like the guy only touched objects he then took with him. Either that or the cops were kind of lousy with the fingerprinting because all that's here seems to be a few smudged partials."

"If there were only a few smudged partials, I'd lean toward someone wiping everything down and missing a couple of spots," Leigh said.

"Cabrera maintains they aren't his prints." Juka looked up from where he sat at the table. "I have the court transcripts. He pleaded not guilty. Said he was never there. Said those couldn't be his prints."

"What other evidence did they have on him?" Leigh asked.

"The few items reported as taken from the house—her wedding rings, a few other pieces of jewelry, and some cash—were never recovered. The murder weapon was a Walther PPK, also not recovered at the scene." Juka scanned the page, flipped to the next, and kept scanning. "What they had was all circumstantial. There were a few prints in the house. The gun was found the next day, tossed into a dumpster a few blocks away. The serial number was filed off so it was deemed stolen."

"This is the ballistics report," Matt said, waving a

sheaf of papers. "The gun was a firm match to the bullets. No doubt at all there. It had some prints on it too. The prints matched those in the house that didn't belong to either of the Kains." He flipped further into the file. "Going forward in time, they don't seem to be finding a match."

"I'm seeing that also," Juka said. "There's a huge time gap that seems to have complicated matters."

Leigh swiveled in her seat to face Juka. "What do you mean?"

"The crime occurred in September of nineteen-seventy-five. Cabrera wasn't arrested until February of seventy-nine. And then the case was tried in the fall of eighty."

"He was arrested four years later?" Matt asked. "Why so long?"

"It looks like there wasn't anything to connect him with the crime."

"Man, this cop was a bulldog." Kiko flipped through her thick file. "At first he focused in on Kain himself, but the evidence just didn't support it. Kain had a clear alibi that day. And then no one else presented as a suspect. But Trooper Bern just couldn't let it go. I have years of reports here. The case went cold almost immediately, but he just didn't give up. He tried to find the woman who Anna met with that morning, but without success. He figured that Cabrera must have wiped down the kitchen, and, in doing so, wiped away all traces of the woman Anna had a cigarette with. Too bad they don't have the cigarettes still."

"Wait." Leigh bent over and sorted through one of the boxes at her feet. "You mean these?" She held up a small plastic evidence bag. Four cigarette butts lay at the bottom of the bag.

Matt snatched the bag from her hand, squinting at the butts through the plastic. "Yeah, those. We can run DNA on them and see who pops up."

Mike rubbed a hand thoughtfully over his neatly trimmed white beard. "You think it's going to be important who a dead woman had tea with almost forty years ago?"

"You never know," Leigh said. "In a case like this you leave no stone unturned. What if this woman is the one person who might have seen something that day but didn't realize it was important." She turned back to Matt. "How fast can that be run?"

"Within the next few days. We should only extract from half of each cigarette butt, though, just in case part of the sample needs to go to the state lab because we actually find something."

"That works. Of course, with our luck, it'll be someone who's been dead for thirty years, but still, it's worth a shot." She bent back over her file.

Matt laid the evidence bag down on the counter before turning back to his own file. He was almost at the end of it when he found the piece of evidence that tied it all together. "This is it. I have what convicted Cabrera." He slid the fingerprint report in front of Leigh. "It was a matter of making the match and connecting the dots. The bullets on scene to the gun and the fingerprints on the gun to the perp. He got arrested for a B & E and that brought him back into the system. His fingerprints were a perfect match to the old case."

"The B & E charge was dropped," Juka said. "But by that time they had him on the murder of Anna Kain. The

entire case was circumstantial. Cabrera swore he didn't
do it, but four years later couldn't provide an alibi or eye
witnesses proving his innocence. He said he was never
there, but couldn't prove it all that time later." He flipped
another page. "Bern did a great job of burying the guy.
Describing the scene of a middle-aged housewife trying to escape, only to be shot in the back by a coward.
That was followed by testimony by Kain himself and the
jury apparently bought it. The defense even put Cabrera
on the stand, but clearly it didn't make a difference. The
jury returned the guilty verdict after less than two hours
of deliberation."

Matt turned to Leigh. Her narrowed eyes were unfocused and one fist absently clenched and unclenched on
her thigh. He touched her arm, drawing her gaze. "What
are you thinking?"

"I'm thinking I'd like ten minutes with this Cabrera."

"You want to go interview a convict?"

"Yeah, just to tie this whole thing up."

"Wasn't it tied up over thirty years ago?"

"You'd think." She reached over to grab her cup and
Matt could see she was buying time, her mind running
a mile a minute as she swirled the coffee in her mug and
took a long, slow sip. Then she set it down decisively and
pulled her phone from her pocket, speed-dialing a number. "Hey, it's Abbott. Can you give me a current location
for a Santino Cabrera? He went up in nineteen-eighty for
murder during the commission of a home invasion." She
tapped her fingers on the counter as she waited. Her fingers suddenly stilled and she whistled. "Okay, thanks."
She set down her phone. "He's in the Souza-Baranowski
Correctional Center."

"Is that bad?" Matt asked.

"It's the only maximum security prison in Massachusetts. It's where the most dangerous criminals in the state go. It only opened in ninety-eight, so he must have started somewhere else and been transferred there." She glanced at her watch. "It's in Shirley, so it's only about an hour away." She flipped her file closed. "I'll contact the warden about heading out there this afternoon."

"Let me come with you." Matt closed his own file and pushed back from the counter. "If you think something is off, a second opinion might be useful."

A battle waged in her mind for a long moment. "You can come with me, but you have to stay in the background. You have this habit of trying to stand in front of me occasionally. I know your intentions are good, but if you do that this time, you'll undermine my credibility and I won't get it back. This is a convict and I'm a cop. The hierarchy needs to be clear from the second he walks in the door. He'll try for the upper hand; you have to leave it to me to keep it."

"Okay."

She pinned him with an icy glare. "Seriously, Matt. This is important."

He raised both hands in surrender. "Understood. Really. I'll stay in the background."

"You'd better." She turned to the room. "Okay guys, I'm going to set this up. I'll try to buy an extra thirty minutes. Give me everything you have on the case. I need to know it all." She glanced at Matt. "Then we'll go hear Cabrera's story and see if they line up."

FIFTEEN: CLIP JOINT

Clip joint: a place of entertainment where customers are tricked and coerced into paying highly inflated prices for inferior or nonexistent goods or services.

Thursday, 4:38 p.m.
Souza-Baranowski Correctional Center
Shirley, Massachusetts

THE ROOM WAS sparsely furnished, with only a table and four chairs. The guard let Matt and Leigh in, and then silently withdrew.

"Well, isn't he a happy fellow," Matt said, frowning at the closed door with a small square window in it.

"This is *not* a happy job, especially in a maximum security prison like this. I've never been in one with this kind of tech." Her gaze drifted up to the small black dome in the corner—one of the facility's many security cameras. "The control center to monitor all the high-def cameras, gates, doors, lighting, etcetera must be pretty extreme. But they've never had a breakout, so something is certainly working right."

"It was hard enough to get in. I have to admit, I kind of thought you'd be able to manage it with a little less effort."

"You just didn't like having to take off your belt and

shoes and going through the metal detector. Even cops have to submit to their entrance requirements. Look at it this way—they had the option of a strip search they didn't exercise. For instance, if they have any suspicion of contraband being brought to an inmate." When Matt's eyes went wide in horror, she laughed. "But you were with me, so there was never any worry." She grinned when his whole body relaxed and he dropped into a chair.

"I suppose I should have guessed they'd want you to turn over your gun."

"The last thing they need is a prisoner overcoming a cop, stealing a gun, and a riot starting."

"Good point. This whole place makes me…" His gaze darted around the room. "Uneasy. I may never speed again."

"You'd have to do a lot more than break the speed limit to end up in here. I'm just glad they squeezed us in. This isn't their normal visiting hours, but the warden made an exception."

Their attention was suddenly drawn to the door as the muffled sound of voices filtered through the glass. The door opened to reveal a wiry older man in an orange Department of Corrections jumpsuit. His salt-and-pepper hair was buzzed short and a scowl split his white beard. Two guards held his handcuffed arms as he shuffled into the room. They led him over to a chair on the opposite side of the table from Matt and unlocked his cuffs before pushing him roughly into the chair. One of the guards left the room, the door slamming shut with a metallic *clang*, while the other guard took up his post beside the door, his gaze flatly fixed on Cabrera.

Cabrera turned unusually light gray eyes on Leigh, his cold stare verging on arctic. "Who are you?" His deep voice carried a distinct north shore accent, even if his skin tone spoke of his Latino heritage.

"Trooper First Class Leigh Abbott of the Massachusetts State Police." Leigh sat down in the chair next to Matt, calmly folding her hands in front of her.

"What does a cop bitch want with me?"

Leigh sensed Matt tensing beside her, but calmly gazed back at Cabrera. "I want to talk about why you're here."

For a brief moment, confusion flashed in those icy eyes, but it was quickly quenched. *You can't ever show weakness in a place like this*, Leigh thought.

"Shouldn't you be talking to Trooper Bern? Isn't he one of yours?"

"He was," Leigh said calmly. "He's retired now. But I wanted to talk to you first. Your case has come up during the course of another murder investigation."

Cabrera swore viciously. "They trying to stick another one on me? I didn't do the Kain woman in the first place."

"That's what I wanted to talk to you about. Your case has fallen into my hands and there are some aspects of it that strike me as…odd. How did you know Mrs. Kain?"

"I didn't," Cabrera snarled, leaning across the table. "Look, bitch, I'm going to say it only once. *I didn't do it.*" One clenched fist thumped down on the table.

"Cabrera," the guard snapped, pushing away from the wall.

Leigh turned around, throwing up a palm to stop him. "Stop right there. I don't need your help. In fact, I'd prefer it if you waited outside, Officer."

"I wouldn't want to leave Cabrera here with a lady."

Leigh stood, pushing back her chair so quickly, it squealed across the tile floor. "I'm a cop, not a lady. Feel free to monitor by camera, but get out. This is a private conversation and this prisoner has rights."

The guard gave her an angry glare, but retreated from the room after pointing an accusing finger at Cabrera. A silent message—*I'm watching you*—and the door closed behind him.

Leigh took her seat again and stared coolly across the table. "Now, can we start again? And how about this time we cut the bullshit attitude? Talk to me, Cabrera. I'm not here for my health, but to get to the bottom of something I have some questions about."

Cabrera looked suspiciously from Leigh to Matt and back again. "Who's he?" He jerked his head in Matt's direction.

"Dr. Matt Lowell from Boston University. He's the scientist working on my cases." In her peripheral vision she saw Matt give a single nod of acknowledgment, but remain silent. "Now, tell me about Anna Kain." She held up a hand as he opened his mouth. "Something more concrete than 'I didn't do it.' When did you become aware of the Kain case?"

"When I was out on bail for a B & E I didn't do either. I was seen leaving the scene of the crime. The only problem was I wasn't involved."

"What was the B & E?"

"Someone lifted some jewelry from a house down by the water in Lynn. I was down in the area, picking up some stuff, and someone tagged my license plate."

"What was the 'stuff'? Were you into illegal drugs?"

Cabrera clamped his lips tight and looked mulish.

"That's fine." She stood. "Come on, Dr. Lowell, if he's not willing to help us, we can't help him."

She was halfway to the door before he stopped her.

"Wait."

Leigh purposely paused for a few seconds before slowly looking around. "Yes?"

Cabrera let out a long breath and drummed his fingers on the table, clearly struggling with himself. "I was getting secondhand baby stuff."

Leigh slowly returned to the table and sat back down. "Can you be more specific?"

"I'd been out of work for a while at that point. No one wanted to hire an ex-con, you know? Even one that was trying to make things right. My woman and me, we had a kid and a second one on the way and we needed some things. Someone she worked with offered us some of their stuff they were done with." The hand on the table curled into a fist. "I was just trying to provide, you know? I was down there picking up some rich lady's cast-offs because her garbage was better than anything I could give my own kids. That's all I was doing."

"And eventually the cops realized that."

"Eventually. And then suddenly none of that mattered anymore because I was accused of being a murderer. And I found out I threw my life away for nothing when my woman took off and took my kids with her."

"You must be pretty angry about that."

"I may be in here, but I'm still their father." Bitterness etched his words like acid. "I've never even seen my youngest." His gaze skittered away, but not before she glimpsed the depth of the pain and loneliness there.

Leigh gave him a moment to collect himself before pushing on. "Okay, let's back up a bit further so I have the whole picture. What about the home invasion you did time for?"

"What about it?"

"Did you do it?"

Cabrera's head drooped. "Yeah."

"How much time did you do?"

"Five years. I was a minor when it happened. Young and invincible. And fucking stupid. I went in at seventeen and got out at twenty-two. I tried to get my life back on track, but no one wanted to hire me. And then everything else happened."

"Your prints matched those found at the scene."

Cabrera leaned back in his chair, crossing his arms over his chest, defiance flashing in his eyes. "Not me."

"You were never there."

"Never."

"But you couldn't prove it," Leigh pointed out.

"Where were you four years ago today? Do you remember what you were doing during two hours in an afternoon that long ago?"

Four years ago she'd been burying her father, but she had to admit that if it came down to a specific day, she wouldn't be able to itemize her actions either. "Probably not. Okay, a different angle. The gun—it wasn't yours?"

"A Walther PPK?" he spit out scornfully. "A gentleman's gun, I'm sure, but too small to be considered a real threat."

"Clearly it was a threat to Mrs. Kain."

"Maybe, but if I'd carried one of those things around, I'd have been laughed out of the neighborhood. Back then it was a .44 Magnum or nothing. *That's* a man's gun."

"So that's what you had?"

"An ex-con on probation? I had nothing." He scowled and glanced sideways before looking back at Leigh. "Okay, I carried a blade because sometimes at night things could get dicey, but not a gun. I was trying to stay straight, stay outside so I could raise my kids. And then they were insisting my prints were on this stolen gun I'd never own in the first place. So I got firearms charges piled on too. And it was all bullshit!" A vein started to throb in his temple and his face flushed with color. "I've been saying for years that I was set up, but no one's ever believed me."

"You have my attention." Leigh leaned forward, purposely closing the space between them to imply intimacy. "Prove it to me."

"I can't goddamn prove it to you!" His fist crashed down on the table again. "If I could, I'd have been out thirty years ago. But no one wants another dirty Spic out on the streets. No one came forward to help me. How am I supposed to prove I've been framed when no one will support my innocence?"

"Then who hated you enough to frame you?" It was the first time Matt had spoken during the whole interview. When Leigh whipped around to face him, he held up a finger. "I know, I'm supposed to stay quiet and just listen, but the scientist in me wants to see the proof as much as you do. And 'when you have eliminated the impossible, whatever remains, however improbable, must be the truth.'" He made air quotes around the phrase. "Sherlock Holmes, *The Sign of Four*."

Leigh gave him a nonplussed stare. "You're flying your geek flag again."

"Proudly. But Holmes has a point. Let me play devil's advocate here. Suppose Cabrera didn't do it. Suppose, like he says, he's been framed. There's an easy way to prove it."

"How?"

"We have the reports and the crime scene photos. The

entire case hangs on linking his prints to those found in the house and on the gun. So let's run them again."

It was so entirely simple that Leigh's jaw sagged open in amazement at her own stupidity.

But Cabrera missed her reaction because he was staring at Matt. "You could take my prints and run them again?"

"Sure. The prints they collected are smudged and not great. Maybe it wasn't a good match. Maybe a second pair of eyes will see something else, or software could match them through current databases to someone else."

Leigh turned back to Cabrera. "Did your lawyer ever demand a second opinion on those prints? Did he supply his own expert?"

"I had a public defender. I didn't have the money for that kind of lawyer."

Leigh swiveled sideways in her chair to face Matt. "Off the books, I can call in a favor and have the prints re-analyzed."

"Why would you do that?" Cabrera's tone was suspicious, clearly the reaction of someone who had learned the hard way not to trust. "Why would you help me?"

Leigh leaned forward so he wouldn't doubt her sincerity. "Because it's the right thing to do. But let me make myself clear. If the prints match a second time, you're in here to stay. And I'll walk away without a second glance."

Cabrera leaned forward, challenge radiating from both his voice and posture. For the first time since he'd walked into the room, the hatred and despair in his eyes was tinged with hope. "Bring it on. They won't match." He drilled an index finger in Leigh's direction. "And that's going to be my proof."

Thursday, 5:12 p.m.
Souza-Baranowski Correctional Center
Shirley, Massachusetts

"Do YOU REALIZE what this means?" Leigh pulled her collar up higher against the chilly wind as they stepped from the prison out into the gathering gloom of dusk. She suspiciously eyed the dark clouds gathering on the horizon; they almost looked like snow clouds.

"If the prints don't match, you mean?" Matt stuffed his hands into the pockets of his leather jacket. "It means he didn't do it."

"More than that, it means it's an unsolved case. God almighty, I thought solving a case from eighty years ago was going to be bad. I think I have a good handle on that one, even if I'm a little hazy on the specifics. But this one—almost forty years ago and truly zero leads. They couldn't solve it four years out, let alone forty."

"If it turns out Cabrera's unconnected, are you going to hand this one off to someone else? You have a pretty full caseload right now."

"No way. Anna Kain is mine now. And so, in a way, is Cabrera. If he's innocent, that man lost his life. We all made mistakes as teenagers, although I admit his was worse than most. But it sounds like he was trying to go straight, trying to be a good father. And he lost it all. Most of his adult years, his lover, and, worst of all, his kids. If he's been wrongly accused, it's my responsibility to correct it."

"*Yours?*" He stared down at her, a frown playing around his lips at her use of the singular pronoun. "You think I'd be willing to stand by and watch an innocent man remain in jail for a crime he didn't commit? When

I can use my knowledge to go back through the evidence and the reports and maybe find something that was missed? Or something that could be discovered using modern tests?"

"That doesn't sound like you at all." She slid her arm through his, her fingers closing over his forearm under the slick leather. "Okay, 'ours.' Because I just can't seem to do a damned thing these days without my team."

SIXTEEN: LEAD POISONING

Lead poisoning: caused by lead acetate (a.k.a. "le▨▨▨ sugar") leached during distillation from ma▨ny ▨▨ ▨d hibition-era stills constructed using lead ¦coil▨ ▨ro- solder. ▨ ▨▨ or

Friday, 10:17 a.m.
Ward Summer Residence
Lynn, Massachusetts

LEIGH PUSHED THE door open with a latex-gloved hand and stepped into the dim house. Inside, sunlight slipped between heavy curtains to tumble over dull wood floors, dust motes dancing in small slivers of brightness before sinking once more into the gloom. White-draped furniture in the front rooms gave the house a shadowed, ghostly appearance. Goosebumps puckered the skin on her forearms, but she scolded herself that it was simply the chilly caress of the ocean breeze winding through the open door.

"See anything?" Brad Riley stood behind her on the front step, craning his neck to look through the doorway.

"Nothing from here." Leigh stepped aside to let him pass and then moved to close the door. She paused briefly, one hand resting on the heavy wood, staring out across Lynn Shore Drive to the churning waves of Nahant Bay. In the distance, Egg Rock Island—once a lighthouse station, now a bird sanctuary—lay at the mouth of the bay where it spilled into the Atlantic. A gust of November wind sent a shiver whispering down her spine, so she pushed the door closed, shutting out the cries of gulls soaring along the beach.

"Split up like we did at Holt's place?" Riley stood in the doorway to the dining room, surveying the ghostly shapes inside. "You take the downstairs, I'll take the upstairs?"

"Sure." Leigh looked past the multi-tiered foyer chandelier shrouded in plastic to the long, curving staircase beyond. It was darker upstairs than on the main floor, even though it was only mid-morning. "You have your flashlight, just in case?" Riley nodded and patted the pocket of his trench coat. Leigh moved to the door of the living room, studying the shrouded shapes. "If this place doesn't pan out as the kill site, I'm not sure where to look next."

Riley drew a pair of gloves from his pocket, pulling them on. "Not his own house, not his workplace, not the girlfriend's. But he certainly died somewhere."

"If his mother hadn't mentioned this place a few days ago, it would have taken property searches to find it." She spun back toward the foyer, feeling a touch of sadness for the house—clearly once a glorious family home, now only a shabby, forgotten relic. "No one's lived here in years, but this was the Ward family home. While Ward was doing business in Boston in the early to mid-nineteen-thirties, his wife and daughter lived here. But the Holts haven't been here for years. As you can see from the 'For Sale' sign on the grass out front, Evelyn is obviously hoping to sell it."

"She may have some difficulties with that if her son

died here," Riley muttered. He found a light switch on the wall at the bottom of the stairs and flipped it on, but the upstairs hallway remained shrouded in darkness. "If I was her, I'd definitely want to get rid of this place before it falls down from neglect. I'm heading up. Yell if you find something." He slowly climbed the stairs, his eyes already scanning for signs of violence as the treads groaned in protest beneath his feet.

Leigh turned back into the living room, moving to one of the windows. She pushed back the heavy velvet curtain, the nap crumbling beneath her fingers. Sunlight spilled through the panes, chasing away the gloom. The room was centered around the fireplace, framed by a heavy, wooden mantel. A faded area rug covered the dark wood floor, partially obscured by furniture and the trailing ends of the drapes. The mantel was starkly bare, yet another sign of emptiness. *Not a home. Merely a house.* She did a slow tour of the room, examining pale walls and even paler sheets, but there was no sign of blood or any evidence that the room had been disturbed in years. Bending, she pulled the sheet from the couch opposite the cold fireplace, revealing dark curved legs and curled arms. The paisley upholstery was now dull and faded, having long ago lost its sheen. She examined the two draped chairs flanking the fireplace before uncovering one. The chair was in a similar style to the couch, but covered in dark, flocked swirls. She dropped the sheet, returning another ghost to the room.

Leigh moved methodically through the room, uncovering and examining each piece of furniture, hope slowly dwindling as each item was eliminated. *Not here.* With a sigh, she turned toward the open door at the rear of the room, already contemplating their next move if this house turned up nothing. Her phone rang, a shrill peal in the silent room, pulling her from her thoughts. "Abbott."

"It's me." Matt's voice was upbeat, a stark contrast to her own darkening mood. "I have the DNA information you wanted."

Leigh stopped at the doorway to the hall. "The cigarettes?"

There was a beat of silence, then Matt's voice returned, decidedly less enthusiastic than before. "Uh, no. We're good, but not that good. Give us another couple of days on that. I'm talking about the autopsy sample from Peter Holt and the recovered tissue from Evelyn Holt. It's confirmed—the remains behind the wall in the speakeasy are those of Charles Ward."

"Funny you'd call and tell me this now. I'm standing in his house in Lynn. The one he left on the morning when he died at the speakeasy."

"What are you doing there?"

Leigh continued down the hall and into the kitchen, which ran the length of the back of the house. "We're still looking for where Peter Holt was killed to see if there's any evidence to link to his killer. We've checked out all the obvious places—his home, work, his girlfriend's— but there's no trace of any of them being the location of his death. We canvassed neighbors around the girlfriend's home. They knew exactly who he was, saw him on a fairly regular basis, but no one had seen him there in the week leading up to his death. He was seen leaving work the night before and security has no record of him re-entering the building after hours."

"There'd be a record of that?"

A floorboard creaked overhead and she glanced upwards. Riley was making his way toward the back of the house. "Key card access after-hours, so, yes. We've gone over his home with a fine-toothed comb, but there's no evidence of blood or a cleanup following a killing."

"We're a week past his murder," Matt stated. "If the murder had been somewhere public, someone would have stumbled over a puddle of blood by now."

"You would think." She quickly scanned the room, taking in the high, airy upper reaches, the tall glassed-in cabinetry, the expanse of dark ceramic tile, and the semi-circular windows letting in light from near the ceiling. "Anyway, back to DNA. You have a positive match on the skeletal remains?"

"Yes. The remains match both Holts', although the match is stronger to Evelyn, as you'd imagine being only one generation removed. But Peter is definitely his grandson."

"Brownie points to Rowe for calling that one ten seconds after seeing that ring."

"The man knows his stuff. Now, this makes the ID official, but it doesn't really clarify anything for us. We know Ward owned the *Blue Ruin*. We know he was killed by Samuel Kain."

"Suspect," Leigh said. "We don't know that for sure." She crouched down in the middle of the room, scanning the dark floor for signs of blood. The tile was brick-red, perfect for hiding bloodstains in plain sight. She made a mental note to come back with the crime scene guys to have them scan for trace evidence if they came up empty.

"But your gut says he did it," Matt insisted.

"Yes."

"Since I've learned to respect your gut, that's good enough for me. So I know and you suspect Ward was killed by Kain. We know Kain's wife, Anna, was murdered but now we don't know who killed her. We know Peter Holt was killed somewhere, and his body was moved to the site of the speakeasy."

"Since we've given up on coincidences for this case, that had to be on purpose."

"So that in itself begs the question: Who knew the speakeasy was there?"

"Kain did. He sent me there in the first place. And by that line of reasoning, so did every member of his family who heard his story about the body."

"But no one actually knew the body was there for sure. No one but Kain. And his own family didn't believe him, which is why it took so long for them to report it. They thought he was just a crazy old man."

"Mostly crazy. But not always, clearly. So the rest of the family is a possibility. But we can't stop there. He likely told the nursing staff, or other visitors. And a lot of people used to go to that speakeasy. Who else might still know about it?"

"Maybe Rowe can find out some specific information. And there's someone on campus, an expert in nineteenth- and twentieth-century history, who might at least know of other resources we could try."

"Abbott!" The bellow came from upstairs, making Leigh jerk to her feet.

"Riley?"

"I've got it. Get up here."

"Matt, hold on." Leigh tore out of the kitchen and back up the hallway, hooking one hand over the newel post to slingshot herself around the corner, taking the stairs two at a time. "Where are you?" she called.

"Here." Riley's voice came from her right as she rounded the corner of the stairs.

Leigh caught a quick glimpse of a shadowed bedroom and a bathroom in shades of white and turquoise as she sprinted by. Riley stood in a doorway at the end of the hall. She slid to a stop at the doorway and he stepped aside, letting her see into the bedroom.

Heart pounding in her ears as she leaned on the door frame, she scanned the room: *Bloodstained wood floor. Blood spatter on dusty sheets and faded walls. A single ragged hole in the plaster. The end of a brass cartridge case peeping out from under the tangled folds of a drape.*

The tinny sound of her name brought her back and she stared down at the phone clenched in her white-knuckled fist, finally remembering it was there. "Sorry, Matt." She had to pause to pull in a breath. "We've got it. Riley found the kill site. It's here in the house." She turned to the younger officer and clapped him on the shoulder. "Nice work, Riley."

Riley flushed up to the roots of his neatly cut strawberry blond hair as he grinned back.

"I knew something was going on," Matt said. "Damn, I wish I was with you instead of only being along for the ride. Tell me what's there. Let me see it through your eyes."

Leigh paused for a moment to take it all in again. "It's a bedroom at the back of the house, probably the master from the size of it. The furniture in the room is draped with white sheeting—a double bed, a dresser, and a wardrobe on the far side of the room. The sheeting over the dresser is covered in spatter and there's a hole in the wall to the left of it."

"The bullet is lodged in the wall?"

"Looks like it."

"Holt was shot right through the thorax. So it's either

JFK's magic bullet again, or the bullet must have hit a rib or two on the way through. Is it intact?"

"I can't tell from here and I'm not setting foot in this room and risk messing up evidence. The Crime Scene Services boys would kill me. But looking at the wall, it's not a nice, neat little hole. It's misshapen and ragged."

"Like from a mushroomed bullet."

"Exactly. Hold on a minute." She dropped the phone from her ear to look at Riley. "You should call this in."

Riley's jaw sagged almost comically for a minute. "Me? But it's your case."

"And it's your find. I don't need the glory, just the results. Get Crime Scene Services on-site. We need answers."

Riley grinned at her broadly. "Yes, sir!" He turned away, pulling his phone from his pocket and moving down the hallway to make his call.

She raised her phone again. "I'm back."

"That was nice of you." Matt's voice was warm with pride.

She dropped her voice so Riley couldn't hear. "I've learned a thing or two watching you with your students. He's new, but he has good instincts. He's a solid cop."

"And he'll get better with your mentoring. I told you he sees you for who you are, not who Morrison says you are. But back to the case. We have the bullet in the wall and spatter where we'd expect to find it. Anything else?"

"I can just see a bullet casing on the floor. Looks like it rolled across the floor and is half-hidden under the drape over the double bed. There's also a blood stain on the wood floor, but it's not as big as I thought it might be considering what Rowe said about the extent of the blood loss. Unless…" She crouched down in the door-way, peering into the room.

"Unless what?" Matt asked.

"Unless there was something else on the floor. I think there was a carpet here. If you look at the floor, the edges are slightly faded whereas the middle of the floor, where the sunlight would come through the window, is darker. It should actually be more faded than the edge of the room."

"So there was a rug that soaked up some of the blood. But the body lay there long enough for the blood to seep through and stain the wood."

Leigh pushed to her feet. "It's also a handy way to transport a body. The house has an attached garage, but he likely didn't want blood in his vehicle."

"And there's no garage at the Adytum Building, so he needed something to cover the body when he moved it. You know, it's kind of odd the way this place isn't cleaned up. He left the bullet, the casing, the spatter. All he removed was the body and maybe a carpet. Why not put more effort into hiding the kill site. Or even coming back later to clean it up?"

"Coming back to clean up could be a real risk if he was spotted by a neighbor."

"Or maybe leaving a mess wasn't a concern for him. Right now you have a scene that's tied to the victim, but not necessarily the killer. Maybe the killer didn't care about leaving blood spatter as long as he didn't leave anything of himself behind."

"That may be true, but he couldn't have walked out covered in spatter himself." Leigh's gaze flicked to the door of the bathroom, just up the hallway.

"You need to check to see if he washed up somewhere."

She strode down the hallway to stand in the bathroom

door. "Already on that. Right next to the master is a big bathroom. And look at that…that might be handy for short-term storage."

"What?"

"There's a big claw-foot tub in the corner. I'll make sure Crime Scene Services checks the sink and tub drains for blood. We want to know exactly what happened here. But for now, Riley and I need to pull out to avoid contaminating anything." She dropped her voice. "You're still okay for five-thirty tonight?"

"I'll be there with bells on. Thanks for the update."

Leigh slid her phone into her pocket and walked back up the hallway to meet Riley, who waited for her at the bedroom door.

"The Crime Scene Services boys are on their way," he said. "They respectfully request we remove ourselves from the premises."

"They told you to get the hell out, didn't they?"

Riley grinned. "Yeah, pretty much. Subtle, aren't they?"

"Never in a million years. Come on, let's go."

Leigh looked back one more time into the room, taking in again all the signs of a brutal death.

Only in her job would this be considered progress.

SEVENTEEN: REAL McCOY

Real McCoy: a corruption of an 1856 Scottish phrase meaning "the genuine article." William McCoy was a sailor who loved boats; he became a bootlegger after his freight business fell on hard times. A designer of luxury speedboats before Prohibition, McCoy turned to running unadulterated and uncut Irish and Canadian whiskeys and rye between Nassau, Bimini, and the East Coast of the U.S. after passage of the Eighteenth Amendment. He was arrested in late 1923 and offered as a defense, "I have no tale of woe to tell you. I was outside the three-mile limit, selling whiskey, and good whiskey, to anyone and everyone who wanted to buy." Convicted, he spent nine months in a New Jersey jail before retiring to Florida a rich man.

Friday, 5:47 p.m.
Abbott Residence
Salem, Massachusetts

"SORRY TO BRING you all the way out here."

The petite redhead glanced up quickly at Leigh and then logged into the laptop already open on the kitchen table. "It's only an hour's drive from Sudbury. And while it would have been easier to show you this in my own office at the SIS, it's not a big deal to do here. I understand wanting to keep this under the radar right now, what with it being another trooper's case and all." She pulled her long hair back into a thick rope, twisting it into a loose bun and securing it with an elastic band pulled from one wrist.

"If we're going to start shaking things up on a case considered closed decades ago, sending a potentially innocent man to jail for all that time, we need to make sure we're beyond certain. I don't want any murmurs getting out that we're even looking until it's already a done deal."

Leigh's doorbell rang, followed by the sound of her front door opening and Matt's voice echoing down the hall.

"Come on back. We're in the kitchen."

Matt appeared in the doorway, unzipping and shrugging out of his leather jacket. "Sorry I'm late. My meeting ran long. Who starts a meeting at three o'clock on a Friday?"

"Someone who doesn't have a life and who doesn't want anybody who does starting the weekend early." Leigh waited while he hung his jacket on the back of a kitchen chair before making the introductions. "Matt, this is Claire Hargrove. She's one of our forensic experts at the state crime lab. Claire, my partner on this case, Dr. Matt Lowell. He's a forensic anthropologist with Boston University."

"I remember you from the Bradford case," Claire said, holding out her hand. "Pulling a burial ground out of thin air from only one bone. Nice work."

"Thanks," Matt said. "And thanks for looking into this so quickly. I was sure we wouldn't get anything back on this until next week at the earliest."

"Once Leigh explained the situation, I thought it deserved some time right away."

"Exactly." Leigh pulled out a chair and sat down on one side of Claire. "Okay, what have you got?"

"I know *you* understand what I'm talking about." Claire pinned her clear blue gaze on Leigh before turning to Matt. "But what do you know about fingerprinting?"

"Mostly what I've gathered from watching crime shows on TV." Matt took the chair to Claire's left. "I don't usually deal with fingerprint evidence because my clients tend to not have skin. Unless we're dealing with mummification, and then there's this trick I can do with fabric softener that would knock your socks off."

"I'm familiar with that trick. And it works surprisingly well. But beyond that, when it comes to actual fingerprint matching, do you know how it works?"

"Only the bare basics."

"Okay, let me give you a quick overview so my explanation makes sense. As you no doubt know, everyone's fingerprints are unique. They're a by-product of the fetal development process, so not even identical twins sharing the same DNA will have identical prints. The skin on your fingers, toes, palms, and the soles of your feet is different from the rest of your epidermis. The raised ridges in those areas amplify the sensation of touch going to the sensory neurons, and the ridged surface improves grip. Those raised ridges have very unique patterns and they give us identifiable fingerprints. Note I didn't say 'identical' fingerprints, because there is no such thing. Like all other skin, ridge skin is flexible, which means no two fingerprints are ever exactly the same. If I took your prints right now, and then fingerprinted you again ten minutes from now, they wouldn't be identical. Which is why fingerprint experts are required."

"Or an automated system."

"The automated system spits out a likely candidate, but the final comparison is still done by human eyes. The algorithms are good, but not as good as us."

"But if two sets of prints in controlled circumstances aren't identical, then the whole process must be pretty subjective when it comes to actual case evidence." Matt sat back in his chair, his face taking on the *I'm a scientist, convince me* expression Leigh had seen many times before.

"It might seem so, but given the correct training, it's less subjective than you think. Still, subjective assessments can be a real problem. Give the same prints to different techs and sometimes you *do* get different answers."

"Would that explain what happened to Cabrera if the prints don't match?" Matt asked.

Claire grinned. "Now you're getting ahead of me."

Leigh couldn't help the small laugh that escaped at Matt's snort of impatience. When he pinned her with a narrowed glare, she returned a sly grin.

Claire glanced from one to the other, her brows slanting together in confusion. "Did I just miss something?"

"I'm just enjoying being on the side of the discussion that knows what's going on for once. Usually it's Matt lecturing me and I'm the one wanting to jump to the end result." Leigh waved her hand at Claire. "Go on, explain it *all* to him." She relaxed back in her chair, a flutter of impatience in her own chest, but she tamped it down, content to wait an extra ten minutes for her answer. It was worth it just to watch Matt squirm with frustration.

"You asked for it, you got it." Claire turned back to

Matt. "Fingerprints themselves can be patent prints—ones visible with the naked eye, usually from a transfer of a substance like ink or blood—or latent prints—prints that are invisible until a tech uses an electronic, chemical, or physical process to visualize them. Most latent prints are organic impressions—sweat from ridge skin, as well as oils from the forehead and cheeks, since people often tend to touch their face." She gave Matt a pointed look. He colored and stopped rubbing his jaw where his chin was propped on his hand.

She pulled his hand free, pushing open his fingers, eyeing the light sheen on his fingertips. "Exactly like that. Leigh, have you got a butcher knife I can borrow?" Matt's wrist jerked in Claire's hand and she laughed, her pale eyes dancing with humor. "Don't worry, your fingers are safe. I'm just trying to make a point."

Leigh rose from the table, selected a wide-bladed, shiny knife from her knife block, and handed it to Claire. Flipping Matt's hand palm down, Claire pressed his fingers against the flat of the blade. She then angled the blade back and forth under the light, revealing the perfect impressions left by his fingertips.

"So basically, the print is an organic slurry of amino acids and fats with some inorganic compounds mixed in." Matt rubbed his hand on his jeans as if self-conscious of the oils there. "How long is it stable?"

"Prints from adults can last for weeks or even months on a nonporous surface. Prints from children have a different chemical composition and a *much* shorter half-life, sometimes lasting only a day or two. Now, as you can see on the knife, we have several lovely prints because I made sure we did. But that's very rarely how it works in real life. Often there are only partial prints, or there's smudging and smearing, or overlapping. Sometimes there's a mixture of prints from different people on the same surface and you have to tease out which print belongs to which person. And there are factors that affect the quality of the print—pressure of the ridge skin against the surface and whether it slips, surface composition and friction, flexibility of the skin, the material being transferred, and the development technique."

"I'm beginning to get an idea of how complicated it is," Matt said.

"And that's only the print itself. When it comes to examining a fingerprint, there are levels of details we look at. The first level is what you can see with the naked eye—the ridges themselves, and the arches, loops, and whorls."

"That I'm familiar with," Matt said.

"Most people are because that's about as detailed as the crime shows go. But within those forms is the second level of detail—ridge pattern deviations, called minutiae, seen at up to ten times magnification. Where the ridge ends, when it splits in two at a bifurcation, where the ridge makes a U-turn in a loop or whorl, that kind of thing. There is a third level at still greater powers of magnification that takes into account pore forms, size, and relative position. When we're running an analysis we go through each level and try to match between prints. If level one checks out, you move to level two and maybe then to level three. The first time something doesn't match, that print is excluded."

"Okay, that makes sense. Can we get into these specific prints now?"

Claire held up a finger to slow Matt down, grinning when his lips flattened into an impatient line. "Almost.

You need to understand one more thing before we start. In the seventies, comparisons were done a little differently than we do them today. Back then, the accepted method of fingerprint matching was to find a certain number of comparison points. For instance, any print matching twelve or more comparison points was considered to be a positive ID in Massachusetts. But if it only had eleven points, too bad, so sad, the print is now borderline. You might get it through court with the help of a second expert's opinion, but it was doubtful. Also, some countries had different standards. One country could convict and send someone to the death chamber on twelve points, but next door, they required sixteen points, so you were a free man."

Matt winced. "Sounds messy. And random."

"It was. But since the late nineties, we've done things a little differently. Now we not only look at the quantity of the comparison points, but we also look at the qualitative aspect. For instance, some ridge formations are comparatively rare. Matching a rare formation carries more weight than matching a run-of-the-mill arch. And sometimes what isn't in the print is more important than what is. So we do a holistic assessment taking into account the number of minutiae and the qualitative aspect of those minutiae.

"Now, let's get into these prints themselves." Claire turned to her laptop and brought up a series of black-on-white fingerprints. "In this case we have two sets of prints, one from the scene and one from the gun. This is the set from the scene. It was on the wall at the door frame from the kitchen to the hall where the body was found. This was photographed right on the wall after being dusted. Back then, the techs would have probably been using aluminum powder. Anyway, the kitchen was likely wiped down because it's basically devoid of prints, even ones we'd expect to find from Mr. and Mrs. Kain. I think the killer was trying to hide his own movements because pretty much the *whole* kitchen was wiped down. It's not like he remembered leaning against the counter-top so he only took care of that area. No, it's the whole thing. Thorough in the extreme."

"Except for this part of the door frame?" Leigh leaned in to study the prints. Three smears spread across the screen, ending in small partial prints.

"Right. The killer was thorough, but was apparently rattled enough to miss these. I've looked at the scene photos. From where the body was found, I think the killer shot Mrs. Kain in the hall and then pulled back to stand in the doorway, probably to watch her die. I'm assuming he's right-handed and holding the gun in his right hand, so he reaches out to steady himself with the left on the wall beside the doorway. See how the print slides for an inch or so, smearing along the wall? Then all we're left with near the doorway are smudgy partials."

"Too smudgy?" Matt asked.

"Not for me." There wasn't a hint of boastfulness in Claire's voice. She opened a new window with several partial prints. "These are prints from the gun. The gun would have been dusted and then the prints lifted off because they'd be hard to visualize on a dark surface."

"They're from the grip of the gun?"

"No, there wasn't anything clear there. A lot of smudges and smears that almost make me think the killer held the gun at some point while wearing a glove. He didn't actually wipe it down—it's not clean enough for that—but he managed to smear any secretions and oils so there aren't any discernible prints. But at some point, possibly while cleaning or loading the gun, he grasped the barrel. And that gave me everything I needed because I got prints that matched the wall—the index, middle, and ring fingers from the print positions. Comparing two unknown samples is harder than comparing a ten-print card to an unknown print, but I'm confident they match. Why I'm confident is because they both show a somewhat unusual formation—a peripheral double bifurcation." She pointed to one of the partials, tapping a short, blood-red nail near the edge of the print. "You see this here? See how the ridge splits into two and then almost immediately splits into two again so it almost looks like a tree branch? That's what I'm talking about. Combine that with the other features, even though they're only partials and not in particularly good shape, and they match." She brought up a new window showing the detailed image of a ten-print fingerprint card, and then swiveled in her seat to face Leigh. "But here's where it gets interesting. They *don't* match Santino Cabrera's prints. For instance, that bifurcation should be right about here." Her index finger circled the edge of the left middle finger print. "It's not."

A hot flush of triumph ran through Leigh, immediately followed by the cold slide of horror for what this meant to Cabrera. And to the system. An innocent man wrongly imprisoned for over three decades. "You're absolutely sure?"

"One hundred percent. I'm not basing this only on that one feature, but on a range of features. The only leeway here is that I compared the ten-print card on file as Cabrera's. If you want to get fresh prints from him, prints that you take so you absolutely know they're his, I'll do the comparison again. But if we're sure the card is right…"

"Then Santino Cabrera was sent away for a crime he didn't commit," Matt finished for her. He sat back in his chair, his expression drawn in a combination of disbelief and discomfort. "I knew this was a possibility, but now that it's a certainty…" He paused, rubbing his palms flat against his thighs before balling his hands into fists. "I'm having a little trouble wrapping my brain around it." He met Leigh's eyes. "What do we do?"

The weight of this new victim settled heavily on Leigh, but she resolutely shouldered it. "We fix it, that's what we do." She turned to Claire. "Which means we have to prove his innocence beyond any possible doubt. I'll get you a second round of prints. Are you on this weekend?"

"No, but call my cell when you have them and I'll meet you. You want to move on this right away, I assume?"

"Yes." Pushing back her chair, Leigh got up and started to pace the length of her kitchen, hands in her pockets, head bent, and her mind whirling. She maneuvered around the room with the familiarity of someone in their own space, but didn't see any of it. Instead, her mind's eye was fixed on the image of the Kains' kitchen. *Small table with four chairs, two teacups, ashtray with cigarette butts, avocado green stove and fridge, paper bags tipped over on the counter, oranges and tomatoes spilling onto the floor. The body in the hallway, sprawled in a pool of blood.*

"She okay?" Claire's quiet voice drifted through her thoughts.

"Yeah. She does this when she's trying to work something out," Matt said. "It helps her think."

Leigh reached her stove, whirled around, and came back. She cast a sidelong glance at Matt. "This works better in your lab; my kitchen's too small. Okay, let's work this through. Beside the fact we now have another murder to solve almost forty years after Mrs. Kain went into the ground, how did this happen? How did we send the wrong man to jail? Were the prints close? Did the tech simply make a mistake?"

Claire folded her lips together, her eyes going ice-cold. "In my opinion, no. They're too far off."

Leigh stopped dead, halfway through another lap of the kitchen. "Are you implying it was done on purpose?"

"I can't definitively say that. But unless the fingerprint tech on this case was drunk or stoned, the only other options are they were totally incompetent or dishonest. This isn't a matter of a difficult comparison and stretching the truth. This isn't the realistic risk we constantly live with of making a bad match. This is a giant leap off the cliff. They simply don't match, not even at level one. And there was no second expert to corroborate a weak match. One tech did the match and Santino Cabrera went away based on that testimony."

"Who was the tech?" Matt asked.

"Joe Emerson. I checked him out. He took early retirement in nineteen-ninety-six, but he still lives in the area."

"I'm going to need to check him out," Leigh muttered. "Is there any way he might have been pressured to give false testimony? By Trooper Bern? By a supervisor? Because he thought he was putting away a 'bad' man?"

"Leigh." The gentleness in Matt's tone made her look up. "You're trying to justify what one of the good guys did because you can't see the good in it. If he purposely made a bad call, there isn't any good to find."

Leigh came back to the table and sagged into her chair, her shoulders slumping. "I know. But I don't like that one of us could do something like this."

"Trust me, I don't either," Claire said, her clipped tone making her displeasure clear. "It gives us a bad name when ninety-nine percent of us put heart and soul into what we do. Part of the problem is the blind faith we put in the system. It allows mistakes to slip through sometimes. No one questions fingerprint techs, and when they're presenting to a jury who doesn't know how fingerprinting works, they can usually find enough similarities to sell it. And if the tech has a good rep, the chances of being questioned on it go down dramatically."

"Our first order of business, then, is to look into the tech, and that includes getting a warrant to look at his financials. Claire, I'll get you fresh prints to work with. Then we look at reopening Anna Kain's murder." Leigh met Matt's gaze across the table, seeing the same resolution there. "Someone got away with this crime and has been living scot-free ever since. It's time to balance the scales."

EIGHTEEN: TWO-WINE THEORY

Two-wine theory: an alternative reinterpretation of 1 Timothy 5:23. Prior to the nineteenth century, the moderate consumption of alcohol was widely accepted by Christians. But as the Temperance Movement gained traction, some churches began to preach that the consumption of alcohol was sinful, and the characterization of alcohol as "Demon Rum" displaced the earlier Christian view that alcohol was the "good gift of God." The Bible exhortation to "use a little wine for thy stomach's sake" caused serious problems for Abolitionists who insisted that the Bible was actually advising people to rub alcohol on their abdomens.

Saturday, 6:27 p.m.
Lowell Residence
Brookline, Massachusetts

"MATT, YOU'RE WEARING a path in the floor. Why don't you sit down?"

Halfway across the kitchen, Matt pulled up short, turning to look at his father where he sat at the kitchen table. "I just thought I'd see if anyone wanted more wine." He reached for the decanter on the granite countertop. "Leigh?"

"I'm good. You topped me up just five minutes ago,"

Leigh said, swirling the wine in her nearly full glass. "Matt, it's going to be fine."

Matt forced himself to lean against the counter, casually crossing his ankles. He felt twitchy, as if his skin was stretched too tight over his bones. "I know. It's just…it's been so long since I saw anyone from the unit."

"I know you don't want to hear it," Mike said "but this is all tied into the PTSD you do your best not to acknowledge."

Matt winced, knowing what was coming, but a quick glance at Leigh had him relaxing fractionally. Leigh had been with him through several recent PTSD episodes and knew his struggles.

"Colin was with you for the worst of your experiences over there," Mike continued. "Somehow, in your head, he's become associated with those memories and the feelings they evoke. But he was doing his duty, just like you. You need to separate the man from those memories."

Matt blew out a breath, letting his head hang for a moment before resolutely straightening. "You're right, of course. The logical part of me knows that I shouldn't be apprehensive about Colin's visit, but the rest of me isn't—" The doorbell chimed down the hallway and his gaze shot to Leigh.

She was already rising from her chair and holding out her hand. "Come on. Let's go meet your friend."

When they reached the front door, Leigh gave his hand a final squeeze and then stepped back to stand beside Mike, who rolled to a stop at the foot of the stairs.

Taking a deep breath, Matt wrenched open the door. A tall blond man stood on the other side, a man so familiar it seemed like it was only yesterday they embraced before Matt climbed into the Twin Huey to begin his final journey home. But this time, instead of desert camo fatigues, a small white clerical collar peeked out from the black shirt he wore under his jacket.

"My God, you haven't changed a bit," Matt said.

Father Colin Reid burst out laughing, stepping forward and catching Matt in an easy, back-slapping hug. "And you haven't changed a bit either. Still blunt as always." The men stepped back and Colin gave him a quick once-over. "You look…good. Happy."

"I think I've found where I need to be. Come on in." Matt stepped back, closing the door behind Colin.

Matt laid a hand on his father's shoulder. "This is my dad, Mike Lowell."

Colin stepped forward to shake Mike's hand. "Mr. Lowell, I've heard so much about you. Matt told some pretty tall tales about your time in the Navy."

Mike fixed a beady eye on his son. "Did he now?"

"Only the good ones, to help keep morale up." Colin's expression sobered. "I'm very glad to see you in one piece, sir. When Matt left camp…we weren't sure what he was coming home to. My condolences on your wife."

"Thank you."

Matt slipped an arm around Leigh, coaxing her forward. "This is Leigh Abbott, the homicide cop I told you about."

Leigh held out her hand to Colin. "Nice to finally meet you. Matt's told me about some of the times you shared overseas."

Colin glanced at Matt as he shook hands with Leigh. "I hope he told you about the many times my killer spike was the only reason we won those beach volleyball games."

Matt grinned. "And here, all this time, I thought it was my serve."

"So delusional." Colin shook his head sadly, as if distressed by Matt's words, but then ruined it with a wicked grin.

Matt held out an arm toward the end of the hallway. "Come on back. Dinner is just about ready. Can I get you a glass of wine while we're serving it up?"

"I'd love one."

Colin and Leigh settled at the table while Matt and Mike finished dinner preparations.

"Your email said that you've settled in D.C., but you didn't say why you were coming to Boston." Matt set a pan of bubbling lasagna on the table beside a large bowl of Caesar salad. "Business or pleasure?"

"Happily now it's a bit of both. But it was originally business. I work for the FBI."

For a moment, Matt simply stared at his old friend in shock. "The FBI? You're Fox Mulder?"

Colin let out a hearty laugh and had a long sip of wine. "No, not Mulder. Remember Dana Scully was the Catholic. But I'm not Scully either. I didn't want to leave the Church. I just wanted to serve God in a way that was fulfilling to me. After being in the service, I knew a life of writing Sunday morning sermons wasn't for me. Life in Afghanistan always seemed to be moments of extremes—boredom as we sat around waiting for our orders, happiness because we'd all made it through a battle alive, or devastation after we lost one of our own. And those long nights, when it sometimes seemed it was just the barest threads of Matt's medical skills and my prayers that kept one of our men from fading for good."

Matt had a sudden vision of one of those nights: The

medical station lights low to allow other patients to sleep. A soldier in the bed, burned, shot, or missing a limb. IV lines and EKG leads running from bloodless skin to beeping monitors. Colin in a chair by the bed, his face pale, dark circles under his eyes, an open Bible in his hands. In those moments when life hung in the balance, Matt couldn't get Colin to leave, so together they stood vigil as if daring the Grim Reaper to take one of theirs. It felt like just the two of them against the world in those moments.

He jolted back to the present as his father nudged his hand with a plate loaded with lasagna. Matt handed it to Colin and continued to pass out plates as his father served dinner. Then he took the empty chair beside Leigh. After Colin said a brief blessing, they all started to eat.

"I knew I needed something a little off the traditional Catholic path," Colin continued, "so I joined the FBI chaplains program."

"The *chaplains* program?" Leigh asked. "I've never heard of it."

"For most of us that are involved, it's a volunteer opportunity. Chaplains across the country work with FBI agents and their families during times of crisis. But they brought me on board to cover a slightly different need. I'm working in the Wounded Warrior Internship Program. We enroll vets that are disabled or on the mend, and bring them in on an internship during their rehab. Some vets join the FBI permanently. Some gain valuable working experience for their transition back into civilian life. I'm there to make sure that not only their physical needs, but also their emotional and spiritual needs, are met as well. And since I was there myself, they don't need to explain to me what they're going through."

"It sounds like an amazing program," Mike said.

"Sure does." Matt set down his fork to stab an index finger at Colin. "But 'fess up. Having an office in the Hoover building has to be pretty neat."

Colin sat back casually, brushing a nonexistent crumb off the sleeve of his black shirt. "It really is."

Matt burst out laughing. "All these years later and you're still full of it." A thought occurred to him as he studied his friend speculatively. "But do you have security clearance?"

Colin leaned in as if they were sharing a secret. "I can't say," he murmured.

"Damn." Matt sat back, shaking his head. "That probably means you have Top Secret clearance. You win, you have the cooler job." The grin slid from Matt's face. "But seriously, Colin, I'm impressed. You did great work with us overseas, and now you're still helping people."

Colin's face flushed scarlet, but he gave a single nod of thanks. "But that's enough about me. Look at you. Ditching medicine and becoming a university professor? I'll bet you didn't see that one coming."

Matt chuckled, remembering how unexpected his own left turn had seemed back then. Looking back a decade later, it had just been a matter of finally finding the correct path. "Not really. But when I came back, I had a hard time readjusting. Dad was recovering from the accident and I needed a drastic change to kick-start things for me. Moving to Tennessee to study forensic anthropology at The Body Farm was the perfect solution. Now, I run a lab with three students and we're working on identifying human remains in the columbarium beneath the Old North Church. When we're not working with Leigh, that is."

"You referred very briefly to that in your email." Colin turned to Leigh. "Your work sounds fascinating. And rewarding."

"It can be, but it can also be frustrating beyond belief. Don't be fooled, this job is a lot more routine than it looks on TV. You know what they say about military service and police work: it's ninety percent pure boredom punctuated by ten percent sheer terror. Matt can now attest to the boredom."

"I can also attest to the terror." Matt flipped up the edge of his right sleeve, briefly revealing the pink, slightly shiny scar that ran along his biceps.

"Is that from a bullet?" Colin pushed the sleeve back up to take a closer look. "I thought you left all that behind when you came home."

"Trust me, I did too," Matt said dryly.

"Solved any cases I might have heard of?"

Matt glanced over at Leigh to find her amused eyes already on him. "Did you hear about Neil Bradford earlier this fall?"

Colin's fork stopped halfway to his mouth. "The serial killer case? That was you guys?"

"It was. That was the first case we worked together."

"Talk about starting things off with a bang."

"No kidding," Leigh said. "And it feels like it's been nonstop since then."

"What are you working on now?" Colin glanced between Matt and Leigh. "Unless you can't tell me."

"Well, I can tell you what my press officer has released. We have two murder victims this time."

"Two? So it's another serial killer?"

Leigh shook her head. "Not unless you have a killer who only kills once every eighty years or so."

"Eighty years?" Colin's eyes snapped wide. "Oh, I get it. That's why you have Matt on board. So, one of the victims is from…the thirties?"

"Exactly. Matt and his team have done their usual magic and we've already identified the victim and cause of death."

Colin's eyebrows shot skyward. "In an eighty-year-old victim? I'm impressed. That was fast work."

"Well, let's just say he wasn't exactly an unknown." When Colin started to ask another question, Leigh raised a hand. "And that's all I can say about it for now. Watch the papers. I guarantee it's going to make a splash when it breaks."

"Now that does intrigue me." Colin pushed his plate back a few inches and lounged back in his chair. "That was amazing."

"Hopefully you're not too full for dad's famous double chocolate cheesecake," Matt said, grinning. "Yes, I remembered your obsessive love of chocolate. But first, let's take our coffee into the living room and let dinner settle before we have dessert in front of the fire."

"Sounds great. But only if you let me help clean up."

As Matt carried plates to the sink, listening to his father good naturedly giving Colin a hard time because guests weren't supposed to do dishes, he felt something missing for a long time settle gently back into place. For too long he'd shut out aspects of his former life from his current existence. Suddenly it was crystal clear that he'd made a mistake in doing so.

Luckily, it seemed that he'd realized that mistake in time.

Saturday, 11:15 p.m.
Lowell Residence
Brookline, Massachusetts

LEIGH TURNED THE corner into the living room to find Matt on the couch in front of the fire staring unblinkingly into the flames. At a casual first glance, he looked relaxed and at ease, his feet propped up on the ottoman before the fire, but her sharp eye caught the telltale signs of tension—stiffly held shoulders and a single index finger tapping a staccato beat on his thigh.

As she circled the couch, she trailed the fingers of one hand across the back of his neck and over one shoulder. "What's wrong?"

His eyes rose to hers as she settled on the couch beside him, drawing her feet up to tuck under her. "Why would something be wrong?"

"I agree, I don't see a need for it, but I can see something's off anyway. We had a lovely evening, yet you're unsettled. What's going on?" She shifted on the couch, cuddling in closer and tipping her head to rest on his shoulder.

His chest expanded on a breath, then slowly released. "I guess it was Colin's visit and all the memories it stirred up. I've tried to put that stuff away for so long that this was like ripping off a Band-Aid."

"And all the memories came pouring out?"

"Sort of. As much as I was looking forward to seeing Colin, I was sort of uncomfortable about dredging it all up again after so long. But it wasn't nearly as bad as I thought it would be."

"He's moved on, just like you have. It's a part of what makes you who you are, but it doesn't define you." She caught his hand in hers, stroking her thumb over the back of it. "Just look at the two of you. He's still a part of the Church, but using his time in the Navy as a springboard for helping vets find a place in the world. You have a foot in both the academic and law enforcement worlds, all while training your students to be conscientious scientists and responsible adults. I like Colin. It's too bad he's heading back to D.C. so soon."

"Yeah, but we're back in touch now. I think today has reminded both of us not to let that connection go. Besides, it's only a short flight between Boston and D.C. Maybe we could do a weekend there soon. When the case is over, I mean."

"That sounds nice."

"You just think he's cute."

"The man is flat-out gorgeous, but he's also a priest. It's a cross we women will just have to bear." She elbowed him lightly, smiling when he chuckled. "But that's okay; I'm pretty satisfied with my current lover. He's pretty gorgeous in his own right." Her teasing tone melted away, becoming serious. "But more than that, he's a smart, intuitive man. One who isn't afraid to step out of his comfort zone to reach for something not only good for him, but good for others as well." She pulled away slightly to study his shadowed face, making a lightning-fast decision. She'd been on the verge for a while now, and he needed her words tonight. "And those are just some of the reasons why I love him."

Matt stilled, the green highlights in his eyes sliding toward dark gold in the firelight as he stared down at her. "Some of the reasons?"

"Oh, I have more than just that. But I wouldn't want a list that long to go to his head."

A smile pulled at one corner of his lips. "He sounds like a very lucky man." He curled a hand around her neck, pulled her in until only a whisper separated them. "Say it again. Say it to me."

She laid her hand over his heart and looked directly into his eyes. "I love you." Under her hand, his chest rose and fell on a heavy exhalation, as if he'd been holding his breath, not sure she'd really say it.

"I love you too. So much."

"You better. Otherwise I'm not sure I could take having Paul-the-smart-ass under foot so much."

She felt his joyful laugh against her lips as he pulled her in to prove it to her.

NINETEEN: HATFIELDS & McCOYS

Hatfields & McCoys: a feud between two families beginning around the end of the American Civil War and spanning three generations. It was sparked by the murder of Union soldier Asa Harmon McCoy by a Hatfield member of a Confederate home guard, the alleged theft of some razorback hogs more than a decade later, and the doomed romance between bootlegger Johnse Hatfield and Roseanna McCoy. Over the years both sides made tentative offers of peace, including squaring off in a joint appearance on the television show *Family Feud* in 1979. The families signed an official peace treaty after the 9/11 attacks, and today Jim McCoy and Mark Hatfield are engaged in a joint venture legally selling moonshine based upon old Hatfield family recipes.

Monday, 10:41 a.m.
Essex Detective Unit
Salem, Massachusetts

LEIGH FLIPPED THROUGH the photos in the file again and took another sip of coffee. The bitter brew burned a trail down to her stomach and she pushed it away in disgust. Someday, she was going to teach these guys how to make decent coffee before one of them became their latest victim. She could just see it on the case report—*Cause of death: Cop coffee.*

She continued going through the crime scene photos from Anna Kain's murder—the kitchen, the hallway, the body—before moving onto the photos taken from other areas of the house.

A small window flashed briefly in the corner of her monitor heralding a new message and Leigh set down the photos and turned to her email.

Satisfaction warmed her at the return message from a local bank. *Finally. Joe Emerson's financials.* The bank had done fairly quick work considering she'd delivered the warrant on Saturday morning and had requested information going back over thirty years. She'd been lucky to have caught Rob Tucker working late on Friday and it had been his lightning-fast skills that had pinpointed the bank in question. First thing Saturday, she'd applied for her warrant and happily waited while the judge promptly signed it, mostly, she suspected, to get her out of his kitchen so he could go back to his family's Saturday morning.

She opened the file, scanning it quickly, her smile spreading as pieces of the puzzle clicked into place. She sent the information to the bullpen printer, and then stood waiting as page after page spewed out. Gathering the papers, she tucked them into a file folder and then into her messenger bag. She glanced at her watch; she'd call ahead of time to make sure they were all in the lab, but she could easily get there before lunch.

Her phone rang, and she reached for it, wondering if Matt had some sort of sixth sense letting him know that she was on to something. But a peek at the caller ID had her abruptly changing gears. She did a quick double check of the bullpen—empty—so she could talk freely. "Hey, Claire."

"Leigh, thanks for getting me that new ten-print card so quickly."

"Nothing like a nice leisurely drive to Shirley on a Sunday afternoon."

"Did Cabrera give you any trouble?"

"Not at all. He's been inside a long time and he's no dummy. I didn't have to say anything for him to know that wanting a fresh set of prints at this point meant that we're on to something. So…are we on to something?"

"We are. For a second time, there's no doubt his prints don't match the crime scene prints. The two ten-print cards match though, so you're absolutely looking at the tech misidentifying Cabrera as the positive match."

"And you think it wasn't really an error, so to speak. You think it was a blatant misidentification."

"I do." There was no hesitation in Claire's voice. "This was a tech with a reputation for being solid. He wasn't a rookie."

"And you're willing to testify to that?"

"You bet."

"Good, because we're going to need you." Leigh started to stack the photos from the Kain house together. The photo at the top of the pile was from the Kain's bedroom and she casually scanned it as she tapped the photos on the desk to line them up. "I'm going to take this to Harper today. By tomorrow the case will be officially reopened and—" Her eyes went wide as her breath froze in her throat. She blinked once, then again, to make sure she was seeing what was in front of her. No, it was still there. *Holy shit. If she was seeing what she thought she was seeing, this changed everything.*

"Leigh, are you there?"

"Yeah, yeah, I'm here. Claire, sorry, something really big just came up. Thanks so much for going over those prints. Can you send me a full report?"

"The report's already done. I'll shoot it over to you right away. Let me know if you need anything else."

"Hopefully we'll have new prints to compare soon. Thanks, Claire." She set down the phone and took a minute to breathe before picking up the photo again. She opened one of her drawers and rummaged for a minute, finally extracting a magnifying glass. Swiveling in her chair for better light, she angled the photo and the lens for better visualization.

She hadn't been mistaken. This really did change everything.

All the connections suddenly started to make sense.

"Coincidence, my ass." She reached for her phone, wedging it between her shoulder and her ear as she packed up the file with both hands. When Matt picked up, she barely gave him time to talk. "I'm on my way. I've got something big. Have everyone there, and I'll see you in an hour."

She left the office at a run.

Monday, 11:58 a.m.
Boston University, School of Medicine
Boston, Massachusetts

MATT BLEW OUT a frustrated breath and closed his laptop. He'd read the same paragraph in a journal article on measurements of the juvenile clavicle using computed tomography three times, and still hadn't absorbed a word of it. He glanced over to where his students were sprawled at their writing stations. They were surfing the web or texting while they waited, but he could read their impatience in tapping fingers and constant fidgeting. He'd called them back from the Old North Church and they'd raced across town, beating Leigh by over twenty minutes at this point.

Leigh came through the door at that moment. "Sorry, I had to make a stop in Salem and then I hit traffic. Of all the days…"

Matt pushed away from his desk to stand. "What have you got?"

"Remember how we're not doing coincidences for this case? This just cements it. It also ties a whole lot of things together." She waved the students over and they all gathered around her. She pulled two case photos from her bag. "Remember this?" She held out a photo of the items recovered from Peter Holt's pocket—his wallet, keys, cell phone, and the pair of antique cuff links.

"You're talking about the cuff links?" Matt said. "The *Blue Ruin*. His grandfather's cuff links."

"Exactly. We've talked about them as being custom-made and Charles Ward's way of subtly thumbing his nose at The Man."

"We have. Leigh, where are you going with this?"

"I'm going here." She handed him the photo of the Kains' bedroom and the magnifying glass. "This is one of the crime scene photos taken at the time of Anna Kain's murder in nineteen-seventy-five. Most of the photos are of the kitchen and hall area, but they also took shots of the other rooms, to use as back up to any potential entry and egress and for any additional evidence. This is the photo of the Kains' master bedroom. Look at the dresser."

Matt took the photo and the lens. He adjusted the lens

to fine-tune the focus on the furniture. *Dark wood. Five drawers. Round handles.* His gaze flicked to Leigh in question.

"Keep going. You'll know when you find it."

His gaze returned to the photo. *Small flat, leather jewelry case on the top. A picture of his family, including a much younger version of Ethel. Some papers. A pair of cuff links. A gold dress wat—*

He stopped cold, his eyes snapping back to the cuff links. "Son of a bitch!"

"You've got it," Leigh said.

"Take this." Matt jammed the handheld lens back into her hand. He snatched the photo of Peter Holt's effects, and strode across the room to the larger, lighted desk-mounted magnifying ring. He flipped it on, studying the two photos side by side.

There was no doubt.

He whirled around. "How in the hell did Charles Ward's cuff links end up in Samuel Kain's bedroom?"

"What?" Kiko hurried across the room to him, slipping the photos from his hands to study them under magnification as he had. "That's absolutely the same cuff link design." She motioned to Paul and Juka. "Come take a look."

The men took their turn examining the photos.

"Can we be sure they weren't mass-produced in some way?" Paul asked. "I know it's doubtful, but can we leap to the conclusion that this is the same individual pair of cuff links?"

"It's not a leap anymore. One of the reasons I took so long to get here is that I stopped in to see a jeweler I know in Salem—Martin Leary. He's done work for our family for years, and I trust his opinion." She drew a small plastic bag from her pocket and poured the cuff links into her palm.

"Is that them?" Juka asked. "The actual evidence?"

"The Real McCoy." She handed one piece to Matt and the other to Juka. "Take a good look. You might even need the magnifying glass again. See the tiny stamp on the back?"

Matt carried the cuff link back to the lit ring, Kiko right behind him. He centered it under the ring, turning it so both he and Kiko could see it clearly. "*Dole and Sons.* Is that a jeweler?"

"Yes. A fairly well-known one in Boston back in the early part of the last century. Martin says that Dole was kind of a legend in the jewelry business back then, known especially for his custom work. Quality work, but expensive. Unfortunately, he and his business didn't survive the Depression and they closed up shop."

"Probably very few had money for custom work like this back then," Juka said.

"And those that did were probably guarding their pennies a little more closely and not making extravagant purchases. But these were clearly purchased before he went out of business, likely in the early thirties. Martin said he'll confirm when the store actually closed."

Matt turned the cuff link over, examining the inlaid blue shapes of the Roman ruins. "Handy, as that helps date the item."

"And, hopefully, reinforces that it's one of a kind. The blue inlays are enamel, popular during the Art Deco period. The gold is fourteen karat."

Matt handed the cuff link to Kiko so she could have a better look and crossed the room back to Leigh. "Okay, so let's think this through. We have what we think is a one-of-a-kind piece that Ward wasn't wearing on the day of his death. We found a pair of black inlaid cuff links intermingled with the remains instead. We assume these cuff links were left at home. So they were in the possession of Mrs. Ward. What do we know about her?"

"Only the bare minimum from doing research on Charles Ward. They were married in nineteen-twenty-five when she was twenty-one and he was twenty-nine. She was from another old money family. In fact, there was more money in her family than his."

"Do we think he married her for that money? We don't exactly know when he decided to get into politics," Matt said.

"It's not outside the realm of possibility." Leigh set her bag down on Matt's desk and propped one hip on the corner. "She was thirty-two when he disappeared and thirty-nine when he was legally declared dead. She died in nineteen-sixty-four."

Kiko returned to hand the cuff link to Leigh. "Can we back up for a minute? I'm still trying to get this straight. These cuff links belonged to Ward, but were not on his body when he died in nineteen-thirty-six, presumably at the hands of Samuel Kain. Then these same cuff links appear thirty-nine years later in Kain's own bedroom at the scene of his wife's murder. Then they disappear again for nearly forty years before resurfacing at the scene of a third crime, tucked in the pocket of Ward's dead grandson."

"These two families are linked in the worst way possible," Juka said.

Matt narrowed his eyes on Leigh, studying every nuance of her expression. "You think they're a message, don't you? An 'I know what you did' from one family to another." The force of that connection struck Matt full force. "You think that someone in Ward's family killed Kain's wife. A revenge slaying?"

"And then tried to pin it on someone else when Bern refused to drop the case," Paul added. "If the case had truly gone stone cold, they'd likely have been happy to let it go, but Bern kept looking so they needed someone to take the heat off them completely. It's devious as hell, but, if you're right, it clearly worked. Now…can we prove it?"

"I got a step closer to that today too." Leigh twisted around to pull a file from the messenger bag. "I have Joe Emerson's financials. He's the fingerprint expert who worked Anna Kain's murder. There seems to be a disconnect between Mr. Emerson's bank accounts, his reported income, and his style of living. New properties, new cars, expensive Ivy League schools for his two children. Yet all apparently on a state employee's salary. He's now retired and winters at his beachfront property in the Bahamas. From nineteen-seventy-nine to nineteen-eighty-three alone, over two hundred thousand dollars was spent on purchases and credit card bills."

Paul whistled. "That's a lot of money now. That's even more money then. But where did it come from?"

"I haven't gotten a handle on that yet, but I have a plan."

"Rob Tucker?" Matt asked.

Leigh nodded. "This will likely be child's play for him. I know he's busy right now"—she met Matt's eyes briefly—"but he'll find the time for it. Mr. Emerson is still in the area, but he'll likely be packing up to head south soon, and it would be so much easier to keep him here than to extradite him from Nassau."

"And if we find out where the money came from, then

we find out who framed Cabrera for Anna Kain's murder. Not necessarily who killed her, but at least who engineered the frame-up," Matt said.

Leigh flipped the file closed. "Exactly. And speaking of the frame-up, Claire called me just before I left the unit. Cabrera's new ten-print card matches his old ten-print card but not the ones from the crime scene. So the case against him has fallen apart. I'm taking it to Harper this afternoon and I'll be asking to have Anna Kain's case assigned to me as it's now officially part of the Ward/Holt cases."

Matt circled his desk and sat down in his desk chair, propping his boots up on the corner of the desk. "Oh, what a tangled web we weave…" he quoted. "So, let's circle back. Kain kills Ward…but we don't know why yet."

"I don't know that we'll ever know that one," Leigh said. "Unless Kain can tell us, there simply may not be enough evidence left to ascribe motive in an eighty-year-old case."

"Then someone from the Ward family kills Anna Kain in retribution for Ward's death and leaves the cuff links as a calling card," Matt continued. "Something that would look innocuous to investigators at the time, but something that Samuel Kain would recognize immediately."

"What if it was more devious than that?" Juka interjected. "Remember when we were going over the case information. Trooper Bern initially looked at Kain for the murder, but he alibied out. What if whoever committed the crime actually wanted Samuel Kain to go away for it, to lose not only his wife, but his freedom?"

"It certainly fits. If you're looking for revenge this would be the ultimate payback. If you kill him, he doesn't hurt for very long. This way, he suffers for the rest of his life knowing those cuff links were left to tell him exactly why his wife died."

"So theory number one is that someone from Ward's family killed Anna for revenge," Leigh said. "But the biggest question is why the huge gap in time?"

"Maybe they didn't know who was responsible for Ward's death until then? Or maybe it was a younger member of the family who had to grow up to commit the crime?" Kiko suggested.

"Could be," Paul agreed, "but I'd be leaning toward the former. For the first few years, they probably held out hope that something had happened and he'd walk back through the door one night. At some point, they had to realize he wasn't coming back, but there was never a body to prove it. But something had to change in the mid-seventies for this to come back to Samuel Kain when no one else even knew the murder had taken place. Surely it would have happened sooner otherwise."

"And then to turn it around all these years later and kill Peter Holt. It's like the Hatfields and the McCoys all over again." Kiko pulled over a wheeled chair from the workstations and sat down. "So then who killed Peter Holt?"

"The real question is which member of that family knew Anna was killed by one of the Wards? If it was common knowledge, then it would be known publicly. But this was private knowledge only. And then, once again, why such a gap in time between the murders?" Juka asked.

"The other issue in all this is whether the person responsible for Anna's death is even still alive," Matt pointed out. "It might not even have been one of the Wards who were 'hands-on.' They had the money to pay for a hit. They had the money four years later to pay for framing Santino Cabrera."

"And that brings up another question of timing," Leigh said. "Why wait four years to frame someone? We know Bern wouldn't let go of the case, but was he finally getting close? Was he about to find something out and they needed to distract him?"

"Is he still around?"

"He is, and it's time I talked to him. We probably can't go back to the beginning and talk to anyone who investigated Charles Ward's disappearance eighty years ago. So this has to be our ground zero for now. I'm going to try and track Bern down this afternoon. He's retired, but still lives locally. And before you ask if you can come, the answer is no."

Matt jerked in surprise, his boots sliding from the corner of the desk to thump dully on the tile floor. "How did you know I was even going to ask?"

"I know you too well." She gave him a twisted smile. "I'm going to go tell a cop there was a crucial error in his case and he sent the wrong man to jail for thirty years. If it was me, I wouldn't want spectators, especially outsiders. I'm trying to leave him a little pride, Matt."

Matt considered her point and nodded reluctantly in agreement. "Yeah, I guess if it was me, I wouldn't want a crowd of people there when someone broke bad news to me."

"Exactly."

"Then while you're working on that, let me see if I can put a little pressure on getting the cigarette DNA results ASAP. I'll let you know as soon as it's ready."

Leigh pushed off from the desk and collected the photos, the cuff links, and her bag. "Sounds good. In the meantime, I'll go back more than thirty years and try to find out what exactly happened to Anna Kain that put the ball back in play again in this family feud."

TWENTY: SPARGING

Sparging: an early step when brewing beer is mixing crushed grains with hot water to convert complex carbohydrates into simple sugars. Sparging, the next step in the process, involves trickling water through the grain bed to extract those sugars. Water of the wrong temperature or pH will extract tannins from the *chaff* (grain husks), resulting in a bitter brew.

Monday, 1:10 p.m.
Bern Residence
Manchester, Massachusetts

"TROOPER BERN, I appreciate you making time for me on such short notice." Leigh took a seat on the couch next to the roaring fire, directly across from a balding older man so slender he bordered on frail.

"Just 'Gary' is fine. I've been retired for eight years now, so calling me by my rank seems needlessly formal. But I'm always happy to help with an investigation." He shifted in his chair, pulling a worn beige cardigan closer around his thin frame. "You weren't very specific on the phone. Just that it was an old case of mine. Which one?"

"The murder of Mrs. Anna Kain in nineteen-seventy-five."

"Well, well. Anna Kain." The hazy gray eyes went unfocused for a moment, lost in memories. "For a while, I thought that was a case I'd never solve. Home invasion. Shooting death. The family was absolutely devastated."

"I've read your notes. You worked that case for a long time." She pulled the overflowing case file from her bag, noticing how Gary's eyes lit up at the sight of it. *Retired, but he misses the old life.*

"You're a cop," he said, his gaze fixed longingly on the folder in Leigh's lap. "You know what it's like when a case sinks its claws into you. This one had its claws into me for nearly five years before I finally put it to bed."

Leigh had to fight to keep from wincing. There was such pride in his voice—for a job well done and a case finally solved. And she was about to shatter that pride. "That's actually what I wanted to talk to you about. I met with Detective Lieutenant Harper earlier this afternoon. We're reopening this case based on new evidence."

"But…" Gary's face went slack with disbelief, his fingers going white where they clasped the padded arms of his wing chair, thin blue veins bulging over the backs of his hands under the pressure. "But I don't understand. That case was closed in nineteen-eighty. We had definitive evidence. We convicted and sent a man to jail."

"Santino Cabrera. I've met with him twice in the past few days. He was never there."

"That's what he always said. But the evidence proved he was lying."

"The fingerprint evidence?"

"Yes. There was definitive evidence that put him in that house at the time of the murder."

"He was never in the house. The fingerprint evidence was falsified."

"Falsified?" Gary's voice cracked as it rose. "How?"

"There never was a match. The fingerprint tech who testified in court either lied or made a grave error." She pulled Claire's report from the top of the file folder and passed it across to him. "See for yourself. This analysis was done twice, the second time with a fresh ten-print card I took myself two days ago."

Gary took the report with a trembling hand and then fumbled with his reading glasses, pulling them from the breast pocket of his cardigan and pushing them up onto his nose. He pressed two fingers to his temple as his face flushed a dull red that sent Leigh's pulse quickening.

She leaned forward, bracing her elbows on her knees. "Gary, are you all right?"

"As a cop, I spent my entire working life trying to do the right thing. And now to learn I may have contributed to helping convict and imprison an innocent man for over thirty years? Give me a minute to absorb it." He looked up over the top of his lenses, meeting her gaze. The bone-deep regret there was like a fist to her gut. "Without the fingerprint evidence, there isn't a shred of evidence to tie him to the Kain home invasion, is there?"

"No, nothing."

Gary's head drooped over his nearly concave chest. His shoulders rose and fell with a sharp breath, but then he raised his head, his eyes clear and resolute. Angling the paper into the light, he quickly read the report. When he was done, the papers dropped limply into his lap. "What have I done?"

"You did exactly what any other good cop would have done. You followed the leads, and you didn't give up. If Cabrera's prints hadn't popped, you would have continued to look for the person responsible."

"But they did pop, as you say. And I thought we'd finally found our man."

"It's clear at this point it was a frame-up, but we're trying to figure out who was responsible and why so long after the murder. The murder occurred in seventy-five; Cabrera wasn't associated with the case until four years later. Why? What were you doing four years later that steered you in another direction?"

Gary slid off his glasses to pinch the bridge of his nose between forefinger and thumb. For a moment he was silent, and then he looked up. "Can I look at that file again? It's been a few years; I'd like to double-check my memory of the investigation."

"Of course." Leigh handed him the file and then sat back as he slipped his glasses back on and flipped through the pages. Some he paused over, some he flipped quickly past. Finally, he came to the mug shot of Santino Cabrera. Leigh recognized the young man in the older man she'd met. His expression hadn't changed much—the anger was there, as was the bitterness. But the hardness that set his mouth and backed his gaze now was absent in this younger portrait. That kind of hardness could only be learned from decades in prison.

He tapped the photo. "I was exhilarated when Cabrera came up. Four years of looking for the right man for the job and coming up empty. And then there he was. His fingerprints placed him inside the house, he had a history of home invasion in the area, had already done time, and looked the part—an angry young Latino, with long hair and tattoos. It wasn't a hard sell to the jury."

"You mention the 'right man' for the job. Did you ever look at any women?"

Gary looked up sharply. "Women? No one ever stood out as a likely suspect."

"But think back to the crime scene. Two teacups on the table, two colors of lipstick on the cigarette butts in the ashtray. You knew someone else was on scene that morning, but you never identified who it was?"

"No. I canvassed the neighbors but no one saw anyone coming or going that morning except Mr. and Mrs. Kain. We knew what time she finished her groceries because the cashier and the grocery boy both confirmed when she checked out."

"And that was?"

"Just before ten o'clock. It was Mrs. Kain's habit to do her groceries on Wednesday mornings promptly at ten a.m. But she was actually early that morning, arriving just as the store opened at nine, and she seemed a little frazzled. Both of these things were out of character."

"When you say 'frazzled,'" Leigh said, "did they think she was afraid?"

Gary shook his head. "Not at all. She said she had an important houseguest coming. When I talked to Kain about it, he was unaware she was meeting anyone that morning. Normally, she did all her charity work in the afternoons and often had ladies over for afternoon tea."

"Do you know what charities she supported?" Leigh asked.

"Yes, there's a list in here somewhere." Gary flipped through the file again, finally stopping on a page. "Here we are. The Lynn Home for Young Women, the Lynn Historical Society, and Ladies Ancient Order of Hibernians."

"I'm not familiar with that last one," Leigh said.

"It's a group for Irish American Catholic women,"

Gary said. "Anna Kain's maiden name was O'Donnell. It could have been any woman from any of these charities. We questioned them all, but none of them knew anything."

"Or at least none of them admitted to knowing anything. If you questioned them, shouldn't there be a list of all their names?"

"There should be. Isn't it there?"

"Not in the file. I went through everything in that file. Twice. And I was specifically looking for information to identify the missing woman."

"Actually, now that I think about it, that list was in my casebook. I'd go back annually to review the case, and that's where I kept that information. Truthfully, I didn't think that woman was important to the case. I thought Mrs. Kain was alone at the time of the attack. If she hadn't been, the second woman would also have been killed or at least injured and would have reported the attack. We always thought it was someone who knew her regular routine. Normally, she wouldn't have been home at that time; she'd have still been out shopping. So someone came through the back door, but then there she was. There was a struggle and Mrs. Kain was shot."

"Why the struggle?"

"Pardon?"

"Why the struggle?" Leigh repeated. "She was past middle age; he was in his early twenties with a gun in his hand. Why would she fight him? They didn't have much in the way of valuables in the house. Why not just stand aside and let him take what he wanted?"

"Maybe she panicked? All I can say is there definitely was a struggle. Groceries were knocked off the counter and there were broken dishes."

"Mrs. Kain was shot in the abdomen first, then five minutes later she was shot a second time. Why the gap in time?"

"We always thought that's when he was collecting the valuables."

"Could be," Leigh agreed. "So then does your theory follow that she wasn't as badly wounded as perhaps your perp thought, she tried to escape, and that's when she was shot in the back?"

"Yes."

"I'm not sure I'm on board with that. What about what was taken? Mrs. Kain's wedding rings, a few other pieces of jewelry, and some cash were all removed from the residence. But what was probably the most expensive piece of jewelry in the house—a pair of antique, inlaid fourteen-karat gold cuff links—was left. Can you explain that?"

"I would just assume they were missed."

"They were left out in plain sight. We suspect they weren't so much missed, but rather left by the killer as a message to Samuel Kain."

"Kain?"

"Yes. Speaking of Kain, did you ever look at him for this?"

Gary's shoulders went stiff and he frowned at her. "Of course I did. You know as well as I do most murders are carried out by people close to the vic. When a wife dies, you always look at the spouse first. So did we."

"But he alibied out."

"Yes. Normally, if he was on a job in town, he'd come home for lunch. That day, he planned to, but there was an accident on-site and, as foreman, he went in the ambulance to the hospital with his injured guy. We looked into it to be sure, but it was just a bad series of events that led to a guy getting hurt, luckily not too seriously. But it alibied Kain for the whole window covering time of death."

"That might have put a crimp in someone's plans."

Gary sat back in his chair, weaving his fingers together and considering Leigh carefully. "You think the murder was committed with the intent of implicating Kain as the prime suspect?"

"I do. You have a family that tends to be fairly regimented when it comes to their schedule. But there were two changes that day. Mrs. Kain changed her own schedule for some reason and then Mr. Kain's schedule was changed for him when an unforeseen accident happened on the worksite." Leigh stared into the flames for a minute, working the scenario through in her mind again. Finally she looked up to find the older man's eyes fixed on her, discomfort and concern etched into the deepening lines of his face. "Gary, please don't take this the wrong way. Times have changed a lot in the last decade. Do you think maybe your viewpoint as a man in the nineteen-seventies might have colored how you looked at this case?"

Gary took off his glasses to peer at Leigh. "I'm not sure I follow. I investigated this case to the best of my abilities."

"I'm not implying anything other than that. But right from the start did you think a man was responsible for the home invasion?"

"Well…yes. Look at the nature of the crime. Home invasions in my experience were always carried out by men, usually young men. Often lower class, often immigrant populations. A violent crime in a nice middle-class neighborhood? It's almost always committed by a man."

"So, taking the nature of the crime into account, was

that why you never pursued the mystery woman? Because it wasn't relevant as far as you were concerned? When you speak of the other woman, it's as not being a victim, but it's never as actually being the killer."

"At least at the beginning, we didn't consider her relevant. More of an irritating loose end we wanted to tie up and couldn't. But then the case went ice-cold. Every year I'd go through the file and my notes again, hoping something would suddenly rise to the top, something I'd missed."

"Except there wasn't anything."

"No."

"So what changed in nineteen-seventy-nine? What set the ball in motion to frame Santino Cabrera?"

Gary raised both hands, spread as if in entreaty. "God as my witness, nothing that comes to mind. Once again, I reviewed the case. And as I did every year, I started making phone calls, re-interviewing people who might have seen something, or known something about Anna's life."

"Was it always the same people?"

"Yes. That list in my casebook."

"Somewhere, in one of those phone calls, I think you made someone worried. You maybe even spoke to the murderer, or someone who knew who it was, and that raised concerns. They'd been willing to let the case lie cold, but when you repeatedly came back to them year after year, and wouldn't let it go, they realized they needed to close the case for good and sooner rather than later. And that was what slammed the door on Cabrera. You don't have that casebook anymore, do you?"

For the first time since Leigh broke the news about the frame-up, Gary brightened. "I do. I kept them all. Mostly for old times' sake, you know? So it's around here somewhere." His gaze skimmed overflowing book-shelves. "I'm just not sure where. My memory's not as… sharp as it used to be."

Instinct told Leigh that what Bern lacked in memory, he more than made up for in determination to right what he now saw as a wrong he was responsible for. "When you find that book, and find that list, would you give me a call? I think I'll recognize one of those names." She stood and extended her card to him. "Call my cell any-time, day or night."

Gary rose to join her. "I'll go look right away. Now… about Cabrera."

She touched his arm lightly, recognizing the anguish and guilt in his eyes. She could only imagine how she'd feel in a similar situation and the thought of it nearly made her physically ill. "I'm taking care of it. We have to go through proper channels, but he'll be released."

"Will you let me know when that happens?"

"You have my word on it."

As Leigh climbed into her car, she made a mental note to get membership lists from Anna Kain's charities at the time of her death, on the off chance Gary couldn't find his notes. She was willing to bet she would recognize one name, at least, on not only one, but both of those lists.

TWENTY-ONE: DECANTING

Decanting: the process of purifying and aerating red wine by pouring off the clear top layer from the potassium bitartrate crystals that have settled to the bottom of the bottle.

Monday, 3:28 p.m.
Boston University, School of Medicine
Boston, Massachusetts

"MATT, DO YOU want something?" Kiko paused with one hand on the open door as Juka and Paul's voices faded down the hallway in the direction of the lounge.

Matt looked up from his laptop screen. "No, thanks. I want to get this report done. I'm expecting to hear from Leigh anytime and I'd like to have it ready for her."

Kiko bounced lightly on her toes in excitement. "This is going to knock her socks off. It's all coming together. I love it when we hit this stage."

"I'm learning to love it myself. It's a lot better than the get-shot-at-by-a-murderous-lunatic stage."

Kiko grinned and mimed taking a shot at Matt, blowing on the tip of her finger afterward. "Been there, done that. It wasn't much fun. Okay, back in fifteen." The door closed behind her with a *thud,* leaving Matt in peace and quiet.

He didn't look up when the door opened again only moments later. "Paul forget his giant vat of a coffee mug?"

"Pardon?"

He looked up to find Leigh standing just inside the door. "Sorry, I thought you were one of the students coming back in. They just went down to the lounge for coffee." He pushed back from his desk as she crossed the floor toward him. "Did you want some?"

"No, thanks." She paused for a second, long enough that Matt second-guessed her and then they were both speaking over top of each other.

Laughing he raised a hand in surrender. "I guess we've both got news to share. Ladies first."

"No way. Not if you have news." She crooked her fingers greedily. "To quote Tucker—*gimme*."

"Only if you're sure you don't want to go first." He tried to look serious but the gleam in his eye must have given him away. He chuckled when she smacked his arm. "Okay, okay, you win, I'll go first." He grinned. "I have the cigarette butt DNA results back."

"I knew it." Triumph laced Leigh's voice. "Have you emailed them to me so I can run the results through the state database? We're not going to have any trouble getting Cabrera released, but having someone else to arrest for the crime would certainly speed things up."

"You don't need to run the results. We've already got a match."

Leigh went stock still. "Who? How? No, wait!"

He stared in fascination as Leigh quickly rooted through her jacket pocket. She extracted her cell phone and started impatiently jabbing keys. "Who are you calling?"

"Rowe. Last time I updated him, he threatened me

with physical harm if I didn't keep him in the loop right to the end of this case." She looked up and pushed a few loose strands of hair behind her ear from where they had slipped from her chignon. "I think he was only half joking." She put the call on speaker and the sound of a phone ringing filled the lab.

"Rowe."

"It's Leigh Abbott. Matt and I have some results back in the Kain case and we wanted you to be in on them if you're free right now."

"I was due at a budget meeting about two minutes ago, but they can't start without me. Make it quick, but I'd love to hear where we are."

Leigh nodded at Matt to proceed.

"Rowe, you're up to date on the Anna Kain murder and how it ties into this case?" he asked. "Specifically the scene of her murder?"

"I am."

"Then you'll remember cigarette butts were found in an ashtray on her kitchen table. Several cigarettes had been smoked by a woman wearing a different color lipstick from anything Anna wore. Back in nineteen-seventy-five, they had no way of tracing who that other woman might have been."

"We certainly can now," Rowe said. "The DNA's been analyzed?"

"Yes. I was just about to tell Leigh that we wouldn't need to actually run the DNA results through the database because we already have the information at hand." He met Leigh's curious gaze. "It was Evelyn Holt. The cigarette butt is a full match to the sample we collected a few days ago."

"We were right all along. They really are the Hatfields

and the McCoys." She sat down heavily on a lab stool, letting her bag drop to the ground.

"Lowell, you're confident in the results?" asked Rowe. "It's not another one of the Ward relatives? It was definitely Evelyn?"

"It was a full match on all fifteen points."

A sound of triumph came from the phone. "That definitely ties up *that* loose end."

"This is still circumstantial," Leigh pointed out, "but circumstantial evidence certainly buried Cabrera. We can place her inside the house, so we can insist on a look at her prints. The prints on the wall might not prove much because her lawyer will argue that she was simply in the house having tea, but any lawyer would have trouble explaining her prints on the gun. As soon as we bring her in, I'll do her ten-print card and we'll get Claire on a comparison right away."

"And remember what Cabrera said about the type of gun? A Walther PPK, right?"

"Right?"

"Not a thug gun. He described it as a 'gentleman's gun,' but maybe in this case, it's really a lady's gun."

"Any idea where she got it?" Rowe asked.

"Somewhere under the table is my bet, based on the filed-off serial number. I wonder where a classy society grande dame like that would have a contact to find her that kind of hardware," Matt mused.

"It's definitely going to be something we'll ask her about."

"How about your news? How did it go with Trooper Bern?"

Leigh leaned toward the phone. "Rowe, you might not

remember his name, but Bern was the investigating officer in Anna Kain's death."

"The officer who put Cabrera away?"

"That's the one. I just met with him and I learned a few things that now should be looked at in a fresh light given this new DNA evidence. For starters, the Kain household was fairly regimented. Anna did her groceries at ten a.m. every Wednesday. Except the morning of her death, she showed up at the store a whole hour early. Bern said she was described by the staff that day as 'frazzled.' From the evidence found at the scene, we can infer that's because she had someone coming over later that morning for tea. Then there's Samuel. His habit was to come home every day for lunch, except on that particular day, there was an industrial accident at his worksite and he ended up going with one of his men to the ER instead."

"Really?" Matt pulled up another lab stool and straddled it backwards, folding his arms across the back. "Kind of makes you wonder if that was where Evelyn's plans started to go south."

"What do you mean?"

"If we're sticking with our previous theory that this was a revenge killing for Charles Ward's death and Evelyn's goal was to frame Kain for the death of his own wife, then she went to some pretty great lengths to set it up. Arranging to meet Anna Kain for tea at a time that would force her to change her schedule, but would get Evelyn into the house early enough that she could kill Anna and then get out. But close enough to the time Kain normally came home during his lunch break to be their number one suspect."

"Except that he didn't come home, and ended up finding Anna hours later with his alibi for the murder firmly intact," Rowe said. "Yeah, I'd call that going south all right." His voice went flat, anticipated boredom creeping into his tone. "Thanks for calling, Abbott. I'd be happy to toss around theories with you all afternoon, but nothing makes true administrators crabbier than a meeting that doesn't start on time. I'm off to go beard the lion in his den. Thanks for keeping me in the loop. Talk to you later." He clicked off.

"Man, I wouldn't want to be in his shoes right now. I hate those meetings," Matt said.

"No one likes them except the accountants. You know, this scenario about Evelyn also explains why Anna was frazzled when she went shopping early that morning. Not only was her morning routine tossed on its head, she had Evelyn Holt coming for tea."

Matt cocked his head uncertainly. "And this would frazzle her why?"

"You're such a man." She patted his arm as if humoring him, and then grinned when his gaze narrowed on her suspiciously.

Her cell rang, interrupting them, and she reached for her phone. "Abbott… Gary, that was fast."

Matt rested his chin on his stacked hands as Leigh listened to her caller, interjecting occasionally with small murmurs of agreement or encouragement. Finally, "That's wonderful, Gary. Thank you. I will. Goodbye." She glanced over at Matt. "That was Gary Bern." Bending back over her phone, she flipped through several screens to her email. "He found his casebook with the lists of charity members he would call every year to follow up on the cold case. He's already scanned the lists and sent them to me. And…here we are."

Matt waited quietly, his gaze on Leigh's bent head

as she flipped through images, scanning down lists of names. Then her body went still and she blew up the image on the screen before slowly raising her head and grinning at Matt. "Well, well...look at that."

"Evelyn Holt on that list?"

"Got it in one. She was a member of the Lynn Historical Society with Anna at the time of Anna's death. We're slowly closing the circle. We've established a connection, and if the fingerprints on the gun match then we not only place her in the house, but we literally put the smoking gun in her hand. Now back to why Anna was frazzled that day. Think how it would have been, especially back them. Anna Kain was a middle-class housewife. No expensive schooling, no rich husband, no big fancy house. An Irish immigrant. And here was one of the pillars of the community coming to her house for tea to discuss a common interest. She may have felt honored, but more than that, I bet she felt pressured. You know how some women are—nothing like company coming over to kick-start a cleaning frenzy. What's good enough for the family is never good enough for a guest, and definitely not a guest with enough money to have a staff to clean for her. Add in that Anna's fridge was probably empty since it was already shopping day, and she was probably totally thrown. And then I suspect that Evelyn showed up early, which also probably put her in a tizzy."

"Why would you say that?"

"Because her groceries were still out. If she'd had time, she would have had a pristine kitchen to show off to her honored guest. But perhaps Evelyn showed up early, maybe even just as Anna was arriving home herself. So the groceries ended up being left on the counter."

"You have to wonder what kicked this all off though,"

said Matt. "We assume that Evelyn found out about her father's death and that's what set this killing in motion, but how was this suddenly new information for her thirty-nine years later?"

"It's a good question. We need to look into what was going on in Evelyn's life then and see if there were any major changes that might give us a clue."

"How are you going to do that without asking her directly? And, obviously, you can't ask her son."

"You'd be amazed what you can find out about a person simply through public records. Family births and deaths. Property changes. Employment records. They tell a story about the lives people lead. And they're a very good place to start."

"So…you started off doubting you'd find a body, and then found two. Then a third murder fell into your lap and that victim became yours as well. And you've already got very strong leads on two of the three murders. Nice work, Trooper."

Leigh tipped her head forward in a small bow. "Couldn't have done it without my team. And that includes Rowe. He's been invaluable during this case. Now we just need to nail down Peter Holt's killer. And I think we know where to start looking there, based on everything else. This whole case has been a tangled snarl of violence and revenge. But we're going to put a stop to it once and for all." Her phone rang again and she glanced at the display. "Hold on, I have to take this." Pushing off the stool, she stepped several paces away.

Matt wandered back toward his desk, trying to give her some small amount of privacy. The conversation lasted less than a minute before Leigh ended the call.

When she turned back to him, she worried her bottom lip between her teeth.

"Who was that?" Her gaze rose to meet his, and he was shocked by the paleness of her face and her shadowed eyes. He took a reflexive step toward her. "Leigh?"

"That was Tucker. He wants to meet with me tonight. Away from the unit. It has…" She swallowed hard and started again. "It has to be about my father."

He stepped closer, running a comforting hand down her back. "What did he find?"

"He didn't say. He just wanted to meet. I suggested my place again since it's close to the unit." Her forehead creased as her brows slid together, her expression perplexed. "He sounded…odd."

"In what way?"

"Like he was trying to convey information without actually saying it. But whatever it is, he wasn't obvious enough for me to figure out his meaning."

"He's a geek. Geeks don't make good spies. But they're great for sussing out information." He leaned back against a benchtop and pulled her back to lean against him. Her body was stiff against his chest, so he settled his hands on her shoulders to massage the tight muscles. "Your shoulders feel like granite. Relax. Try not to worry ahead of time because there may be no reason. Wait until he has a chance to tell you what he's found."

Her weight shifted against him as she settled in closer, letting her body lean into him. "Easy for you to say. Will you come?"

"Of course I will. And whatever it is, together, we'll come up with a way to deal with it. Tucker's on board now too, and he might have some ideas on how to handle whatever he's uncovered. So let's hear him out and we'll go from there, okay?"

"Okay."

The lab door banged open and Kiko, Paul, and Juka pushed into the room. Kiko broke into a broad smile when she saw Leigh, although Matt couldn't tell if it was the sight of Leigh leaning intimately against him or because she was excited about their results.

"So, did Matt tell you about the DNA?"

Ah. The results. "I told her."

"Isn't it great?"

Matt dropped his hands from Leigh's shoulder as she pasted on a smile and stepped into the group of students. Their infectious enthusiasm buoyed her and within minutes, her smile was relaxed and genuine and her shoulders were loose. Matt watched her carefully, feeling his own tension dissipate slightly as she bantered easily with his students. All was well.

For now.

TWENTY-TWO: BOOTLEG

Bootleg: the illegal transport of alcoholic beverages; in modern times, an audio or video recording of a performance that was not officially released by the artist or under other legal authority.

Monday, 7:13 p.m.
Abbott Residence
Salem, Massachusetts

"SOMETHING TO DRINK?"

Tucker glanced at Leigh as he nudged his sneakers against the wall behind the door. "Have any beer?"

"She does because I keep a few in her fridge." Matt appeared in the kitchen doorway. "Can I get you one?"

"Could really go for one, yeah."

"I'll join you. Leigh?"

Leigh tried unsuccessfully to quiet the nerves that jangled with Tucker's need for alcohol. She raised her mug of tea. "I think I'll just stick with this."

"Okay, back in a sec." He disappeared into the kitchen.

"Come on into the living room." Leigh led the way down the hallway and Tucker immediately dropped into the same chair he'd occupied several days earlier. He blew out a tired breath and ran his hand through his hair, further disarraying the bright orange strands.

Not wanting to start the discussion until Matt came

back, Leigh opted for shop talk. "If you have some spare time, I could use a hand on the Anna Kain murder."

Tucker glowered at her from under his eyebrows. "When do I ever have spare time, Abbott? You guys work my fingers to the bone." He wiggled ten digits in her direction. "See? Practically nubs. But I'm sure I can manage what you need."

"You're a real trooper, Tucker." A beat of silence passed. "Pardon the pun."

"Ha ha. Cop humor. You should do stand-up. But lay it on me."

Leigh wrapped her hands around the mug, warmth flowing into her ice-cold fingers. "I need a comprehensive background search done on Evelyn Holt."

Tucker rolled his eyes until only the whites showed momentarily. "Child's play, Abbott. Where's the fun in that? You could even give it to Delancy and he could do it." Matt entered the living room and handed him a bottle of Samuel Adams. "Nice choice, thanks."

Leigh shifted sideways slightly, balancing her mug on one knee as she made room for Matt beside her. "How about a comprehensive background search starting from say…nineteen-seventy-five?"

Tucker froze with the beer partway to his lips as his gaze snapped up to hers. "Now that's a little more challenging. Not impossible, but a little something I could sink my teeth into. Email me the specifics of what you're looking for and I'll get on it first thing tomorrow." He brought a hand down heavily on the manila envelope in his lap. "So…this stuff."

Leigh's stomach did a queasy flip-flop just before Matt's hand closed over hers, his fingers cold from holding two beer bottles. She laced her fingers through his and tried not to hold on too tightly. "Did you find anything?"

"Yeah, you could say that." Tucker took another slug of beer, then reached forward to set the bottle on the coffee table. He shook some of the contents of the envelope out into his lap and selected the top sheet. "Let's start with this—the phone log and the highlighted number. You're right, Abbott, it's from a burner phone. I tracked it back to a phone sold at a mom and pop convenience store in North Salem. Paid for in cash. And from that point on, the trail goes mostly cold. Now, I ran some searches based on the phone log you got, and a lot of the calls were to known dealers in the area."

"Which makes it look like it was used in the local drug trade, but we don't know who it belonged to," Leigh said.

"That's my take. These no-contract phones make it easy for perps to do business with each other. Lay down your fifty dollars cash and get a phone with a new number and unlimited talk and data for the next thirty days with no way to connect it to you. By the time the cops are on it, you've already tossed it away and moved on to a new phone and a different number. Wiretaps need never concern the tech savvy perp because the cops never have enough time to get a warrant and start listening in. And fifty dollars as the cost of doing business without getting caught is a steal of a deal for these guys. I tried to finesse out a little more information, but when they're all using the same short-term communications strategy, it's not easy, at least in this abbreviated time frame. And, speaking of North Salem…" He pulled the photo of Nate Abbott and the unknown man under the glowing *Bruno's Tavern* sign from the pile. "We have this photo. I scanned it and extracted all the available biometric data from it.

The lighting and the graininess of the security footage certainly made that job a particular challenge."

Leigh's heart plummeted. *You knew this would be hard, even for Tucker. He can't pull answers out of thin air.* "So you couldn't get anything from it."

Tucker pinned her with a flat stare. "Did I say that, 'O ye of little faith'?"

She bolted upright, leaning forward. "You got something?"

"I used the one side of his face to generate a three-dimensional image and, from that, I got a match. It's only a ninety percent probability, which is pretty damned poor, but it's the best I could manage with what I had to work with."

"Ninety percent sounds not bad, until you realize you might be sending someone to jail with a ten percent error rate," Matt said. "That's *way* too high."

"It certainly is. But considering who it is and how he fits into the scheme of things, I suspect it's correct." Tucker pulled a mug shot from the pile. "This is Thomas Dawlin." The photo showed a man in his early twenties with three days' growth of beard and dark, messy, unkempt hair that fell into hard eyes. "Dawlin's rap sheet is as long as your arm. Drug possession to distribution to a little B & E on the side to finance some of his own habits when dealing didn't do the trick. He did time and went through rehab and supposedly came out a new man."

"And was my father meeting with him because he had his finger on the pulse of the Salem drug community?" She looked over at Matt, hope rising. "We can make contact with this guy. Confirm that it was him meeting with Dad and then find out why. We know Dad was investi-

gating at least one death in the drug community; maybe
he was using Dawlin as a C.I."

Matt swung around to Tucker. "Can you track this
guy? Give us current whereabouts?"

"Oh, I can give you current whereabouts on him.
North Street in Salem—"

Leigh stiffened as Tucker's tone set off warning bells,
bracing for the blow she instinctively knew was coming.

"—in St. Mary's Cemetery. Dawlin was gunned down
shortly after this picture was taken and just a couple of
weeks before your father's death, Abbott. I'm sorry."

"Goddamn it," Matt muttered. "*Another* dead end."

Leigh tried to block out Matt's voice. He was trying
to help, but his frustration only wound her tighter until
she was struggling to breathe. She pulled her hand free,
camouflaging the action by shrugging out of her sweater
and laying it over the arm of the sofa as if she was too
warm. But chilled to the bone, she picked up her tea and
cradled it in both hands, keeping herself separate, struggling to hold herself together.

She sensed Matt's gaze, but continued staring down
into her mug until Tucker's voice broke into her thoughts.

"I do have more for you in that photo than just a dead
end."

Her gaze snapped up to his. "What else?"

"I analyzed the structure of the photo itself. I can tell
you with one hundred percent certainty the photo was
tampered with. In fact, your father was never there at all."

Oxygen suddenly flowed into her lungs as tension
sluiced off her like a waterfall. "You can prove it?"

"Would I say I was one hundred percent certain if
I was just guessing? Yes, I can prove it. Someone else
was in the place where your father is now standing in

that shot. When you analyze the photo at the pixel level, there are issues around the image of your father—missing pixels, cloned regions that were repetitively copied to fill in some of the blank spots, and blurred regions to hide the fact the lighting around your father was slightly different than it would have been had he actually been standing there. Without a doubt, the image of your father was pulled from somewhere else, added to this location after the original person had been removed, and then the attempt was made to hide the fact the image was photoshopped. To the average person, with the naked eye, it wasn't a terrible job. For real photo analysis software and the wizard who knows how to use it, it was a joke."

Leigh sat back against the couch cushions, letting her head fall back, relief making her muscles lax. "He wasn't there. And we can prove it. The only thing that's too bad is we don't know who was really there. Or could your fancy software tell you that?"

"No. But I wondered the same thing. So I did a little investigating. Kind of a field trip for a guy like me who never leaves his keyboard."

Matt saluted him with his beer bottle. "You found the camera, didn't you?"

"I did. And it was an interesting experience, let me tell you." Reaching into the envelope, he pulled out a VHS videotape. "But I also came home with this baby."

"What the—" Leigh shot upright and her mug cracked down on the table. "Tucker, you're a geek, not a cop. You can't go out gathering evidence. We don't have a real case. You didn't have a warrant."

"Whoa. *Whoa.*" Tucker frowned and extended both palms to Leigh. "Slow down there. You asked for my help. I'm giving it to you."

"And I appreciate that, but you're supposed to do it from the safety of your office. You don't belong out in the field."

"What was I going to do? Send you? I knew what I was looking for. I didn't need any help."

Matt laid his hand on Leigh's arm, holding steady when she shot him an infuriated glare. "Leigh, let him finish. Tucker, how did you get that tape?"

Tucker sat back, propping one foot up on the coffee table and linking his hands behind his head, like he didn't have a care in the world. "I figured out where the camera must have been from the angle of the shot and I went down there yesterday to look around. The camera is on this little family convenience store, run by an old guy— one of the tinfoil-hat-paranoid groupies, if you ask me. Anyway, the camera is mounted on the front corner of the store angled to record the front door on one side and most of the parking lot in the rest of the frame. But, from its location, one side of the frame catches the front of *Bruno's Tavern*, which is kitty-corner across the street.

"It's a beautiful new camera and it gave me great hope we'd be successful so I went inside to talk to him. And he proceeded to dash my hopes against the rocks when he told me this was his new system, replacing an ancient VHS system the year before. But I took one look around his store"—Tucker's lip curled in distaste—"which was a jumbled mishmash of pretty much anything you could imagine buying anywhere, and took a chance. I asked if he had any of his old tapes, and the old pack rat said he did. Not all of them, but the bar across the street was known to be a hot spot for drug activity and it wasn't uncommon for the Salem cops to come in wanting his security tapes. He always provided them, but he always made sure he made personal copies just in case."

"In case of what?" Matt asked. "They were his security tapes, not an accusation he was involved."

"Remember how I said he was part of the tinfoil-hat brigade? As far as he was concerned, they were his property and if The Man was involved and wanted his tapes, then he wanted copies because clearly there was something someone was trying to hide in that content. Truthfully, I think he thought Perry Mason was going to call him up on the stand and he'd have to testify about aliens invading and didn't want to be caught unprepared. I don't care why he did it, he just did. And he must have been asked by the cops more than a few times because he had two full boxes of copies." He brandished the tape in the air. "And this one was in there, matching the date stamp on the photo. My analysis software found the exact frame used in the photo sent to you." He held out his hands as if to say *ta-da!*

"And?" Leigh repeated his gesture. "What did you find?"

Tucker's lips twisted. "You take all the joy out of the reveal, Abbott. What I found is that the photo's been tampered with on about every level possible. And not well done, either. When you get to the analysis stage, errors and inconsistencies abound."

"What do you mean?"

"Well, the time stamp was right, which was a blessing or else tracking this down would likely have been a whole lot more work on my part. But the image was different. And intact. Run that same frame through the software and the picture is pristine. We've got the original."

"Who was the perp talking to?"

"And that's where we hit a snag." He pulled a large black and white photo from the envelope and handed it to Leigh.

The photo was identical to the one she'd received, except for the man facing the camera in the place where her father had been. The fur-trimmed hood of his parka was pulled up over his head, throwing his face into shadow. Only his chin and the edge of his lower lip were dimly lit by the flickering neon sign over his head.

Matt leaned over, studying the picture in Leigh's hand. "Looks like a man to me. From both the style of the coat and the mental eminence."

Leigh pulled back a few inches, staring at him in confusion. "The mental what?"

"Mental eminence." He tapped a forefinger gently against her chin. "Right here." Picking up her hand, he pressed her fingers against her chin, rubbing up and down. "Feel how flat that is? That it's nearly a vertical line from your teeth to the lower edge of your mandible? That's typical of females." He moved her fingers to his chin and repeated the motion. "Now, feel how my chin projects forward? That protuberance is typical of males." He released her hand to tap the photo. "It's in no way a sure thing from one grainy, dimly lit photo and a single data point, but that looks like a man to me."

"So we think it might be a man, but other than that, it's yet another dead end." Leigh tossed the photo onto the coffee table in disgust.

"You know, the number of dead ends in this case has to make you wonder," Tucker said. "Everything seems to lead nowhere. We have untraceable numbers, dead convicts, and unidentifiable suspects. Everything that is, until we get to the third delivery."

Leigh's gaze flicked up to meet Tucker's. The look on his face sent a shiver racing through her—caution mixed with…was that fear? *Whatever he's got, it's bad.* She took a deep breath and sat up straighter, squaring her shoulders. *Get it on the table. We can't deal with what's in the dark, only with what we bring out into the light.* "What about the third delivery?"

"At first glance, everything seems consistent. It really is a series of drug busts. As I'm sure you could tell from the files themselves, those are the public access records of the cases. Names of the victims and any personal information have been redacted. But the investigating officers are there. So I looked closer. Two of the three files are exactly what they seem."

"Which two?" Matt asked.

"The Palmer case and the students from Salem U."

"Which leaves the case with the dead child," Matt said. "What's not right there?"

"Well, the paper copy looks good. It matches the file as it exists in the state police database. The problem is— it doesn't match the case reports from your father's hard drive."

Leigh froze. "You pulled data off the drive?"

"Yes. Some of it was a bit of a challenge. A lot of the files had been deleted and some I only recovered pieces of; it's an old drive. But the file containing this particular report I recovered in its entirety." Tucker picked up the fat file. "This case was supervised by your father as the unit sergeant. The officer assigned to the case was the late Trooper Robert Mercer."

"And we're back to the dead ends," Matt said.

"You would think. It's certainly what the official record shows."

"But…" Leigh pressed.

"But that's not what your father has in his report."
Tucker paused and swallowed. And then met her gaze
full-on, his eyes shadowed and serious, all hint of humor
gone. "Leigh, you need to be prepared for this. For what
it might mean."

More than his warning, it was Tucker's use of her
given name that made the breath freeze in her lungs. *How
can you be prepared when you don't how far the fall will
be?* She gathered herself. *Whatever he throws at you, you
can handle it.* "I am." The words were supposed to come
out strong, but even she could hear the tremor in them.

Matt sidled closer, taking both her hands in his. He
nodded at Tucker. "Go."

"The official record has been changed. I'm not sure
when, and I can't swear by who, although you can read
between the lines. The report on your father's hard drive
identifies a different investigating officer." He paused for
a second before plowing on quickly, as if needing to un-
burden himself. "The case was investigated by Trooper
First Class Daniel Kepler."

For a moment, Leigh only heard whistling in her ears
as her whole body went numb. Matt's grip could have
broken her fingers and she'd never have noticed. "Kepler?" she croaked.

"Kepler." Tucker threw himself back in the chair, his
face a palette of conflicted emotions. "For God's sake,
Abbott, our sergeant could be the one responsible for
all this."

Trooper First Class Daniel Kepler. The man who had
donned the mantle of Sergeant Nate Abbott following his
death. The man who was her direct supervisor.

Yanking her hands free, Leigh surged to her feet, striding away to stand in front of the painting above the mantel, fighting for serenity as her thoughts tumbled over each other.

Her father, murdered in his prime. Kepler as the investigating officer on scene, ordering other officers to keep her away. Kepler who could have doctored evidence or suppressed it to cover his own guilt, and none of them would have been the wiser. Kepler who took her father's place as the unit's sergeant. Kepler, welcoming her to the unit when she joined the following year. *Your father would be so proud.* Kepler, whose orders could mean the difference between life and death on any given day.

Stop!

Leigh let her head drop and gave herself a moment to push everything out of her whirling brain. *No more panic. Think it through logically.* Her eyes rose back up to the painting, but instead of finding the laughing girl or the puppy frolicking through the surf, her gaze landed on her mother's signature in the corner. She focused on that signature until her heart stopped racing and it was no longer such an effort to breathe.

"This doesn't feel like Kepler to me," Leigh finally said, her back still to the men. "He's a hard-ass, but he's an honorable man. If he has a problem with you, he doesn't whisper it behind your back; he bellows it in your face. This kind of skulking isn't Kepler's style."

"Maybe you don't know him as well as you think." It was Tucker's voice, his words slightly muffled as if he was curled inwards and talking into his chest. "You think that secret deliveries aren't his style, but we have no idea what the endgame might be in all this. Whoever is playing this game isn't playing it for kicks. He's playing to win. And using a method that's not his normal M.O. could further obscure his identity."

"He's right, Leigh." Matt spoke from behind her and she latched onto the quiet logic in his tone. *There lies sanity.* "This is a deep game started years ago. Maybe it doesn't strike you as his style now, but maybe it was then and he's being forced to follow through on it."

"Could Kepler have had a hand in your father's death?" Tucker asked. "He certainly benefited from it since he was immediately promoted into your father's position."

Leigh had to hold herself back from snapping out a response. Her gut was telling her it was all wrong. "Someone had to step into that role, but there wouldn't have been any guarantees that he'd get it. Killing a commanding officer in hopes of taking over his position in the unit is nothing short of insane."

She turned back to face them. Tucker was folded up in the chair, his feet propped up on the edge of the coffee table, his shoulders hunched up around his ears and a miserable expression on his face. Matt sat exactly where she'd left him, but he was swiveled on the couch with one arm thrown over the back facing her. Keeping his distance and letting her settle, but still keeping watch.

She moved to stand behind the couch, slipping her hand into his and squeezing in silent thanks.

"You okay?" he asked.

"Been better." She blew out a breath. "Honestly, I need time to think this through. My gut says it's not Kepler, but maybe that's years of him training me to see something that isn't there. I can't depend on anything he's ever told me now. I have to look at him like a suspect. But I have to do it while he's still my commanding officer and has the power to send me into a situation that could erase me if I get too close." She looked up at Tucker. "You're safer than I am, but you need to keep your head down. Don't take any more chances. We don't know how he might react if he's orchestrating this and finds out we're onto him."

"I can be careful, Abbott. But we need to know more. If he's really responsible for this…"

"I know. But I won't have your life on my hands. You have to be beyond careful, Tucker. You're on record with the tinfoil-hat guy as wanting information. The moment you try to pursue which cops wanted which tapes, you could get flagged in a big way. It's a whole new ball game now."

"Don't I know it," he muttered.

Leigh's gaze fell on the fat file in Tucker's lap. They needed answers and they needed them now. And they had to find a way around the dead ends and the dead witnesses. Someone had to know something.

They just needed to figure out who.

TWENTY-THREE: LOW WINES

Low wines: the liquid produced by the first pot still in the distillation process. The low wines flow into a second still where they are redistilled to produce colorless, high alcohol spirits.

Tuesday, 5:34 p.m.
McDermott Residence
Lynn, Massachusetts

LEIGH TOOK A SEAT on the overstuffed floral couch. "I appreciate you all taking the time to meet with us again."

"No trouble at all." Barb slipped past Matt with surprising agility and settled beside Leigh, sitting so close that Leigh shifted closer to the armrest to ease the pressure against her side.

Matt struggled to keep his grin from showing as he chose the armchair across from them. Ethel, David, Craig, his wife, Muriel, Connor, Heidi, and Eric all filed in and took seats. Leigh looked incredibly uncomfortable as she unsuccessfully tried to maintain a little professional space and distance from the woman who was clearly basking in the novelty of being involved in a police investigation.

Matt settled back in his chair, adopting a casual pose as he scanned the room. He had his marching orders as outlined earlier by Leigh, and was ready to act on them.

"I want you to come with me to the Kains this evening."

Matt shrugged out of his lab coat and hung it up. "I can do that. Do you need something in particular?"

"Actually, yes. I'm hiding the real reason for the visit behind the pretense of breaking the news of Santino Cabrera's innocence. But what I really want to find out about are the cuff links. And while everyone is watching me, I want you watching them. Between the two of us, we should be able to keep an eye on the whole room."

"Because you think one of them has to know about the cuff links."

"And be responsible for Peter Holt's death, yes. Samuel Kain must have found them after his wife's death, but we know he wasn't capable of carrying out Holt's murder and then moving his body. So the question is—who acted for him? Who killed Holt and then planted the cuff links as a message to Evelyn?"

"This does have an 'all in the family' kind of feel, doesn't it?"

"It does. So we need to figure out who's responsible. Exclude no one." When he started to speak, she lifted a hand to stop him. "I know what you're thinking. We're moderately safe in it not being Ethel because of her age and frailty, or Barb because she's not in physical shape to lug around a body. But any of the men could have managed it."

"So could any of the younger people. Heidi's not that robust, but remember the body was in a rug. She could have dragged it."

"Good point. And keep a particular eye on Eric. I don't like his attitude. There's something about him that's...unsettling."

"Barely banked violence. Yeah, I picked up on it too."

"Watch them all carefully, but keep him in mind in particular."

"You don't think he's too obvious?"

"Sometimes the obvious ones are that for a reason."

"We wanted to stop by to see you all personally," Leigh said, bringing Matt back into the present.

"You have more news about the body you found in the speakeasy?" Barb asked, leaning in even closer in her eagerness.

"We've progressed nicely in that case, but actually, I need to speak with you about Anna Kain."

Barb drew back several inches in surprise, and relief at the additional space flashed across Leigh's face for a fraction of a second before she recovered and smoothed her features. "Grandmother?" Barb asked. "What news could you have there?"

Matt followed Leigh's gaze across to Ethel. The older woman sat across the room in a high-backed armchair, her face pale and one trembling hand spread over her sternum.

"We've recently discovered there was a terrible miscarriage of justice done in nineteen-eighty," Leigh said gently, ignoring everyone else in the room to speak directly to Anna's only surviving child. "The man arrested for your mother's murder, Santino Cabrera, was not guilty of the crime."

The room exploded into pandemonium. David shot to his feet, his face flushed, shouting that they'd made a mistake. Both Craig and Connor asked questions over each other while the women chattered anxiously among themselves. Eric mouthed a single crude epithet, his dark eyes narrowed on Leigh. Only Ethel remained silent.

Leigh pushed to her feet and held out both hands. "Please, everyone calm down, I can answer all your questions."

The furor finally died down until David's was the only voice. "How could this have happened? I was there. There was a trial. There was definitive evidence and Cabrera was convicted. It didn't even take the jury long to make the decision. It was a convincing case."

"It might have appeared to be convincing, but the truth of the matter is that the fingerprint evidence was what convicted him, and that analysis was incorrect. Cabrera was never in the house. He's innocent."

"You're sure?" Heidi asked.

"Absolutely. It's been verified by one of our top fingerprint experts."

"So that man… He's been in jail for over thirty years for *nothing*?"

Matt recognized the horror in her tone; he'd felt the scrape of it over his skin himself. *So many irreplaceable years lost…*

"Yes. We can't fix the fact that he's lost three decades of his life, but we can get him out of there as fast as possible so he doesn't lose any more."

"Then who is responsible?" Ethel asked. "Who killed my mother?"

"We actually have a few leads on who that might be." Her gaze flicked to Matt and he gathered himself, knowing that she was about to drop the bomb.

"Like what?" Connor asked.

"Does anyone recognize these?" Leigh pulled a small evidence bag from her pocket and held it up. Inside, the antique gold glowed dully.

Barb leaned forward. "What's that?"

"They're cuff links. They were found at the scene of your grandmother's murder."

Matt quickly scanned the family spread around the room. Most of them sat forward in their chairs, squinting at the small bag Leigh held. Only Eric gave it a quick glance, and then his gaze darted away to study Leigh instead of the evidence.

"I don't understand," David said. "You don't see it so much today, but back in the seventies, men still wore cuff links. Finding a pair of Samuel's doesn't tell us anything."

"But they're not Samuel's." Leigh moved to stand in front of him, extended the bag so that he could see them better. "Do you recognize them?"

He shook his head. "But men often don't notice stuff like this."

"True, but most women do." Leigh turned back to Barb. "Have you seen these before?"

"May I?" Barb took the bag, studying them closely. "No, never. Mom?" She passed the bag to Ethel.

Ethel angled them toward the light, running the pad of her thumb over the inset blue stones. "They're lovely. And quite old, I think, from the style. But I've never seen them before."

Leigh waited as the small evidence bag was passed around the room.

Matt studied each person as they accepted the cuff links. Some were openly curious and took time to study them, like Craig, who commented on the local jeweler. Some were dismissive, like Eric, who glanced at them, shrugged noncommittally, and handed them off immediately.

"Have you shown these to Great-Grandpa?" Connor

asked. "I'm not sure showing them to us is that useful. If anyone could shed light on them, it would be him."

"Only if you caught him on a *really* good day," Barb muttered.

"It's true, we could ask him, since they were found in his bedroom. But since he couldn't have been involved with Peter Holt, I thought I'd ask this group instead."

"Peter Holt? Isn't that the man who was found murdered last week?" David asked. "I saw something about it in the paper."

"Yes, his body was found downtown." Leigh held up the bag. "These were in his pocket."

There was a moment of stunned silence, before Craig finally spoke. "Are you suggesting there's a connection between Grandmother's death and the death of this Holt fellow? We don't even know the man. How can there be a connection?"

"I'm just exploring all possible avenues," Leigh said calmly, plucking the evidence bag from Heidi's hand and sliding it back into the pocket of her jacket. "What I can tell you is that these cuff links appear in crime scene photos from Anna Kain's death, and then were found on the body of Peter Holt. They're unique pieces, so there's no mistaking them."

"Maybe they were Great-Grandfather's cuff links and he sold them," Connor reasoned. "That would be why none of us recognize them. Perhaps they've been gone for years. He could have sold them through a jeweler or a pawn shop. Or perhaps he gave them away. Either way, there's no connection to us."

Not in a million years, Matt thought. *Not considering their provenance. They aren't just pieces of jewelry; they're harbingers of death.*

"He could have," Leigh said, her tone casual. "But I need to exercise due diligence." Hands on her hips, she studied the room. "I need to know your whereabouts during a two-hour window from ten p.m. a week ago Thursday until midnight on Friday." She flipped open her notepad and pointed at David with the end of her pen. "Starting with you."

They went slowly around the room, each person providing detailed information. The alibis came fast and furious—the married couples were home with each other; Ethel was alone in her room at her retirement home, but the staff would attest that she never went out; Connor was at a private astronomy viewing at the High Rock Tower observatory; and Heidi was working the evening shift at a local bar—all except for Eric, who sullenly announced that he was out "for a drive" after he and his ex-girlfriend had a fight that evening.

Leigh flipped the notepad closed and nodded to Matt that the interview was over. "Thank you all for your time. When I learn anything else, I'll be sure to let you know."

Tuesday, 6:07 p.m.
McDermott Residence
Lynn, Massachusetts

MATT AND LEIGH were silent on the walk back to the car as Barb and David stood on the front step, unmindful of the cold air streaming into the house through the open door behind them. It was only after they'd both climbed in and Leigh pulled away from the curb that she let out a long breath. She glanced over at Matt, his profile lit by splashes of light as they sped down the street. "So, did you spot anything that set off warning bells?"

"I think the announcement of Cabrera's innocence honestly caught them all off guard. If one of them knew about it ahead of time, I didn't catch any sign of it. I could have missed it, or whoever it is might just be damned good."

"I didn't catch anything then either. So how about once I showed them the cuff links?"

"Things are a little trickier there. The only one to show real disinterest was Eric. While everyone else was staring at the cuff links, he was staring at *you*."

"I did a run on him because I didn't like his demeanor. He's had a few dust-ups with the cops before. Drunk and disorderly behavior, a bar fight or two, that sort of thing. Nothing so far that would hint at something like this, but most criminals start with small stuff and then it escalates from there."

"His focus on you could also represent general caution with the police. If he's got a record, even for minor stuff, he might feel that we're automatically looking at him."

"We *are* looking at him. Especially since he's the only one with no alibi. Of course, I'm going to check out everyone else's. And I'll look at the married couples carefully since they alibi each other."

"You've done a nice job of keeping the two related deaths disconnected. If they'd been paying attention, someone should have put two and two together. But because you've been able to keep the speakeasy out of the news since Charles Ward's murder isn't really a current police case, they know about the hidden body there, but haven't connected the physical location with Peter Holt yet."

"That's not going to last though. I could bet money on the fact that at least one of them is looking into the details of Peter Holt's death as we speak. And once they realize that it's all in the same location, the puzzle pieces are going to start to click into place for them."

"Except Peter Holt's killer already knows all about it," Matt pointed out. "It's the reason he left the body there. Another private message to Evelyn Holt: My mother/grandmother/great-grandmother died…and now you're going to pay."

"The real danger here though is that now the killer knows that we know those details. I'm walking a delicate line here; I'm trying to push one of them into revealing something about themselves, but not so hard that they run."

"Or go completely off the rails and try to kill Mrs. Holt herself, or even you. You need the killer off-balance so they do something stupid and tip their hand, I get that. But even if they don't, we'll still figure it out. We're close, Leigh. The person we're looking for was in that room. I could feel it."

"Me too. So close and yet so far." Her phone rang and she pulled it out of her pocket, glancing quickly at the screen. *Rob Tucker.* She handed it to Matt. "Can you answer that and put it on speaker?" She waited while Matt connected the call. "Tucker, I'm here with Matt, and you're on speaker. What have you got for me?"

"I'm fine, Abbott. It's been a good day. Thanks for asking. How about you?"

"Blah blah blah, Tucker. Now cut to the chase."

"See what I mean, Lowell? See how she rides my ass?"

Matt laughed. "No doubt about it, she's a slave driver." He winked at Leigh. "Now, what have you got?"

"Awesome, now you're doing it too. Fine. Abbott, I think I might have what you're looking for. There weren't any big changes in Evelyn Holt's life in nineteen-seventy-five. No births or deaths in the family. No new employment. No change in taxation to indicate significant income adjustment. But what I did find was something that others might have skimmed over and missed."

"You're amazing, Tucker. It's why I asked you. Now spill."

"You could bruise a guy's delicate ego, Abbott."

"Delicate, my ass. It would take more than me to put even a tiny dent in yours. Now, what tiny, yet significant, thing did you find?"

"Evelyn Holt applied for, and was granted, building renovation permits for the house in Lynn in May of nineteen-seventy-five."

Leigh glanced at Matt, who stared back, one eyebrow cocked in interest. "The Ward family house? The one where Peter Holt was murdered?"

"The same. Abbott, she found something, I just know it. She didn't act for years, but then suddenly, she goes after Samuel Kain's wife? For most minor fixes, you don't need a permit. But you do if you're doing a major renovation. My guess is they took out floors or walls to update an older home and she found something that helped her figure out what must have happened to her father—maybe something he'd hidden away—and went after Anna Kain in revenge."

"Tucker, you're brilliant. I owe you one."

"It's worth it all just for you to stroke my ego like this. I'll shoot the details to your email. Gotta run. Over and out." He clicked off.

Leigh smacked the steering wheel in jubilation. "He's good, you can't deny it."

"Nope. And another loose end potentially gets tied off.

We don't know what she found, but for the first time the huge time gap between murders makes sense."

Leigh checked the car's clock. "I want to check on the info Tucker's sending, but then I think it's time to go bring Evelyn Holt in for questioning. You free first thing tomorrow? You can't sit in on the interview but you can certainly observe."

"If I'm not, I'll clear it. I don't want to miss this. You're going to nail her to the wall and I want to watch it happen."

TWENTY-FOUR: 190 PROOF

190 proof: the highest concentration of alcohol in any alcoholic beverage. Above 190 proof—ninety-five percent alcohol by volume—the liquid draws moisture from the air and self-dilutes.

Wednesday, 9:49 a.m.
Essex Detective Unit
Salem, Massachusetts

LEIGH LOOKED UP from a stack of paperwork at the sound of a soft tap on the metal edge of her cubicle. Matt leaned against the wall, his leather jacket slung over his shoulder, hooked over two fingers.

"Good morning."

"Oh, damn."

He fixed her with a pointed stare. "Should I have shown up bearing coffee as a bribe? I thought we were meeting now."

"We were and bribery isn't required. I just got caught up in something else right at the beginning of shift and I haven't had time to go down to Boston yet to bring Evelyn in for questioning. Sorry, I should have called you to let you know, but I lost track of time."

"Luckily I cleared my morning, so I'm flexible."

"Thanks. Let me just pack this up for now and we'll go." Standing, Leigh started to stack her papers and was sliding them neatly into her file folder when her phone rang. "Trooper Abbott."

"Trooper, it's Hilary Boxall."

Silence stretched across the line as Leigh tried desperately to place the name.

"I'm Evelyn Holt's assistant," the woman continued.

The image of the willowy, perfectly coiffed blond in a white blouse and black pants bloomed in Leigh's mind. "What can I do for you, Ms. Boxall?"

"I found your card in Mrs. Holt's desk…"

When the woman paused overly long, Leigh deduced it wouldn't be a short conversation and waved Matt into her cubicle. He leaned a hip on the corner of her desk, his jacket tossed carelessly over one knee as he fixed on her face, trying to follow the conversation from only one side.

"How can I help you, Ms. Boxall?" Leigh pressed.

"It's not me, it's Mrs. Holt." The words came out in a rush, stress accentuating the final hard consonant.

"How can I help Mrs. Holt then?"

"She left about twenty minutes ago in a flurry."

"And this concerned you in some way?"

"Mrs. Holt is *never* in a flurry. She's one of the most composed and controlled people I know. Something is very wrong."

"Hilary, I need more." Leigh hoped the use of the woman's first name would not only calm her, but would coax a more intimate sharing of information. "What put Mrs. Holt into this 'flurry'?"

"She got a phone call. I don't know who it was from—a man, I can tell you that much since I answered the phone—but I can't tell you anything more. I don't think it was someone she's close to because the voice was unfamiliar."

Leigh reached for a pen and her notepad. "Young? Old?"

"I'm not sure. And there was no number on call display."

"When was the call?"

"Just before she left the house. She took the car, for God's sake!"

Leigh stared up at Matt, perplexed. This level of alarm seemed a little over the top. "This is unusual?"

"Yes. Boston traffic can be intense, so Mrs. Holt prefers I drive her most of the time. But she made it very clear she was going alone this morning, even though she seemed very agitated."

"Are you concerned she's going to have an accident?"

Hilary gasped. "I never even thought of that. What if she does?"

Leigh's mental image of the holier-than-thou assistant disintegrated into that of a huddled and terrified child. "Hilary!" Her voice came out sharply. Matt stiffened beside her. "Stay on point. Why are you so concerned?"

"I listened in on part of the conversation." The confession came out as a whisper. "She was arguing with him. I couldn't hear the whole thing, but I heard things like 'What right do you have to demand that of me?' and 'I'm a Ward and you're nothing but the by-blow of a street rat.' The last thing she said was 'I know what you did, and you'll pay.' Then the phone crashed down and there were doors slamming and a *clang* and then she tore out of the house. It's the *clang* that really worries me."

"Why?"

"I'm pretty sure that's the sound of her gun safe slamming shut. It's hidden behind some false books in the den."

Leigh surged to her feet, Matt following suit in alarm, his jacket tumbling to the floor. "Where did she go?"

"I don't know, but I think she's meeting someone

somewhere. There was a pad of paper on her desk. On it were three letters—HRT—and the time—ten o'clock."

Leigh covered the mouthpiece with one hand. "HRT," she hissed at Matt. "What could that stand for?"

"Heart rate turbulence? Hostage Response Team?"

"It's more likely a location of a meet."

He shook his head. "I've got nothing then." His eyes lost focus and she knew he was desperately running through local landmarks and businesses, trying to match the letters.

"Trooper, are you there?"

Leigh dropped her hand from the mouthpiece. "I'm here. Hilary, what does Mrs. Holt drive?"

"A silver four-door Lexus."

"Leave this with me for now. But I want you to call me if you think of anything else or if Mrs. Holt comes back. My cell number is on that card. I'll be in the field so call me there."

She hung up and quickly filled Matt in, his face growing more and more concerned. "You think she's gone after someone?"

"I'm certain of it." She paced several steps away before rounding on him. "Did I make a mistake last night?"

"In revealing the cuff links? I don't think so. You had evidence that connected one crime scene to the next, limiting the number of people who could have been involved. You had to question those people."

"And I didn't have enough to bring anyone in and possibly be able to hold them. I wanted to shake things up, but I didn't want it to go this far."

"Maybe it's unrelated. Maybe she just had a charity emergency of some kind or a friend is sick. We don't know enough yet, so don't jump to conclusions yet."

"She took a gun with her. What other conclusion should I be jumping to?"

"Okay, you got me there. It looks bad." He picked his jacket up off the floor and shrugged into it. "What next then?"

"I think we need to find out where all the Kains are. If what we suspect is correct, one of them is on the move and won't be in touch with the cops. And we need to do it before Evelyn gets caught in the crossfire."

"If revenge is what our missing Kain has in mind, that might have been the plan all along."

"Maybe, but it's not happening on my watch." She instinctively laid a hand on her badge and her service weapon, making sure she had everything she needed before grabbing her jacket and stepping out from the cubicle.

"Hey, Abbott." Riley's head popped over the top of his cubicle on the far side of the room. "I was hoping I'd catch you. I've been following up on confirming alibis for the Kain family for a week ago Thursday."

"Yeah?"

"I think I just hit pay dirt."

With a head cock at Matt to follow, she met Riley in the narrow corridor between the cubicles. "What have you got?"

"I started with Heidi Kain. She was working that night and multiple people can attest to it. But Connor Kain either lied to you, or he's not telling the whole truth. He said he was at a private viewing at the observatory that night. The head of Lynn City Development is in charge of who has access to the tower and when. There was a private viewing that night and Connor was asked to attend, but he backed out at the last minute and had someone else cover for him. I've still got a few more names to check, but I thought you'd want to know right away."

"You know, if you take a minute to think this through, he makes sense," Matt said. "Connor's the one with the closest bond to Samuel. Closer apparently than even his own daughter, who talked about their 'special connection' and how Samuel was the one to get Connor started in astronomy. Something that was such a strong love it became his career."

"Think back to what Connor said last night," Leigh said. "He was the one who tried to lead us away from the family group by suggesting the cuff links had been sold years ago."

"He expected to be so peripheral that you'd never look at him. He probably never thought he needed an alibi to hold up so he didn't make sure from the start that he could prove where he was that night. He had no idea you would tie the cuff links back to Anna Kain's murder and point the spotlight right at his whole family."

"Until last night when I made it clear I was looking exclusively at them. But why would he kill Peter Holt?"

"Because of that bond with his grandfather? Somehow he not only got a hold of those cuff links, but he also found out what they represented. And just like Evelyn killed Anna for both revenge and to make Samuel suffer, he did the same thing to her. You know, when you look at it like that, Eric doesn't make sense as the killer. He's capable, we've both felt that, but he isn't involved enough in the family to give a damn. Certainly not enough to risk a life sentence if he ever got caught."

"But Connor would. Damn it, I let myself get distracted by the obvious. And maybe now the time gap between Anna's and Peter Holt's deaths makes sense too.

It's because his great-grandfather doesn't have long to live. Connor's killing in his great-grandfather's stead, so he wants him alive to know he's taking care of family business."

"He probably also knows Samuel has very little time to recognize what his favorite great-grandson did for him at the rate his mental capabilities are degrading."

"So then if we assume that call was from Connor, what could he say that would draw Evelyn out?"

"Maybe he told her he had information about her son's death? Or maybe he told her he knew she killed Anna and she had to meet him or he was taking his information to the police?"

"No big threat there. He couldn't afford to shine that kind of spotlight on himself right now."

"You know that and I know that, but Evelyn probably isn't thinking too clearly right now. She's still grieving over the loss of her only son."

"She may also feel she has absolutely nothing to lose anymore," Matt pointed out. "Remember, this is a woman who's killed for revenge before. If she knew she was talking to the person who'd killed her son, I don't think she'd hesitate to kill again. And we know she's armed."

"Which is something Connor doesn't know. So… HRT. That's the key. What does that mean to Connor specifically?"

"That one's obvious," Riley interjected.

Leigh turned to him. He'd been so quiet and she'd been so focused on Matt and their discussion that she'd forgotten Riley was there. "Do you want to share it with the class?"

"Sure. HRT is High Rock Tower. It's where he said he was the night of the murder."

Realization poured over her like a bucket of icy water and she slapped an open palm against her thigh in frustration. "Of course. He'd direct her to somewhere familiar to him to finish this off. He knows we're going to figure out it's him. He's got nothing to lose." She met Matt's gaze. "People with nothing to lose are extremely dangerous."

"That's a combat lesson I learned years ago. Leigh, the note said ten o'clock." His gaze flicked to the clock on the wall. "We're not going to get there in time."

Digging into her pocket, Leigh yanked out her notepad and scribbled down Evelyn's name, address, and the make of her car. She ripped off the sheet of paper and thrust it at Riley. "Find out the plate number for this vehicle and put a BOLO on it." She gave his arm a quick squeeze. "Good work. Thanks."

They left the office at a sprint.

TWENTY-FIVE: DÉGORGEMENT

Dégorgement: the traditional method of removing dead yeast (lees) from champagne by popping the crown cap and letting the carbonation push the plug out from the neck of the bottle. Before the process was invented circa 1815 by Madame Clicquot Ponsardin, traditional champagne was cloudy.

Wednesday, 10:27 a.m.
High Rock Tower
Lynn, Massachusetts

"Hang on."

Glancing sideways at the hard set of Leigh's jaw, Matt reached for the grab bar above the passenger door just as they careened around the corner onto Circuit Avenue. Leigh hit the gas, gunning it uphill, charming clapboard houses streaking by in a blur of blue, yellow, and beige. Another sharp curve and then the closed loop at the end of the avenue came into view. Beyond, High Rock Tower stood atop the rocky rise, a dark shape backlit by the brilliant, cloudless late autumn sky. As they quickly closed the distance, Matt could make out the architectural details of the tower. Built of reddish granite, its corners and trim lined with gray stone, it stood on a cliff, towering more than two hundred feet above sea level. Arched windows with granite railings circled the second floor, with smaller arches on the third, leading up to the crenellated observation deck. Topping the tower was the silver dome of the observatory.

"Look." Leigh took one white-knuckled hand from the wheel to point at the cars parked at the far end of the curve. "The silver four-door sedan. That could be Evelyn's." She groped in her pocket for her phone.

"Definitely. The other could be Connor's. The observatory's probably not open this early, so no one else is here. Pull in behind them. We'll have to go on foot from there."

Leigh pulled to a stop behind the cars, unbuckling her seatbelt even as she called it in, giving their location and requesting backup while grabbing a spare pair of cuffs from the glove box. Then they were both out and sprinting along the sidewalk, hurdling over the short wood rail fence at the edge to race along the grassy hill leading up to the tower. Glancing upwards, Matt caught a glimpse of movement through one of the upper arched windows before he had to pull his attention away as they leapt onto the walkway.

They took the long rise of steps two at a time, only slowing near the top as they approached the unlatched double doors at the entrance. They stopped under the patinaed copper plate above the doors commemorating the September 1905 dedication of the tower. One firm pull and the door swung silently outward.

Matt grabbed her arm before she could move through. "Careful," he whispered. "I thought I saw movement on the third floor. Someone's inside."

Leigh nodded, pulling her gun from the cross-draw holster on her left hip. "Stay behind me."

They crept into the quiet darkness of the tower. Inside,

the unadorned granite walls enclosed a massive brick column filling the center of the space. Leigh indicated the open door and together they stole into the brick cylinder, where a metal staircase wound clockwise up the tower. Normally illuminated by lights installed high on the inside wall, the shaft was mostly dark, lit only by natural light filtering down faintly from above. Leigh started up the staircase, moving silently from tread to tread, ignoring the metal handrail and keeping hold of her weapon, while reaching out to trail the fingers of her left hand over the rough brick as they ascended. When they reached a small open window to the tower, they stopped briefly, but only silence greeted them before they continued up into the damp chill of the stairway.

They came to an open door partway up. Across from the doorway, arched windows and a granite balustrade opened out over downtown Lynn and beyond to the Atlantic Ocean, the wind whistling unimpeded through the tower.

Matt suddenly froze, closing his eyes. *Was that a voice?* It was hard to tell over the moan of the wind, but, if it had been real, it was gone now. He opened his eyes to find Leigh staring at him curiously. He simply tapped his left ear and she nodded in understanding.

They continued upwards another half turn before Leigh abruptly stopped. This time there was no mistaking the voices, no matter how faint.

"How dare you lay hands on me?"

Their eyes met. *Evelyn.*

They doubled their pace, choosing speed over silence. Past the door that opened out to the third floor of the tower and further up toward the upper deck, the sound of voices growing louder.

Matt grasped Leigh's arm, stopping her just inside the open door at the top of the stairs. A small revolver lay on the ground just inside the door frame. *Evelyn's gun, almost certainly. Connor must have forced her to drop it and now had the upper hand.*

Outside, the gusting wind scuttled small dried leaves around the deck of the tower, piling them into the corner of the stone wall opposite the doorway. But over the whistling of the breeze, raised voices were clear.

"You killed my great-grandmother. Shot her in cold blood. Waited while she died." Connor's voice, fury driving his words.

"She was collateral damage. Samuel Kain needed to pay for what he did."

"What he did? He avenged his mother!"

Her head still cocked toward the conversation, Leigh quickly picked up the revolver. She flipped the cylinder open, eyed the six bullets inside and closed it again before sliding the gun into the pocket of her jacket.

"An alcoholic who drank herself into the grave? That was her choice." Disdain was thick in Evelyn's tone.

"Your father *poisoned* her and probably other customers with bad booze. For money. It was always about money." Disgust crept into Connor's tone. "He lined his pockets with their money and when they died, he didn't care. You're still living on that money, which makes you as guilty as he was."

Leigh motioned to Matt, indicating that he should go to the right, while she took the left. They went through the door together, splitting to circle the central tower housing the observatory and its telescope. Hugging the brick wall and leading with her gun hand, Leigh quickly disappeared from view. Matt assessed the open steel staircase that faced him. Curving around the center brick column, it led up to another door, one Matt assumed led directly to the telescope. Running up the first four steps, he vaulted over the railing, landing lightly at the edge of the crenellated wall that surrounded the tower. Downtown Boston spread out in the distance, and Matt automatically noted the familiar landmarks, from the Prudential Tower in the west to the Customs House Tower and beyond in the east.

Quickly pressing himself against the tower wall under the staircase, he inched forward. The argument continued uninterrupted and he knew that Leigh was balancing her desire to learn as much as possible with her need to end the killing.

Another few feet forward, Matt caught a glimpse of Connor and Evelyn, his pulse skipping as he realized Connor's plan. Connor had the older woman pressed up against the granite wall at one of the low crenel openings, her body bent back over the edge of the wall. A pistol was thrust under her chin, forcing her head back even further.

One good push and she would tumble over the wall and fall onto the jagged rocks below. An "accident" with no trace back to him. The circle finally closed.

Suddenly Connor bellowed, "Great-Grandpa! Are you watching? I'm doing this for you!"

Matt's gaze snapped to the buildings spread out before them down the hill, quickly finding a low brick building several blocks away. Everything abruptly clicked into place. Unconcerned with concealing his own identity, Connor had chosen this place for his final kill, within sight of the old man's room at Saint Joseph's Nursing Home. One final act of love for a beloved mentor before he died.

Was Samuel lying in his bed and watching even now?

"That old man lost his mind years ago," Evelyn hissed. "He probably doesn't even know you exist."

She gasped as the gun jammed harder, digging into the soft flesh under her chin. "Don't say that," Connor gritted. "He's a better person than you ever were. And now he'll watch you die."

"Connor, stop." Leigh's voice carried both authority and calm as she stepped forward into Matt's view, gun pointed unwaveringly at Connor's torso. His gun jerked in surprise at the sight of her, but otherwise he gave no reaction. "Let me handle this. I know she killed Anna. Let me take her in. She'll spend the rest of her life in jail. Murdering her isn't the way."

"It's *her* way," Connor said, his gaze fixed on Leigh. "Revenge is her way. This would be justice." He started to back away, dragging Evelyn along the wall, ignoring her cry of pain as skin scraped across granite.

Matt pulled back further into the shadows, knowing he was in full view now and not wanting to make Connor feel cornered—cornered animals could be unpredictable. Leigh's gaze darted toward him, a quick flick unnoticed by Connor.

"But it's over so quickly this way." Leigh inched forward slowly, maintaining the distance between them. "My way puts her in prison for the rest of her life. I can do it too; we have definitive proof."

Connor's gun wavered, dropping slightly "What proof?"

"We have her DNA from a cigarette in Anna's kitchen ashtray and her fingerprints were found at the scene. Connor, let us handle this."

Good job—distract him with the promise of retribution, but don't mention his own part in Holt's death.

"We know she killed Anna to get to Samuel," Leigh continued. "We don't know why, but that hardly matters at this point because we know she's guilty. It'll be such an open and shut case that any jury will convict her." Leigh's careless tone made it appear that she considered the motive inconsequential, but Matt knew she was actually fishing for information.

"It was justice," Evelyn spat, struggling against Connor's hold. "Any jury would understand that. Samuel Kain was a nobody who tried to rise above his station by killing my father. A congressman. A *Ward*. But when no body was discovered, there was no crime to investigate."

"So you took matters into your own hands." Leigh spoke to Evelyn, but her gaze stayed fixed on Connor. "Connor, let her go. Let me do my job. Your satisfaction, your great-grandfather's satisfaction can come from knowing that she'll spend the rest of her life in jail. No servants, no gourmet meals. No personal assistant. A life of having nothing after having it all. Think of how she'll suffer. It's over. She's done."

Connor faltered in that moment, relaxing his grip on Evelyn, his face a study in conflict and confusion as brain and heart battled over the greater justice.

Matt saw the effect of Leigh's words on Evelyn, realized they were backfiring in a way she hadn't anticipated. She was trying to bring Connor closer emotionally; instead she was driving Evelyn to desperation. Evelyn, who had no gun to defend herself, would consider that there was only one way out at this point.

"Stop!" He bolted forward, already seeing desperation settle into resignation and acceptance on Evelyn's lined face. She wouldn't live out the rest of her days disgraced and penniless. It simply wasn't the Ward way.

Evelyn took advantage of Connor's indecision, shoving him hard. He stumbled backward, fumbling the gun in his already loosened hold. He tried to tighten his grip with both hands as Leigh leapt for him.

Matt ignored Connor, leaving him to Leigh, knowing that between the two suspects, she'd consider Connor the imminent threat because he had a weapon. She didn't even consider the danger Evelyn posed, but he did—the danger to herself.

Evelyn was already scrambling up onto one of the crenels, only a mere four feet off the ground. Glancing over her shoulder, her eyes went wide as Matt darted around Connor and Leigh, heading straight for her.

She closed her eyes and launched herself out into the swirling wind, spreading her arms wide as if asking her father to accept her sacrifice.

"Not so fast!" Matt hurled himself against the wall, impacting with enough force that pain stabbed through his ribs. Chest pressed flat to the top surface of the battlement, he reached out, catching Evelyn's leg milliseconds after she pushed off, his hands scrabbling desperately to gain a hold over slick stockings. He clamped down hard, automatically digging the toes of his boots and his knees into the wall for leverage as she slipped ever further through his grasp. The vicious wind whipped at her body, tugging her through his fingers.

He was losing her.

With a grunt of effort, he held on desperately as his grip finally caught just above her ankle. With a cry, Evelyn's body jerked out of free fall, slamming painfully into the granite wall, the shoe of her free foot spinning away to clatter onto the deadly jagged rocks of the cliff face.

With a groan, Matt started to pull her up. She wasn't that heavy, but laid out flat over the wall, his elbows extended into thin air, he had no leverage. His muscles started to shake with the effort. *One inch. Two. Three. You can do this.*

Then she started to fight him, twisting from side to side so that it was all Matt could do to maintain his hold, forget about lifting her to safety. A thought briefly flashed through his mind—*if you want to die so badly, I could oblige you.* But medics saved lives, no matter what. They went to the wall to save them, even if it meant literally.

"Leigh." Her name hissed through gritted teeth, barely loud enough to be heard over the scream of the wind.

A metal click sounded behind him, followed by scuffling, but he couldn't turn around to look without risking his already tentative grip. He tried her name again, louder this time.

Then she was beside him, taking in the situation in a glance, fitting her smaller body into the crenel, reaching out and catching the flailing stockinged foot. Immediately, the strain on his shoulders eased.

"Let's bring her up slowly," Leigh said. "Slow and steady."

Evelyn struggled against them, but little by little, they dragged her back onto the deck, ignoring her cries of pain. Being dragged over a rough granite wall would still be less painful than falling nearly ninety feet onto the rocks below.

Finally pulling her over the parapet, they dumped her unceremoniously onto the stone floor. Leigh pushed her onto her stomach, securing her arms behind her before rolling her face up.

Leaning against the wall, panting from exertion, Matt studied Connor, who sat against the far wall, his arms secured behind him and his head resting on his upraised knees. A quick scan found Connor's gun in the corner of the stone wall where Leigh must have kicked it before subduing him.

Leigh leaned on the wall beside him. "Good catch. Lightning-fast reflexes. I didn't see that coming."

"You were too focused on Connor." He stopped to breathe in, breathe out. "I was watching her. When you were dangling the carrot of her horrible existence in front of him, she was realizing the same thing and decided she wouldn't live with that. I could see it in her eyes. So when you went for him, I went for her. Almost missed her too, but got lucky in the end." He eyed her torn and bloody stockings. "It was close though. Thanks for the hand. When she started to struggle, I thought it was game over."

"Happy to be of service. Helps me too, actually. Much less paperwork now."

He grinned at her. *Cop humor.*

"And now I can reward you by taking the night off to say thanks properly."

His grin widened wickedly.

In the distance, sirens wailed, quickly drawing closer. Leigh leaned over the balustrade and peered down before turning to smile back at Matt.

The cavalry had arrived.

TWENTY-SIX: SABRAGE

Sabrage: a ceremonial method of opening a champagne bottle by striking the neck with a saber.

Friday, 3:56 p.m.
Shirley, Massachusetts

"So, SAMUEL SHARED the whole story with Connor, not with the intent of sending him out for retribution, but because I think he wanted someone else in the family to know why his wife was killed. His lucid moments were growing fewer and farther between, and he knew he didn't have much time. Sharing the story also gave him someone else to help carry the immense weight of his own guilt," Leigh explained. "He was close to Connor, so he was the obvious choice. I don't think he intended the killings to continue."

"If he had, he likely would have continued himself," Matt said. "He must have known as soon as he found the cuff links that Evelyn had to be responsible for Anna's death since she was the only Ward left. He had years to go after her or her family if he wanted to. He didn't, so either he didn't want to attract attention to himself, or maybe he felt that to continue would only put his family in more danger and losing his wife was enough."

"Connor didn't see it that way. Samuel was generations older, but they shared a bond of like minds and interests.

Samuel set him on his chosen career path, and Connor felt this was the ultimate way to repay him—doing the deed that Samuel couldn't do without revealing himself."

"Would it really have been a problem at this point?" Paul asked from the backseat, where he was wedged between Kiko and Juka as the forest flanking Route 2 streaked by.

"It's not like he'd even survive long enough to go to trial," Kiko agreed. "Or if he did, how could he testify? He's the only one left with any actual knowledge of that time, but he's not lucid enough to be a reliable witness."

"Even if he was convicted," Juka said, "he'd only serve a fraction of his sentence and likely not even be cognizant of it."

"Not to mention that I bet Samuel thought the score was settled when he killed Ward," Matt said. "Ward's life for his mother's."

Leigh slid him a sidelong glance. "That's vigilante justice. That's not how we do things in this country."

"But sometimes it's really that simple, especially when you're up against someone like Ward. Someone with money and power, who can buy his way out of trouble, especially back then."

Leigh took her eyes off the road long enough to drill him with an appalled stare. "Do you actually condone what he did in that speakeasy?"

"Condone...no. But do I understand why he did it? Sure. If someone untouchable murdered my mother and I knew that she'd never see justice, would I try to make my own? It's a gray area. I'm not sure what I'd do."

Paul reached forward to tap Matt on the shoulder. "A word of advice, man. You're talking to a cop, who's going to see it in black and white. Stop talking now before you bury yourself."

"Speaking of the speakeasy, there's a place where Connor went wrong," Kiko said.

Leigh met her eyes in the rearview mirror and Kiko grinned sheepishly as she purposely changed the subject to keep her boss from digging an even bigger hole for himself.

"What do you mean?" Juka asked.

"He left Peter Holt's body there as a message for Evelyn. I'll bet he purposely left his ID on him so there was no way to mistake in the message who he was. The only problem was that the most important part of the message didn't get through, at least not right away. Connor learned the location of the *Blue Ruin* from Samuel, but clearly Evelyn didn't know about it, so the significance of the body dumpsite was lost on her."

"Until she saw the cuff links," Paul said. "Only then did it all make sense. She had to know the Kain family was responsible for her loss, but she didn't know who, specifically, until Connor panicked after realizing his alibi wasn't going to hold up and Leigh would figure out it was him. But what I want to know is how she figured out that Samuel Kain killed her father?"

"We got a lot of the story from her yesterday in interview. She was doing major renovations to the house in Lynn in nineteen-seventy-five," Leigh said. "When they ripped out the floor of Ward's office, they found a floor safe. She had it drilled and discovered a bunch of Ward's business papers and account books. He'd made note of threats from Samuel Kain over a wrongful death."

"He was a politician," Paul pointed out. "He was probably covering his ass in case he got sued. But that still doesn't point the finger at Samuel."

"It doesn't. But she recounted a story back from when she was very young. Sitting at the top of the stairs, watching her father meet with someone in the front hall. A very angry young man, she recalled. The man wanted restitution following the death of his mother. He even threatened to kill Ward before he got thrown out. Ward shouted at him that he'd never be anything other than a dirty bricklayer. Evelyn was certain that man was Samuel Kain."

"That was forty years after the death of her father," Matt scoffed. "How could she be sure it was Kain? The memory of a small child from so long ago?"

"Apparently he mentioned his mother's name—Nora. Kain's mother's name was Nora."

Matt made a sound that fell somewhere between a snort and a laugh.

Leigh held up a hand to placate him. "I'm not disagreeing with you. I also found it hard to believe that she killed Anna Kain based on a few vague documents and the wisp of a childhood memory. But, in fact, she was correct. She never went to the police because her father's body was never found. No proof of death, no actual real evidence, no investigation. So she took matters into her own hands, and then used the family fortune to pay off Emerson to ID the wrong man, ensuring that the cop who wouldn't let the case drop stopped looking at her."

"How do you know all of this?" Kiko asked.

"By this point in the interview, Evelyn was giving me any info on Samuel Kain's guilt she could, both in her own defense and in an attempt to bury Kain. The most disturbing thing to me was that sending an innocent man to jail for decades didn't bother her at all. She described

Cabrera as a dangerous criminal who was better locked up in jail than free on the streets collecting welfare. The fact that he lost decades of his life and missed his children growing up didn't faze her in the least."

"What about Peter Holt's death?" Paul asked. "You figured out he was killed at the Ward family home in Lynn, but how did Connor actually get him there?"

"Connor was banking on what he considered to be a rich person's love of money. In the end, it served him well. There was a 'For Sale' sign on the front lawn when Riley and I went to search the house. It didn't take much work on Connor's part to find out that the listing price was too high—against the realtor's recommendation—so it wasn't moving. He cold-called Peter, posing as an agent of a local auction house specializing in moving exclusive properties. Peter told him the house belonged to his mother, but Connor explained that he wanted to run the idea by Peter first and even offered Peter a 'finder's fee' if he'd be willing to help convince his mother that auctioning the property was the way to go. It wasn't an unlikely proposal since some of these auctions can gross twenty-five percent or more for the auctioneer, plus hourly fees. Also, because of the auction process, the final sale price can exceed the asking price, so it's worth it to them to go out and drum up business. Peter certainly bought it. He had access and agreed to show Connor the property. Evelyn never knew anything about it. It proved to be the last mistake Peter would ever make."

The sun was just setting behind the trees at the edge of the property as Leigh pulled the car into the half-full parking lot in front of the Souza-Baranowski Correctional Center. "Also speaking of the *Blue Ruin*, you remember what Rowe told us about how the government deliberately poisoned industrial alcohol to keep people from drinking it? That's what Ward used to dilute his real Canadian, Jamaican, and European booze. Kain's mother was just one of many casualties of the practice." She killed the engine. "And here we are."

Paul leaned forward, peering through the windshield at the two huge structures sprawled behind the low-slung building outside the sky-high razor wire fence. "Whoa. That is *not* where you want to spend twenty years of your life."

"Trust me, it's not where you want to spend even a week of your life," Matt said.

"It looks…" Kiko seemed to be at a loss for words. "Foreboding. Tiny barred windows surrounded by deadly fences. It must be miserable inside."

"It's not good. Remember, it's a prison, not a day spa. We're not rewarding people for committing serious offenses." Leigh opened her door. "Come on. Cabrera is supposed to be released at four."

"I still can't believe you got him out this fast," Paul said. "I mean, the justice system just doesn't work that way."

Leigh paused to turn to the backseat. "It does in a case like this. D.A. Saxon arranged for a judge, Cabrera got counsel assigned to him, and then there was an immediate court session to release him. When the evidence is this black and white, they don't drag their heels. Everyone does what they can to release the wronged man immediately. And since no jury is required, everything can be arranged quickly. It really can happen in a matter of days."

They climbed out just as another car pulled into the parking lot. The engine died and a man and woman got out. The woman opened the backseat and leaned in, straightening a moment later holding a baby in a padded, pink, footed onesie. Turning she spotted Leigh. After a moment's conversation with the man, they both started toward the group.

Matt leaned down to murmur in her ear. "Are those Cabrera's kids?"

"I think so. I talked to his daughter on the phone a few days ago. She's never met her father and wasn't sure she wanted to." Leigh eyed the woman, who appeared to be in her early thirties, as she quickly closed the distance between them. "I think she changed her mind."

"Trooper Abbott?"

"Yes."

The woman shifted her baby to her other shoulder, freeing her right hand to shake. "Sofia Cabrera. Thank you for your call the other night. I know I wasn't very receptive to your idea initially, but maybe I just needed some time to think about it. This is my brother, Luis." When the man behind her continued to hang back, his dark eyes darting suspiciously from side to side, she grabbed his arm, hauling him forward with surprising strength for such a small woman. "Luis, we've been over this."

"Don't like cops," the man mumbled.

"And this cop isn't here for you," she retorted.

"Mr. Cabrera, it's good to meet you. I'm so glad you came to meet your father. It will mean a lot to him." Leigh extended her hand, waiting patiently while Luis weighed his options before finally shaking her hand, whipping his hand from her grasp as quickly as he could. She turned to Sofia. "I'm glad you both came. It will mean a lot to him."

"I thought a lot about what you said. That he was innocent of this crime. And while he'd been found guilty before, he'd been trying to straighten out—for us—when he got into trouble. Mom always made it clear that he didn't love us enough to stay straight, but you tell me that's not true. It's going to be difficult to try and change the beliefs of a lifetime, but if you're right, then he deserves the chance to prove himself."

"Good for you. I think your father will need you now, perhaps more than he's needed anyone else in his life. It's not the same world he left over thirty years ago. He's going to need someone to help him find his way."

"I think I'd like to try."

"Look!" Paul pointed to the door of the correctional center as it slowly started to open.

Cabrera stepped out into the fading sunlight. Someone had given him street clothes to wear. The baggy jeans, plaid shirt, and worn jacket didn't fit perfectly, but they were clean and neat. He was clean-shaven now, the scruffy white beard gone, revealing a lined face.

Sofia gasped, her hand rising to cover her mouth.

"You okay?" Leigh asked.

Sofia nodded several times in quick succession, the movement bouncing the baby on her shoulder. "He looks so much like Luis. But old. So old."

"His life here hasn't been a picnic. But your being here will likely make this easier on him." Leigh looked back at the man staring at them from across the space. "Do you want me to take you over and introduce you?"

"No, we can do this. Luis, are you coming?"

The other man jammed his hands in his pockets, hunching his shoulders and shaking his head.

"You're a fool then. Come on, Maria, let's go meet Grandpa." She started across the parking lot.

"Gutsy gal," Matt murmured.

"That she is," Leigh agreed. "I think she takes after her father."

Sofia stopped feet away from her father. "Papá?" Her voice was uncertain and a slight tremor ran through it.

"Sofia?" Cabrera's gaze swept over her, taking in every feature and hesitating over the small form in her arms. "Is that you?"

A tiny nod was all Sofia could manage, and then she rushed forward to throw her free arm around her father. Cabrera froze for a moment, stunned and unsure how to react. Then his arms slowly came around the daughter he'd never met as his eyes closed in bliss.

A hand rubbed comfortingly up and down Leigh's back and she looked up into Matt's smiling eyes. "You did good, Trooper."

"We did good. We couldn't have lived with ourselves if we'd sat back and done nothing. It's not who we are."

"Amen to that."

Sofia pulled back, self-consciously wiping her eyes. Shifting the baby from her shoulder, she held out the small form to her father.

Cabrera glanced uncertainly from his daughter to the baby and back again. "It's been a long time since I've held a baby." His gaze flicked to the dark man standing apart from the group.

"No time like the present to practice, abuelito. Meet your granddaughter, Maria."

Cabrera hesitantly took the baby, holding her awkwardly at first until some old reflex kicked in and he adjusted his hold, settling her against his chest. Fascinated, the baby stared up at him with a nearly identical pale blue gaze. "She has my eyes."

As if in response to his words, the baby reached up, tapping her fingers gently against his freshly shaven chin.

Kiko gave a small sniff and Leigh glanced behind to see her staring at the trio, blinking furiously.

"Are you *crying*?" Paul asked incredulously.

"No." Kiko contradicted herself with another sniff. "The sun is in my eyes, that's all."

"Uh-huh." Paul's look clearly said *I don't believe you* but, with a grin, he turned back to the family tableau before them.

"Luis." Sofia was standing in front of her brother, hands on her hips. "We've been over this. Now stop being a stubborn ass."

Luis's shoulders inched higher and his gaze dropped to his scuffed work boots.

"It's okay, Sofia." Shifting the baby more securely into the crook of one arm, Cabrera stepped forward, grasping his son's arm. "You were just a tiny boy the last time I saw you. But I still see that boy in the man you are now. I'm sorry I wasn't there for you growing up." He threw a glance at Sofia. "For both of you, but I'll do whatever I can to make amends for that now." He paused when his son didn't move and continued to stare at the asphalt between their feet. "Luis, look at me."

The younger man's head rose reluctantly, his flat gaze meeting his father's.

"It wasn't my fault I was taken from you, but it doesn't change the fact that you lost your father, a hard thing for a boy at any age. I can't bring back those years, but I can try to be that father now. Please let me try."

Luis remained stock still for a moment, and then gave a subtle jerk of his head. Satisfied his father stepped back.

A dark sedan attracted Leigh's attention. It pulled

into the lot only a few cars away. A frail older man climbed out.

"Uh-oh."

"What?" Picking up on the stress in Leigh's voice, Matt leaned in. "Who's that?"

"That's Trooper Bern." She laid a hand on his arm. "Stay here. I need to go smooth the waters."

But Cabrera had already seen the older man and was handing the squirming baby back to her mother. "You've got some nerve coming here, Bern." He crossed the parking lot in ground-eating strides, standing at the end of the gap between the two cars, blocking Bern's path. "Get the hell out of here. You're not wanted."

But the older man straightened and Leigh could see the bearing of a police officer slide back into place. "I may not be wanted, but I came anyway. I owe you an apology." He held out his hand. "I was so focused on finding who killed Anna Kain that perhaps I didn't stop long enough to question the evidence that came into my hands. If I contributed to putting you here, to keeping you here when it's now clear you were always innocent of her murder, then I'm sorry. In my need to find justice, I was blind to your plight. You never wavered from your innocence, but I wasn't listening."

Leigh reached the men, putting out a hand to stop Cabrera from stalking further forward. "Cabrera, you need to know that Trooper Bern played a significant role in your release by providing the information that led to the apprehension of the real killer. He was determined to right whatever wrong he may have done. More than that, it wasn't his fault. We know who falsified the evidence that put you away, and that person is being brought into custody as we speak. It was a reputable witness who was paid off."

For a moment, Cabrera only stared down menacingly at the retired trooper, who still stood with his hand extended in greeting.

Heart beating faster as the silence stretched and the tension rose, Leigh started to calculate if she could successfully leap the corner of the hood of Bern's car to get physically between the two men. Cabrera was heavier and likely stronger than she was, but she still had the advantage over Bern's frailty. She laid her hand on the warm hood of Bern's car and started to gather herself when Cabrera slapped his hand into the older man's. It wasn't a warm handshake; it was terse, and, from the wince on Bern's face, it was overly hard. But it was a start. Cabrera dropped Bern's hand and strode back to his family without a backward glance.

Bern gave Leigh a short nod of thanks and a sheepish smile before he got back into his car and drove away.

Leigh wandered back to Matt and his students. "I thought things were going to get dicey there for a moment."

"You and me both. You were going to get between them, weren't you?"

Leigh blinked innocent eyes up at him. "Would I do that?"

The look he gave her told her he could see right through her charade.

She laughed. "Okay, I would. And nearly did. But it all worked out. You can tell that Cabrera is trying to make a fresh beginning. Some areas of his life will be easier than others, but he's trying. It's a good start." She caught Sofia's eye and raised a hand in farewell, receiving a bright smile and a wave in response. "Let's leave them to their reunion."

They returned to Leigh's car, the students piling into the back again.

"So Emerson's been caught?" Matt asked.

"Riley should be picking him up right now. Mr. Emerson will be enjoying at least the next several years of his retirement as a guest of the Commonwealth of Massachusetts."

"Hardly seems fair after the harm he caused."

"I agree. And even though there will be a handful of charges—from perjury to accepting bribes, and maybe a few others the D.A. will throw in—it still won't equal Cabrera's thirty plus years inside."

Matt looked through the windshield to where Cabrera stood with his son, daughter, and granddaughter. "At least he's trying to make up for lost time right away. I wish him luck."

"Me too. He's had a hard life and deserves a break now. I think his granddaughter is going to give him the strength to start over again. New life, new beginnings."

"Especially since he missed Sofia growing up. She's given him the gift of experiencing that through her daughter."

As she pulled out of the parking lot and onto State Road, Leigh found herself reviewing the case. So many years of death and revenge. From a callous poisoning, to decades of targeted killing meant more to wound the living than to punish the victims. One killer's life was nearly at an end. Two others would pay for their crimes. And the man who had been sorely wronged finally tasted freedom again for the first time in decades.

Sometimes when you couldn't change the past, changing the future had to be enough.

An image bloomed in Leigh's mind of Cabrera gazing down into the identical eyes of his granddaughter, years of hard prison life falling away under the gentle touch of baby. Her team was responsible for that.

Smiling, Leigh ignored Paul's pleas from the back that she turn on the lights and siren so they could get the full "perp experience" from the back of a cop car as she turned toward home.

It was enough.

* * * * *

ABOUT THE AUTHORS

A SCIENTIST SPECIALIZING in infectious diseases, JEN J. DANNA works as part of a dynamic research group at a cutting-edge Canadian university. However, her true passion lies in indulging her love of the mysterious through her writing. Together with her partner ANN VANDERLAAN, a retired research scientist herself, she crafts suspenseful crime fiction with a realistic scientific edge. Their three previous Abbott and Lowell Forensic Mysteries include *DEAD, WITHOUT A STONE TO TELL IT*; *NO ONE SEES ME TILL I FALL*; and *A FLAME IN THE WIND OF DEATH*.

Ann lives near Austin, Texas, with three rescued pit bulls. Jen lives near Toronto, Ontario, with her husband and two daughters. You can reach her at *jenjdanna@gmail.com* or through her website at *http://www.jenjdanna.com*.